Mary Clayton was born and brought up in Cornwall, and read History at Oxford University. After university she went to America as a Fulbright English-Speaking Union Fellow to Ann Arbor, Michigan, where she taught in the History Department. She has lived in America, Denmark and Italy, but now spends much of her time in Cornwall.

As Mary Lide and Mary Lomer, the author has written historical novels and sagas.

Pearls Before Swine

Mary Clayton

HEADLINE

First published in 1995
by HEADLINE BOOK PUBLISHING

First published in paperback in 1995
by HEADLINE BOOK PUBLISHING

10 9 8 7 6 5 4 3 2 1

ISBN 0 7472 4862 1

Printed and bound in Great Britain by
Cox & Wyman Ltd, Reading, Berks

HEADLINE BOOK PUBLISHING
A division of Hodder Headline PLC
338 Euston Road
London NW1 3BH

To James and Ron –
for providing the ambience,
and for giving advice with the writing –
with love and thanks.

Prologue

There was no moon on Bodmin Moor and, after a week of storms, even the animals had come down off the tors. Except for the moaning of the wind there was no noise; except for the slash of rain on grass and gorse nothing moved. It was not a night to be abroad, not a night for casual wandering.

Even by day the moor is remote and isolated, the spine of central Cornwall where rocks stick out like bare bones. Yet the farms and villages which border it have become used to its wild aspect, its treeless wastes, its streams and bogs. Farmers farm the adjacent fields, hikers climb the rocky hills, campers nonchalantly set up tents in the circles of old Iron Age forts – until this one June evening.

The old stallion heard the sound first. Ears pricked, he trotted to the edge of the incline and stood looking northwards, head to the wind. Presently, as the sound grew closer and crystallized, the mares broke from the herd, their foals running long-legged beside them. Following their example, next the sheep stampeded, milling aimlessly as if being rounded up, then bounding away in great staccato leaps.

The sound was unexpected, having nothing to identify it, yet grating on the nerves like fingernails on slate. It

1

came spiralling off the highest moors, to the right of Bolventor, muffled by the fold of hills, then breaking out as the land flattened, gradually settling to a sustained, uneasy rhythm like a workman's hammer.

Down the rough-hewn path came the tap, sharp and irregular now, the rap, rap, rapping of stumbling feet, pumping like pistons. Who or what had caused their frantic flight, it was impossible to say, or to whom they belonged, whether big, small, young, old, man or woman; whether living or phantom. The mist parted to let the figure through. And terror ran beside it.

And when once more the noise of its passing had diminished, when ponies and sheep had steadied back to their grazing, only then did a last cry echo through the night and ebb away into darkness . . .

The body was found next morning . . .

Chapter 1

Bad Ted found it. That wasn't his real name, as he was careful to inform the local police when he'd been revived with tea and biscuits and was able to speak. His real name had long been forgotten. But he didn't like this new nickname, no, he didn't, although he'd first pretended to. 'They gived it me,' he said.

He was a spry old man, elegant in his way, clean-shaven, although his chin was nicked by dull razorblades. He wore a tattered scarf of silk and nosegays of weeds. Meadowsweet, fool's parsley and ragged-Robin decorated the collar of his coat like wreaths, and tufts of straggly hair sprouted through the holes in his knitted cap like bleached grass. But it was his boots he was especially proud of, discarded riding boots, which he kept polished with dubbin; even as he spoke he kept trying to wipe the mud and slime off on the back of his leggings.

He was what in the old days had been called a tramp (before they were up-marketed into 'New Age Travellers'), and was proud of his ability to survive on his own without help from a Welfare State. Had he been born a Red Indian he would have been in his element. He was a familiar figure on the moors, with his own established routes, appearing and disappearing regularly like some migratory bird, following his own sense of seasons. He'd spent the night in Bestwick's barn, so he said, with Bestwick's permission. It was only recently he'd teamed up with the 'Travellers', as they called themselves, had camped with them up near Bolventor, had in fact parted from them that same night. And glad of it.

'Didn't mean to join them in the first place,' he told Derrymore, the local policeman, who listened to this preamble with stoic resignation. 'Just stumbled on to them. Came back one day to a spot I liked and there they was, in their van, lording it like the place was theirs, swarming out like a pack of curs: men, women, little children. Asking this, asking that – how do you manage this?, what's that for? – made a fellow feel some grand. Even gave me a fair share of their grub. But that didn't last long. When they'd sucked out all my secrets, or thought they had, they used me for a fool, and there's the truth.'

He scratched his head under the cap. 'Never said I was a saint,' he protested in answer to Derrymore's quizzical look. 'All right, I've stolen some when I had to eat – you can call it trespass if you like. But never did nothing wrong, ask anyone, never cut down living trees, never killed a living thing, never harmed a living soul. That's why they called me Bad Ted, see, because I weren't.'

He settled his cap firmly on his head. ''Course,' he said, again in answer to Derrymore's questions, 'they was younger, different. From the beginning didn't like their jokes. The one called Meg, she was the one to watch. "Come on now, Bad Ted," she'd say, "strut yer stuff." Always one to make a mock she was. But Hal, he were all right in part. Made you toe the line, though. "Communal loyalty" he called it: they was a community. When he talked like that I was off. What was "community" to me?

That's why I took to tramping in the first place.'

Resettling his clothes, he stretched his legs to admire his boots. 'Then there was always argie-bargie, see; they was always on the move, restless like. So last night, I'd had enough. Spent the evening in the Jolly Miller, used to know it well, good for a free beer or two and a seat afore the fire. Why not?' he added, somewhat self-righteously. ''Twasn't the weather to be out if you could find somewhere dry out of the wet. At closing, when Bestwick made his offer, I jumped at the chance.'

He winked his small eyes, black like sloes. 'Just this once, Bestwick, says, if his missus didn't find out.'

'That's the Bestwick here and present now,' Derrymore said, writing carefully, young, and anxious that his first murder report would be mistake-free. 'Owns a small-holding up St Breward way, I believe—'

'Right,' Ted broke in, in full spate, not liking interruptions, and, free of the Travellers, glad to revert back to plain Ted. 'Know Bestwick well, I do, and done him a few favours in my time. Many's the drink I've had with him. But these days when he's drunk he's scared of his missus. So I said I'd help him home and spend the night, if he'd give me work. A good day's work tomorrow, I said, that'll set us right.'

He winked again. 'Common sense,' he said. 'A hard woman, his missus; where drink's concerned, a demon. But soft if you get on her right side. A day's work shows respect, and respect goes a long way with her. Show respect, tip yer hat, work a bit, there'll be a square meal at the end with perhaps a second or third free night thrown in for good measure. Three things I swear by,' he said, suddenly proud: 'never outstay yer welcome, never foul yer own nest, never expect something fer nothing.

'Them Travellers have none of that,' he continued, aggrieved. 'Bloody arse-kissing they called it, bloody toadying up, as if the world owed them a living.' He fell silent here, as if brooding.

'And Hanscastle Farm?' Derrymore prompted.

'Well,' said Ted, 'the work wasn't to my taste, but that's the luck of it. "Could do with a hand after the rains we've had," Bestwick said, "up at Hanscastle." Didn't tell me exactly what, of course, not then, that is . . .'

'And when he did?'

'I was surprised,' Ted admitted. 'Didn't even know he knew the place, let alone made use of it. But there, Bestwick's secretive like that. Lots of irons in lots of fires – part-gypsy, see. Said he'd not be up until later himself, sleeping it off, I thought, but to get myself there sharpish like, and when I did I'd see what needed doing. Would have cleared off double-quick if I'd knowed what I know now, and no mistake.

'Would have run a mile,' he repeated, his face contorting with the memory. 'Wish I had. Never a hot pasty worth the price, not even one made by Bestwick's missus.'

At first light, he explained, he'd set off. Shouldering a pitchfork and 'borrowing' a piece of sacking against the morning chill (both items he swore he meant to return), with a bag of cheese and bread and a bottle of tea slung across his back, off he'd plodded across the moors towards the farm to see what Bestwick wanted done.

And in answer to Derrymore's question, 'Yes, I guessed Bestwick was up to something shady. Drunk or sober, Bestwick's a schemer. A gypsy, see. But small-time. Nothing big or evil. Bestwick's missus'd make sure of that. And no more a murderer than I am.'

Lingering now upon the first part of his journey, as if

reluctant to come to his destination and what he'd found when he got there, the old man continued to describe how the day had started, promising fine after all the rain. Although the trees around the barn still dripped and the grass underfoot was soaked, already the rising sun shone through the morning mist, a real Cornish morning, the weather changeable as a woman. No, he hadn't hurried, he'd paused every so often to take a gulp of tea and look round. Well, wasn't that the way life was meant to be: free, part of God's creation. If he'd been younger he'd have stripped off and run naked through the grass as he used to do as a lad and had taken to the open. When a fox crossed his path – the only thing he'd seen that morning – its brush, glittering like a new penny, ruddy in the sun's first light, had brought him close to tears.

'Suppose not many of you young 'uns know a real June morning,' he said, wiping eyes watery with emotion. 'Up at four to enjoy it. And I don't suppose you remember Hanscastle Farm. Proper place it was in the old days. Used to be good too fer a night's lodging. Farmer Hansard (no relation to the place) always made me welcome. Was a religious man, see, believed in God, believed in helping others.'

He shook a warning finger. 'Much good religion did him. Didn't help when the clay-works took his land, bought it out from under him for a song: old mining rights, they said. Killed him, that clay-mine did. And for what? The mine closed down again, all turned to waste, breaks your heart,' he said.

'Farmer Hansard used to claim his land'd been farmed since ancient times,' after a while he continued. 'Used to be an old fort on the hill, he said. What do they call it – some Iron Age place? Expect it's buried under the sand-tip now. And the way I went, off the moors, down a dip of tree-lined stream that starts up near Bolventor, well, the stream and trees are still there but everything beyond is buried under sand as well, fields and hedges all gone as if they never existed. Farmer Hansard used to boast he could plough a furrow so straight you could take a ruler to them fields and never lose an inch. Poor soul, he'd turn in his grave to see the mess them clay-works left 'em in. And all for no good purpose.'

For a while he remained obstinately silent, as if musing on the unfairness of the world. 'As for the farmhouse,' eventually he went on, 'take more than a clay-mine to shake it down. Still got its original slated roof and good granite walls. And those door lintels, ever seen lintels so thick? To tell the truth, with the early sun glinting on the window-panes, from a distance off, you'd say it hadn't changed and was like it was when Farmer Hansard was alive.'

He shook his head. 'But when I came down the hill I saw the fences had all fallen down and the orchard was overgrown in brambles, with branches of dead apple trees sticking out, like arms.'

Once more he paused, as if the squalor had silenced him, as if the piles of rotting wood, the unidentifiable farm equipment, the broken-down machinery and rust-covered tractors had defeated him. As if the effluent from the pig-sty still spread its unmistakable stench. For the final insult, the final shock, was finding what the farmhouse was being used for now – as a pig-sty, for Bestwick's pigs.

What happened next had about it the sense of the inevitable, a sense of *déjà vu*, a personal tragedy. Picking his way gingerly, Ted approached what had been the inner yard and peered over the wall. When he had seen it last it had been a simple cobbled yard, sloping up to the farmhouse door. Edged with flowers and surrounded by a fuchsia hedge, it was where Farmer Hansard had held evening prayers three times a week, obliging all his workers and their families to take part, even to the singing of the hymns. 'Always went meself,' Ted said. 'Never saw no harm in it.'

Now the workers and their cottages were gone, the flowers and bushes were gone, and the yard was swamped by slurry from the pigs.

The rains had turned the slurry into a bog from which an occasional bubble burst; in the morning heat a faint steam swirled above it, like some hideous stew. Three porkers, gigantic sows, stretched on the step of the open farmhouse door, their eyes closed, their snouts raised to the sun in blotched pink bliss. Other pigs, smaller, snuffled along the edges of the wall, over their hocks in thick green ooze, while the oldest male, a giant of a fellow, wallowed in the deeper slime where the ground ran down to a drain, obviously blocked.

If clearing this was the work Bestwick had in mind, there was work enough to keep someone for days. Beggars can't be choosers. Ted set down his burdens, observed detachedly, drank some more tea and resolved to wait until Bestwick himself showed up.

'Odd things pigs,' he now added. 'By nature clean. Shouldn't have to live in filth. That courtyard hadn't been cleaned in weeks, wasn't just the rain. But Bestwick's like that. Starts a thing, goes at it for a while, then can't keep it up. Of course I wondered how he came to keep pigs there; of course I knew farmhouse and farm didn't belong to him, but that didn't worry me then. And yes, I did wonder what he meant me to do with the pigs after I'd cleaned the place up. Butcher them, I thought, else he wouldn't bother to put in an appearance himself. And yes, I did think, well, aren't there rules these days, always rules of some sort, about housing and feeding and such? Something on the sly here, I thought, something underhand. Bet no one knows he keeps them here, not even his missus. Look at that fat monster there, I thought, must cost a fortune to keep it fed. As long as a man is tall and twice my size, not a creature I'd like to meet on a dark night.'

He gulped his tea. 'It were the sows,' he said. 'They rolled apart and came awake. Snuffled, sensing out the air, squealing, struggling to their feet. Watching me with their small pig eyes.'

Now he was reliving it all, the way their cloven hooves stepped daintily from one clot to the next, their slender legs, out of proportion to their weight, picking across the brown crust, cracking it apart like icing on a cake. At the lowest slope, where the corners of the walls met, he saw what he still could not, would not, speak of – the shadow of a something. A shadow that seemed to rear up from the ooze as they threshed towards it, a shape like a log of wood, or a sack of meal, or a truncated human form, even as it sank back into the slime again.

When, at a little past nine o'clock, Bestwick drew up his ancient lorry with a shriek of brakes; when, slowly, nursing his aching head, he clambered down, removed his knives, brushes and pails, then as slowly waddled towards the house, whistling under his breath, he found Ted half over the wall, flailing with his pitchfork at the pigs, and shouting for help in a voice that was barely recognizable.

Inspector John Reynolds, ex-Inspector Reynolds, of the Devon and Cornwall Constabulary, prematurely retired to become a successful author of detective mysteries, heard the news the next evening. Although he lived in St Breddaford, the nearest village to Hanscastle Farm, and although, because of former and present professions, he might be supposed to be interested in crime, he'd actually spent the day in happy ignorance, across the river in Plymouth, discussing plans for a new book with his editors. Returning home late, glad to be free of urban rush (although most of his career had been spent in the city), he had immediately come out into the garden to enjoy the late sun, the contrast with the previous day's gale complete. Typically Cornish, he thought: one moment wind and storm, the next placid tranquillity.

Reynolds was tall and athletic, looking closer to forty than fifty-five. His face was thin, the cheekbones prominent: his was the sort of face that holds rather than gives away secrets, hiding its thoughts under a bland exterior. Beneath the close-cropped hair, however, there lay a brain known for its subtle ingenuity, and his deep-set eyes were capable of intent and penetrating scrutiny – as many offenders had learnt to their cost.

He had given up all that. It was gardening that now occupied most of his time. Together with book-writing, it had become the focus of his life, his inner sanctum, his solace since his wife had tormented and deceived and then left him six years ago to what had gradually subsided into outwardly accepted bachelorhood. He stook looking about him, rocking slowly back and forth on his heels. The scent of roses filled the air; he breathed deeply. Here's contentment, he thought. And he settled down to an hour of retying of battered plants before tackling a new chapter. A voice, hailing him from the roadside, broke in on his absorption with all the unwelcome force of a bucket of cold water.

At first he couldn't make out who it was, the figure

obscured by the leafy growth of the wistaria; then, as the gate creaked open and he heard heavy footsteps up the path, he recognized the village policeman, Constable Derrymore, a young man of sizeable build and girth, as became the local wrestling champion.

Derrymore removed his helmet and rubbed his hand through thick cropped hair that stood on end like hedgehogs' bristles. His face was weary, making him suddenly seem older than he was. 'Brutal business this,' he said, in so lugubrious a voice that John Reynolds felt sorry for him. 'What is?' Reynolds asked. And thus received his first tidings of what was to become an even greater obsession – the finding of a body at Hanscastle Farm, left for pigs to eat.

His immediate reaction was anger, not so much at the crime itself but at the realization that even here in his quiet retreat, ugliness should have followed him. Afterwards he was almost ashamed of his self-centredness, typical of normal citizens confronted with sudden and violent abnormality. But, he excused himself, it was after all now as a normal citizen, as a normal resident of a small Cornish village, that he was reacting to crime. And even Derrymore's repetition of the word 'Brutal', followed by the observation, 'Never heard the like,' suggested the village policeman also considered it a personal affront.

Reynolds knew that feeling well. He'd felt it every time a new case had come across his desk, even though he should have become hardened. To a rural policeman, used to minor rural crimes, this one certainly would have come as a shock. He looked at the younger man with growing compassion and, giving in to the inevitable, resigned himself to a blow-by-blow account. And when Derrymore had told him all the details, all those released to the public that is, he couldn't resist asking for more, difficult to do in the circumstances without emphasizing his own professional background. But after all, he told himself, I suppose most people in the village know who I am, although they never mention it, with true Cornish courtesy ignoring what they think I want ignored. And I don't suppose Derrymore's ever given me a second glance, except as an older man to nod to in passing, a newcomer who minds his own business and whose only interest is in growing flowers.

'I suppose it is murder?' Reynolds now said. 'Seems to me no one can fall into a pig-sty by accident. Unless blind drunk, or drugged.'

To his surprise Derrymore answered freely, suggesting that he did know more about Reynolds than Reynolds had given him credit for. He put that thought aside for further investigation. 'It's murder all right,' Derrymore was saying, looking grim. 'When the story first came in, a telephone call from Bestwick, I couldn't make head or tail of it. Bestwick was bleating on about his pigs, no blame to them, he said; he fed them the best swill, shouldn't have been hungry and so on. But the last few days the weather'd been so bad he'd skimped on it, a rough track up to the farm and he was afraid of being bogged down. As for Ted, you know Old Ted, the village tramp, when I got up there he was huddled under a piece of sacking beside the wall, pitchfork in hand, as if he was afraid of being eaten himself.'

He paused, as if reliving that moment. 'Anyway, when it all came out, what they were doing there, and what Ted thought he'd found, after we'd driven the pigs back into the house – Bestwick uses the house itself as the sty, by the way; dreadful state it's in, of course – we got down into the muck. Ted was right. It was there, the body. Or what was left of it.'

13

'Any clues to identity, male or female, that sort of thing?'

'Not yet.' Derrymore shook his head. His face grew even sterner, as if he were fighting down some memory. 'Not from the remains, that is, although after pathology's finished we should know more. And that's another problem,' he burst out. 'If the murderer's local – and he has to be local, only a local would know the place – presumably the victim's local too. And if it happened last night – couldn't have been earlier else there'd have been even less of the body left – why has no one come forward to report someone missing?'

His voice trailed off, perplexed. 'As for the remains,' he continued after a while, 'well, I can't say it was easy looking, but I could tell that before the body was tipped in, someone had hacked off the head.'

That grisly piece of evidence certainly would not have been revealed to the general public. But Derrymore was insistent that he was right. 'I've seen things like that before,' he said. 'No doubt about it. Just luck the body hadn't been, well, completely destroyed, if you get my meaning. And just by chance really that it was found anyway. If it hadn't stopped raining, I suppose Bestwick wouldn't have bothered to go up there in the first place, certainly wouldn't have decided to do any cleaning out, although God knows it needed it.'

Both men were silent then, as if contemplating the full horror. 'As for choosing the slurry as a hiding place,' Derrymore concluded, 'not many people know pigs eat human flesh. I didn't. And I'm not sure Bestwick did. As I said, he was in some thrash about that.'

'What about Old Ted?'

Derrymore stopped for thought. 'Ted might,' he conceded. 'That's the sort of thing Ted might know. He's been around the moors off and on since I was growing up, fond of birds and animals and all; used to feed them until they were tame.'

Confidence was coming back into his voice as he spoke again of things he was familiar with. 'But since apparently Ted found the body, it wouldn't make sense to call attention to it if he'd hidden it. As for Bestwick, well he was well and truly drunk last night, and there's plenty at the Jolly Miller who'll vouch to that. And to hearing him ask Ted to help him home. But if Bestwick were in a state to put the body there, the same difficulty stands: why set Ted up to do the finding? No, I think they're both in the clear. Except . . .'

He frowned. 'Except of course there's no knowing where the murder itself took place, could have been anywhere. But you'd need some way of getting the body to the farm. You couldn't have carried it far.'

'Tyre marks?' By now it seemed easy, almost natural, for Reynolds to ask. And as easy for Derrymore to answer. 'There're plenty, all over the place.' Derrymore made vague gestures with his arms. 'Seems Bestwick was so upset that when he drove out to make the phone call he couldn't steer straight, almost went in a ditch, making it difficult to see if other vehicles were involved.'

'Any theories as to why Bestwick was so nervous – apart from the discovery, that is?'

'Myself, I suspect he's afraid of something else,' Derrymore said. 'Probably he was just planning a butchering on the quiet, that's what Ted thinks, and doesn't have the proper permits. Actually, I doubt if he even has permission to use the farm at all: it still belongs to the clay-works.'

As if answering other unspoken questions, 'Oh yes,'

Derrymore added, ticking over things in his mind, 'one other thing. Ted's taken up with a group of Travellers, said so himself. Some of them have been camping rough on the moors. But they've been there for ages, doing no real harm. And yes, you're right, sir, there's no way anyone could have got up there, by accident I mean; even less likely last night, after the storm. And in daylight, although you can drive up to the farm buildings from the main A-road, they're still a long way up a stretch of what passes for a lane. Behind it, there's only moor and clay-tips.'

He was done. Not a bad summing up, Reynolds thought; better than I would have imagined. And he's put his finger on some of the problems, couldn't have been more concise myself.

'Come inside for a cuppa,' Reynolds said on impulse, although not without a qualm, for he'd been looking forward all day to these quiet moments. Reluctantly restoring his tools to the garden shed, and shedding his boots, he led the way indoors as if, in the past, he'd been used to village policemen popping into his home for a chat. Yet so unprepared was he for company that for a moment, once he and his 'guest' were installed in the living room, with its comfortable litter of papers and books, he was at a loss how to continue, the truth being that having been given the facts of the murder he had had enough. What did murder matter to him now? He was done with it. Invented, book-contrived crime was his only interest these days . . . Fortunately, Constable Derrymore solved the impasse for him.

Derrymore, who had followed and seated himself with a bemused look, as if still lost in his own theories, suddenly came to with a start, as if he were conscious of some grave irregularity. He pushed back the chair and heaved himself upright, standing very stiffly to attention, his hands by his sides and his helmet tucked under his arm.

'I'm here about something else,' he burst out, turning very red. 'Nothing to do with Hanscastle at all. Shouldn't have burdened you with Hanscastle, my apologies. Actually what I've come for is, well, it's a request. With your permission, sir,' he added even more formally. I'm in for it, Reynolds thought, half amused, half irritated, but there, can't blame the chap.

Appreciating the young officer's dilemma, reading embarrassment in Derrymore's open expression, again despite himself Reynolds felt sorry for the young man and tried to put him at ease.

'That's all right, Constable,' he said with a wave of his hand. 'We're off duty here. So what's the request?'

He wanted to make the younger man comfortable but suspected he was failing. It's all in the tone of voice, he thought, surprised his had so quickly reverted to the way it used to be when he was in charge of many such investigations. And the truth was, for all his feeling sorry for Constable Derrymore and wanting to put him at ease, underneath he was still irritated: irritated that his peace had been disturbed, irritated that his private façade had been broken through, irritated that the real world with its real problems had been thrust back on him.

But it seemed it wasn't Reynolds' official manner that made Constable Derrymore redden (as much as the younger man's natural ruddy complexion allowed, that is). In fact, it wasn't so much Reynolds' reaction at all as the nature of the 'request' that the young officer now felt obliged to reveal.

'It wasn't my idea,' Derrymore was hastening to explain, stuttering a little in agitation. 'And I'm sure there's

17

nothing to it, but she insisted. And when I told her that she should talk to the Devon and Cornwall big-shots they've already called in to deal with Hanscastle, "Not good enough," she said. "I want Reynolds," begging your pardon, sir, Inspector Reynolds. And when I must have stared at her as if she expected me to pull you out of a hat, "He lives in the village, you . . ." she said, well, she wasn't exactly polite and was so insistent I thought I'd not argue.'

He didn't explain who the 'she' was: he didn't have to. There was only one 'she' in St Breddaford whom everyone knew and feared (although Reynolds himself had never met her), who would have the gall to insist upon such special treatment as if it were her right. Lady Rowan of Rowan Court would be more than insistent, Reynolds thought, remembering things he'd heard of her, more than 'impolite'. She'd probably threatened Derrymore with instant demotion if he didn't immediately do as she said. If Derrymore's had a run-in with Lady Rowan, he deserves all the sympathy he can get.

'She said you were the best,' Derrymore was still struggling with explanations, 'said you'd know how to handle it. And although it's irregular like – I mean, I didn't like to intrude before, sir, and don't like to intrude now, but agreeing she was right, I mean about the best, I said I'd try.'

Having got over what for him was the most embarrassing part, he obviously felt freer to felt his enthusiasm show. ' "Fancy," I'd said to Mum when you first came. "Inspector Reynolds moved down the lane from us and me having read all his books and loved every one." That last one, involving the container ship now, I thought it was a classic.'

He smiled. 'But I wasn't going to let on to Lady R that I knew all that. "Very good, madam," I told her to keep her quiet, "just as you say, madam, three bags full, madam, lick your boots, madam." But only if you don't mind, that is.'

He broke off as Reynolds also stood up and looked at him. They were about the same height, although the younger man was much broader, and had a similar soldier stance. He's been in the army, Reynolds thought, look at the cut of his hair, look at the way he holds himself. Like me he's seen action just as I did in the Middle East, Ireland perhaps in his case. He isn't just your normal village policeman with a mind as flat as his feet, isn't all bluster and fuss, would probably do well in a real crisis, involving real danger.

That observation altered his original decision to refuse. 'Why didn't she ask me herself?' he said. But he knew that answer too. Lady Rowan gave orders to others as if she were a medieval lord, expected them to be carried out like royal commands, wouldn't know what refusal meant.

Constable Derrymore's expression tightened. 'She said it was better this way,' he said, 'nothing official, like, all low key.'

He broke out, 'Damned if I know, sir, that's the truth. First off she rang the office, left a message asking me to call, said it was to do with the, er, crime. I thought she was talking about the body in the pen, even knew who it was, perhaps. And for my part, I'll admit I was glad to hear her voice, if only to know she was alive. Not that I bear her ill-will, not my place to, but if there's anyone in the village who's gained ill-will, she has.'

He looked at Reynolds squarely, without subterfuge. 'Especially after what happened in the village itself, last night,' he said. 'That's what she was really on about. Seems she'd called a village meeting, special like, she said. Everyone was invited, including you, she said. Says you didn't turn up, as you ought to have done, says it's a pity you didn't, else none of this might have happened.

'I'm only repeating what she said,' he added apologetically. 'She's no right to put the blame on anyone. Well, her meeting didn't go according to plan. Instead it degenerated into what she called a slanging match, everyone at odds with everyone else. Then, presumably when they'd all gone home, sometime in the middle of the night someone took an axe to her flower-boxes and smashed them flat. The boxes she had put up around the green,' he added hastily, as in turn Reynolds stared at him. 'Last year, remember? When she barred the village from using it, even the pub, and turned the whole thing into what she called a Medieval Pleasance, her fancy name for a garden. The whole village was up in arms.'

Reynolds did remember. One could scarcely forget. Even though he'd made it his policy to keep himself apart from village life, Lady Rowan's ongoing quarrels with St Breddaford had loomed too large to ignore. Especially her main area of controversy – the large square of common land in the middle of the village, used for grazing cattle in olden times, and now, in more modern ones, as far back as collective memory went, for soccer and cricket; great for sitting on, of an evening, outside the Fox and Goose, beer mug in hand. Lady Rowan's unrelenting pursuit of it, her determination to take over this innocuous piece of turf and use it for her own purposes, and her inevitable success, had long dominated village gossip. Together with the final closure of the pub, it had undoubtedly won her the undisputed title of most hated woman in the village, as well as winning first place for St Breddaford in a Beautiful Britain contest.

'Made a right old hash of those flower-boxes,' Derry-more was saying, not without a trace of satisfaction, 'although she had her gardeners out first thing to clear the debris up. Cleared away the evidence too, along with the bits, but that's by the by. She insists the smashing of the boxes and the hiding of the body in the pig-pen are linked, but isn't willing to explain how, not to me at any rate.

'Well, you know what she's like, sir,' Derrymore went on, after a suitable pause. 'Eccentric, if you get my meaning. Before I went to see her, I'd already guessed she'd be after something unusual. And she'd never have asked for me in the first place if she hadn't wanted to bypass higher channels.'

This assessment of his own insignificance didn't seem to bother him, as once more he paused, after what was obviously, for him, another very long speech, still standing stiffly to attention. 'Of course, I ought to have passed the whole thing up the official chain like, but I had my doubts. And I thought, well, I didn't want her, Lady Rowan, to go making a fool of herself with outsiders.'

And he wouldn't, Reynolds thought; he'd be protective of his own, even protective of an old busybody who's caused more trouble in St Breddaford than I'd like to count.

As if guessing the former Inspector's thoughts, Derry-more added, 'And then there was the temptation, sir, if you know what I mean, talking to you on the quiet like, even if it's a bit peculiar . . .'

His voice trailed off again. And again Reynolds felt a thrust of sympathy, remembering suddenly what it was like to be young and honest and enthusiastic, when it was still possible to indulge in hero worship, however much you later discovered your hero's feet were made of clay.

'Don't know much about flower-pots.' Reynolds' voice was deliberately dry. 'Murder's more my line, you know.'

Derrymore looked suitably abashed. 'I've not had much to do with Hanscastle myself actually,' he now hastened to explain. 'Not after the first original alarm that is. The others took over double-quick; set up an Incident Room in an empty sweet-shop.'

He enunciated the word carefully, by syllables, 'In-ci-dent', as if he were suspicious of it. 'A man called Clemow is in charge. Chief Inspector Clemow.'

For the first time he sounded aggrieved. 'I expect you know him, sir, a shortish chap, about your age, curt like. Suggested I go back to filling forms and leave the rest to him.'

He broke off, obviously wary of saying too much. And for a moment Reynolds felt his own face stiffen. The name was one he hadn't heard in a while, didn't want to hear.

'And what do you think the smashing of the flower-tubs means?' he asked.

Derrymore shook his head. 'Damned if I know,' he said again. 'And damned if I can see a link.'

'Except perhaps the same axe was used,' Reynolds mused. He set down his mug. 'Right, thanks,' he said in a tone that showed he had made his mind up and decided it was time to finish the interview. 'But that's the name of the game, isn't it, Constable, the hopes we all live on, the "perhapses", the "whys", the "ifs".'

Smiling, using the 'we' deliberately, he led the way to the door, opened it. Feeling Derrymore's hesitation behind him he said, as if in afterthought, 'And don't worry about Lady Rowan, we'll deal with her.' He didn't add a last 'if' – 'If we can.'

Chapter 2

After Derrymore had gone, Reynolds stood at the garden gate looking down the lane towards the village green. It was too dark to work in the garden, but there was still light enough to see the little bridge over the stream which gave the village its name and, beyond it, the outline of the twelfth-century church with its quaint off-kilter steeple. He could hear the ducks along the river banks and, if he listened carefully, catch the fret of the water through the long rushes. Otherwise there was no sound. He remembered now how on his return there had been no one about; no one walking dogs or gossiping over back fences; no children playing in the street. On a fine evening they should all have been out, gathered round the green, like they used to be when he had first come here. But it isn't just the shadow of murder that's left the village frightened and empty, he thought; other things have changed it too: the estate agent's 'For Sale' sign swinging in place of the old Fox and Goose, half the line of little bow-fronted shops shut down, mortgage companies' repossession notices bristling at every other cottage window. In the two years since I've come here, the old peace and the old tranquillity have gone, killed by the current economic recession. And, along with it, that rural innocence that I've always loved, Lady Rowan's so-styled 'formal garden' part of the process, replacing the easy and simple with the contrived and artificial.

And I chose to live here, he thought, even more moodily, in a village I discovered by chance and always liked but never, thank God, had any dealings with in my former work. I bought this place with the proceeds of my books, probably the last real sale here before the slump. Although London bred and city reared I settled down easily to country life. For me, St Breddaford used to be the perfect place for a writer who likes to watch unobserved and take notes without being disturbed. I don't want it to change.

Depression growing, he returned to the house, slouched down in a chair before the empty hearth, even desire to start his book lost. The sense of malaise was familiar, too familiar, like a darkening of the sun, like a headache one can't quite locate. If he let his mind wander, if he sat here vacantly without set parameters and goals and deadlines, there was only one thing which could fill the vacuum – his hand almost reached for it, his mouth was dry for the taste of it, his body craved for its oblivion. And he knew where he could get it. Starkly he could see it on the empty shelf in the hall cupboard, the unopened whisky bottle which he had put there the day he had moved in as a memorial and a challenge.

No one knew it was there, of course, and certainly no counsellor of the AA (of which he was now a lifelong member) would approve such a flaunting of the rules of total abstinence. It was his way of fighting back, a cocking of the nose at the vice that had almost ruined him, although no one perhaps even knew how vicious the fight had been, certainly no one in his former life. Except perhaps his wife. And the man who'd gleaned the information from her.

He forced his fingers to relax. Here was the real reason for his gloom, the real fact that had dominated his thinking since Derrymore first mentioned the name. I like Derrymore, he thought. He's young, of course, untried, but there're the makings of a good police officer, if he can be rescued from obscurity before it's too late. And he's honest, a novelty these days. But, however unintentionally, Derrymore had opened old wounds. Even Derrymore's expression when he first spoke of Chief Inspector Clemow, even Derrymore's words – 'Curt like. Suggested I go back to filling forms' – had both suggested Derrymore's chagrin and recreated Clemow with all his obvious faults. In the past Clemow had often blundered badly in professional relationships because of misplaced scorn, had ridden roughshod over inferiors. In his new position of authority there was no reason to think he'd changed. He'd have no time for village policemen or village life. And to Reynolds' own surprise, already in this case he was beginning to feel protective of both.

But there was much more to it than that. 'I expect you know him,' Derrymore had said. Know wasn't the word for it, Reynolds thought. Once Clemow and I were friends. We worked together, there wasn't much I didn't know. I had the ideas, he kept my feet on the ground, our partnership worked as well as most – but that was before he had an affair with my wife.

I could forgive him that, he now thought with the detachment of time. He wasn't the only one, nor the first. And she did the chasing. Sometimes I even think I can forgive her. If she cajoled, insisted, and then, having got him, put ambition into his head, it was out of some twisted need to get even with me. 'You're married to your work, I don't count.' How many times had she thrown that taunt at me, he thought, how many times found solace with other men? But the others weren't close companions, professional associates who could use the titbits of information she fed them. Although I can only guess at that, he thought, I have no proof.

Reluctantly now, he gave memory full rein, back to the past when he was still Inspector Reynolds of the Devon and Cornwall Constabulary and Clemow had been his second-in-command. 'I congratulate you, John,' Clemow had said, when rumour of Reynolds' probable promotion to Chief Inspector had first been raised. 'I'm for you, one hundred per cent. You're the man for us.' He'd smiled, a smile as false as his words, ambition as strong as lust. For Clemow, cuckolding a superior had not been enough. First Reynolds' wife, next Reynolds' new position, a position Clemow himself so burned to have that he had betrayed his friend behind his back, belittling his achievements, casting doubts upon his competence, even to spreading nasty rumours about his private life, including his drinking problems – only to find out, too late, that Reynolds, already offered the post, had turned it down.

How did I ever have the guts to do that, Reynolds wondered; good job, even if I'd come to hate it, good income, all chucked over for something I didn't even know then would work? Just thank your lucky stars, he told himself, that it did work, that's all you need to know. Three bestsellers isn't bad going. But at the time Clemow needn't have bothered to smear your reputation, everyone thought you were mad anyhow. All that was over with. Reynolds' wife had left him, certainly not wanting to exchange one policeman for another, weary of men in general, a clean break. The only good turn she ever did me, Reynolds thought; her surgical precision had been his salvation. Reynolds himself had refused promotion, had resigned, had given up drinking whisky and moved on to make a success of writing books. The way had been left free for Clemow to have what he had schemed for. Nothing of that mattered now – why then, this evening, had betrayal still rankled so?

He took a deep breath, faced the unpleasant fact. Faced too the equally unpleasant fact that the man who had betrayed him was here, in his own bailiwick as it were, as intrusive as any murderer. The first time he had let Clemow have what he wanted. Was he now to lie down a second time and give up?

He took another breath, sat up, flexed his shoulders. He knew himself well enough to know that he'd give his right arm to outsmart Clemow and get his own back. And already in one sense Clemow had made a false move, was at Reynolds' mercy, since presumably, although Reynolds knew of Clemow's presence, Clemow didn't yet know of his. You've got the start on him this time, Reynolds thought, his fighting instincts aroused. Revenge is the real name of the game, beating him at his own job. And it's revenge that'll prompt any interest in this case and give this proposed visit to Lady Rowan a special zest.

Focus on the lady then, he told himself, in so far as she's the only lead you've got. Admit you're curious about her too – about what she knows, or doesn't know, what real information she's got. And, more important, why she's selected you for the telling of it!

He didn't find her interest flattering as he had been flattered by Derrymore's. In his mind he'd already classified Lady Rowan as a snob, for whom no doubt all policemen were beneath notice, a sub-species, the sort of woman who'd not use flattery for nothing. There's something she wants in return, he thought, and I want to know what it is.

Careful now, he warned himself, you aren't involved. You've no call to make professional visits, even less to meddle. Yet even as a private citizen he had the right to be troubled. A crime had taken place on his doorstep; there were things about it which didn't add up, pieces of the jigsaw that didn't fit. Why, for example, throw the body into a pig-sty to be eaten but first cut off its head? And why hide a body in a sty at all, with miles of open moor on all sides?

He grinned, all depression gone. Old habits died hard. It's being trained to do a job, he thought with a wry shrug, a bloodhound, never letting go. Seeing the lady may be only a surveying expedition, if you want to call it that, a testing of Clemow's position, a proving of why Clemow isn't the right man for the job – at base it's also the satisfying of an instinct, one you've often had before, that you're on to something worth investigating.

And with that observation he went happily to bed, the spectre of his old temptation reduced to what it was, merely an unopened bottle on an empty shelf.

Chapter 3

Although some miles away, Rowan Manor lay within the boundaries of St Breddaford Parish and was set in a secluded valley, much still forested. As Reynolds drove along next morning, he noted with pleasure that the trees were native beech and oak rather than those ubiquitous firs whose plantations ruined so much of the Cornish countryside. It was another fine June day, the sunlight dappled through well-kept glades, no wild underbrush here, no spreading bramble thorns. On every side the signs of good management showed: coppicing cleverly managed, fences newly painted, stone hedges painstakingly rebuilt; obviously since Lord Rowan's death there had been no loss of care. She should concentrate on this, he thought, and leave St Breddaford alone. Derrymore's right, most of St Breddaford has good cause to hate her. And hate is a tricky beast. No one knows that better than I do, the depths to which it can submerge itself, the energy, the venom it can unleash when it finds an outlet. But to kill for a village green, that doesn't make sense either, not unless Lady Rowan is the victim. And what Lady Rowan can know, or tell, of any murder, or of any possible murderer... he shrugged. At least, he thought, as he turned in the driveway (noting as he did so the arrogance of its new name, Rowan Manor, written large on the gate-posts so it could not be missed, instead of the Doomsday Trehance of its former owners), the old busybody can't threaten me as she did Derrymore. Busybody, however, no one would deny – but sometimes even unwittingly busybodies drop pearls before ... Hastily he blocked out the end of the quotation as inappropriate.

The manor had belonged to the same family for centuries, had been purchased by the Rowans a mere couple of decades ago. Like the name on the gate the drive was also new, relocated to give the best of views across a rolling park. Drive and parkland were twigless, leafless, presumably raked clean after the storms. A Herculean task. Along the gravel edge unusual flowering bushes and shrubs had been massed. How had they been moved when mature, Reynolds wondered, and at what cost, so many plants and so varied that in straining to identify them he almost missed the turn off to the house.

One branch of the drive led presumably to the servants' quarters in the rear; the other curled in front where a Rolls was parked. Reynolds drew up beside it, climbed out, his own car suddenly dwarfed. And he felt dwarfed too by the building, not so much by its actual size but by its aura of antiquity, although from the exterior it was hard to tell how old it really was, its chimneys, twisting above a slate roof, possibly Elizabethan, its façade added afterwards in the eighteenth century. A flight of shallow steps of indeterminate date led to the front door; tubs of flowers (she seemed overfond of them, he thought) brightened stones grey with age. When the highly polished bell chimed, its peal seemed to echo through vast empty rooms, along vast empty corridors.

But when the door was opened – and, true to expectation, a butler opened it – to his surprise Reynolds found himself inside what must have been the original medieval hall, its wooden beams and oak panelling certainly authentic. A fire smouldered in the wide central hearth, there were even two large dogs, hounds he supposed they should be called, asleep on the floor. Nothing had been spared in this recreation of the past, from the fraying tapestries to the uneven paving stones.

'You approve of my house, Inspector?'

Lady Rowan, he presumed it was Lady Rowan, paused on the stairs, leaning on the carved oak banister of the sixteenth century. She was dressed in some kind of flowing garment, misty grey shot with green; the material floated behind her as she herself seemed to float down the steps. He had the impression of someone tall, slender, with reddish-grey hair wisped in braids and knots like some Florentine statue. He had a glimpse of grey eyes, large, set wide apart. Not a classically beautiful woman, he thought, too tall and thin and commanding for that, yet in her way beautiful. And certainly not your average old busybody, certainly no old hag; if anything she seemed overflowing with energy into what looked like becoming an increasingly vigorous middle age.

'Not what you expected,' she was saying, meaning the house, but from the ironic tone she might have guessed what he had been thinking about her. 'Now come and see my gardens.'

Without waiting for a reply, without even pretending to wait for one, she led the way through doors on one side of the vast fireplace, along a back corridor. Reynolds followed her, confused, off-kilter. It wasn't often he was as wrong as this. Out again into the sun, the blinding light making him blink. And then, as vision cleared and he took stock of where he was: here is the true heart of the manor, he thought as he still followed her along neat paths edged with box, through the famous arched yew hedge, across clipped lawns where fountains played and roses bloomed. But it was by the herb-beds beyond that his fancy was caught, as every visitor's must be, he thought, the intricate plants entwined and interlaced, their fragrant leaves, dew-soaked, stretching towards the sun.

Lady Rowan stopped as if to breathe. 'My favourite place,' she said. Then without preamble, 'The true medieval world. It's not put on, as some think. I feel it in my heart.'

Her sincerity was so apparent he had no fault to find, although her voice had a slightly hysterical timbre, almost dramatic, that he should have found irritating, but didn't.

'And I know no one else with your ability to make sense of the senseless,' she was saying. 'Like this unspeakable crime.

'I warned of it, of course,' she said, and now she did turn melodramatic, threw up her arms as if about to prophesy. 'Two nights ago. This is what will happen, I said, if we don't act fast.'

She gave an exaggerated shudder. 'So who do you think destroyed my handiwork, the sum of all my efforts, my lovely green?'

Reynolds didn't say anything, watched her as she walked up and down, or 'floated' again perhaps was a better word, like some earth goddess, he thought, stooping now and then among the beds to straighten a bent stalk or remove a faded leaf. He thought of his own tattered flowers and his slow, laborious progress. Here's the difference, he thought, a simple man's garden compared with that of a rich woman. She must employ a score of men.

And for a moment a pang not so much of envy but of longing possessed him. He paced beside her, his shadow compact, upright, beside her nebulous one. Only when they came to the end of the last bed did he say, softly for him, 'You didn't bring me here just to talk of damaged flower-boxes.'

She swivelled round, her gaze suddenly penetrating. 'You'd better come inside,' was all she said and, abruptly turning, led the way back. Again he followed. This time she took another route across the lawn, entering the house through a side door that gave on to a smaller room, what could have been called a study except for its completely feminine furnishings from the soft swirls of curtains to the carefully positioned Dresden ornaments. A tray with two cups and a silver pot of coffee was set on a low table. She seated herself before it, a swift swirling motion, and began to pour. He had the oddest feeling that he had passed some test, that she had had the coffee prepared in case he did; that, conversely, if he had failed, he would have been shown the door, and there would have been the end of it.

She didn't say anything for a while, leaned back against the brocaded silk of her chair, her coffee cup in her hand. He noticed that it was shaking slightly. He too leaned back and prepared to wait.

What she said surprised him. 'I've known who you are since you came here. I presume you prefer to live incognito, as is your right. But I've read your books, Inspector, and I know you're the man I want.'

He stamped down the temptation to ask, 'For what?', let her go at her own pace.

'You must understand something,' she went on after a while. 'I've not always been in the circumstances I'm in now. When I married Lord Rowan, then Mr Malcolm

Rowan, he was a much older man, and I was an art student, with a flair for colour and a firm belief that I would be the century's Michelangelo.'

She sounded almost rueful. 'Not much chance,' she said, 'but he made up for that. He was very rich, I was poor. Suddenly I had the means to have whatever I wanted, go where I wanted to go, do what I wanted to do, live where I wanted to live.'

She paused again. 'St Breddaford is very dear to me, the place we finally chose to settle in. A special choice, made from so many possibilities. And the selection itself dependent on one thing alone – the certainty that for the first time in my life, free from all restraints, I could indulge an artistic freedom that I hadn't had since student days.'

Once more she paused as if to collect her thoughts. Strange, Reynolds thought, that in her own home she seems almost hesitant, less forceful than I'd imagined. Perhaps that's the effect of an older, dominant husband. He made a mental note of that.

'I don't know if you can appreciate what I'm trying to explain,' Lady Rowan was continuing. 'It's not granted to many, that perfect freedom. And in this house, these grounds, I was in touch with what I'd always been looking for. Call it history if you like, a rapport that goes beyond mere liking, an attunement, a melding, that unites past and present. It costs money, of course,' she added with a little smile, 'the recreation of the past isn't a simple matter. But there was always plenty of money. And when my husband died I resolved, in my way, to expand beyond the manor grounds to include St Breddaford, retrieving for it the beauty it deserved.

'Of course I know they say I'm wrong,' she added. 'I know they claim common land is just that, land used in

common – I'm not stupid. That doesn't mean they have
the right to turn it into an eyesore with their dogs and
balls. And the manor always had the privilege of closing it
off if it were misused. Myself, I think a proper garden a
better asset than a muddy scrap of grass.'

Rather a high-handed view of medieval history, Reynolds thought, as well as inaccurate. *But I'm not in a position to debate with the lady. Let her speak for herself.*

'And of course I'm not just talking of the flower-boxes,'
she next burst out, 'I'm not that stupid either. Although I
think their destruction is symbolic of the way people think
and act these days. Barbaric, vicious, taking their anger out
on inanimate objects until they find something animate to
destroy instead. I know I'm not exactly popular,' she went
on. 'I know I'm thought vain and silly, too fond of my own
way. But I'm not as insensitive as people like to pretend. I
do have feelings, strange feelings. I've always had them,
ever since I was a child. I know that what I feel, have felt
for a long while, is not imagined.'

She knotted her fingers together, as if willing them to
hold still. 'There's a peace in this place that comes from
balanced harmony,' she said, 'a rightness that belongs to
time. I sense it in the marrow of my bones. But there's also
evil, Inspector Reynolds, old evil, come to life again. And
after that meeting it's been loosed abroad.'

Once he would have passed her remarks off as hysteria,
a change-of-life dementia such as many women suffer
from. Subtly he would have given her assurances, spoken
blandly, the adult equivalent of pats on the head. In his
former profession he'd heard it all before, not much had
escaped him. It was to her credit that he took her claim
seriously.

'Suppose you tell me about it,' he said, as if he had all

the time in the world, as if there was nothing he wanted more than to listen to some crack-pot theory that she seemed determined to impose on him. But it wasn't quite like that either: he'd seen the intelligence behind the chatter, he'd sensed the genuine effect of fear.

At first it came out in fits and starts, how after her husband's death she'd been lonely, had wanted more to do; the manor, which had been her main interest for so long now, having been virtually restored to how she wanted it. He noted that she spoke only of her dead husband, the older Malcolm who had obviously indulged her; presumably there were no offspring, no doted-upon child perhaps to fill a vacuum. He gave a quick look round. No pictures in silver frames, no portraits, nothing of human family interest.

He knotted his brows in effort. Had there been gossip of a child now dead, or had he imagined it? That would fit, he thought, childless women are noted for their self-absorption. It dawned on him that although he knew much, too much, about Lady Rowan's public life, he knew correspondingly little about her private. Like a modern Lady of Shalott, she'd lived apart, locked up here in her ivory tower, only venturing out, in her case, to cause mischief. He glanced at her with added interest. If that was so, he'd a lot to learn just by listening to Lady Rowan speak about herself, let alone waffle about invented dangers.

As if she saw his glance and interpreted it; as if again she guessed his thoughts, she gave a little laugh. 'What does a lonely woman do, you'll ask, to keep herself occupied?' She made a moue. He caught a glimpse, a flash, of what she must have once been when she was young, an art student, on fire to reform the world. 'The beautification of St Breddaford's village green may not seem much to you,' she went on, 'but it was my life-line.'

And so her new objective had been born. Yes, she knew she was obsessive; yes, she knew she had gone at it tooth and nail, she was like that; yes, she knew she had made enemies, was criticized for going too far. That business about the green being common land had caused all sorts of difficulties she hadn't imagined when she'd begun. But if you aren't committed, if you don't push, you won't be successful; you have to be strong. And so again, two nights ago.

The meeting had been of especial importance, concerning as it did the saving of the whole village as it now existed. 'A life-and-death matter.' She used the term deliberately. 'A life-and-death venture I took upon my own shoulders because no one else would.'

The meeting should have been a routine affair, called as usual by the village chairman, one Peter Burns, the village schoolmaster. A complete nitwit, her scathing look implied. The discussion should have been equally minimal, a report of the latest bingo drive and a reading of the minutes. Given the rainy weather, she supposed few would have bothered to attend. It was to avoid that possibility she had taken it upon herself to write to everyone personally, had herself delivered the hand-addressed envelopes, deliberately stirring them into action, goading them into it. 'Someone's got to whip them up,' she said, as if speaking of some lumbering beast of burden.

Most members came. At least those who counted, the more influential ones. *Although you didn't bother to*. She didn't actually say so, but again he felt the reproach.

He thought, 'By influential you mean people *you* can influence! Or frighten into compliance. No wonder you didn't expect open revolt.'

'Do you know, at this very moment, how many empty properties there are in St Breddaford?' she next asked. She addressed Reynolds in what he supposed was the same manner she'd used on her original captive audience. She reached behind the sofa, took out a briefcase, presumably also carefully placed in readiness, emptied it on the table, spilling papers out. 'All over Cornwall villages plastered with "For Sale" signs,' she said. 'All sorts of reasons given for the economic depression. What I blame is greed. If people hadn't been so eager to sell in the first place, if they hadn't demanded and been paid such outrageous prices, our village wouldn't have been swamped by the outsiders who were the only ones who could afford to buy. And then, when prices fell as they were bound to and the outsiders abandoned us in droves, we wouldn't have been left in this dreadful predicament.'

Here she'd paused as if expecting rebuttal, as if she wanted Reynolds to put up counter-arguments. He had none. By and large he agreed with her, although he was sure there were other reasons, more complex ones, contributing to the present economic decline. As if disappointed, she went on, slowly, but without hesitation, 'A half-empty village, a dying village, inhabited by old men and women, that isn't the true St Breddaford. The true St Breddaford's a vital place; for over a thousand years it's thrived. There was a crossing of the river here before the "Doomsday Book". And I for one refuse to be blackmailed by outlaws who want to destroy us, hold us to ransom, rob and pillage. Outlaws who've never done a day's work in their lives, terrorizing us, making us prisoners in our own homes.'

Reynolds was startled; she might have been talking of ninth-century Vikings. She is mad, after all, he thought, quite barmy. Derrymore was right to have let this one ride.

Once more he composed his expression, allowed her to talk on. There must be more to it than this, he thought, there must be some significance. And sure enough she was coming to it.

She didn't mention the 'outlaws' again directly, didn't exactly elucidate on who or what they were, continued to talk of them obliquely. Reynolds thought at first she was speaking of some vague danger she didn't really want to identify, then decided finally she must be talking of squatters, those homeless people (more than usual these days) who had been known to force their way into empty houses and stay there under the protection of some old law that they claimed gave them this right. But whatever she meant, apparently it was fear which had caused her to call the meeting. And having put the same fear, and the thought of all those empty properties, those falling prices, into her audience's heads, she had been gratified that everyone had responded, at first, in the way she meant.

Like a hound baiting its quarry (her choice of phrase), she harried the audience to give tongue: who had an empty house next door, who an abandoned property repossessed by the mortgage companies; how disgraceful it was for people who paid cash on the dot, who never asked for credit. And, more to the point, who had been burgled recently, who had had their house broken into, whose car had been stolen, whose garden defiled, as Miss Polrose, the elderly postmistress, had primly put it.

'I let them talk and when they were done I had them eating from my hand,' Lady Rowan was saying. She spoke calmly, as if there could be no other possible conclusion. 'When they were ripe to listen, I gave them my proposal. I'd had it prepared before and brought it to the meeting for them to sign. And when that's done, I told them, there'll be no more danger from empty houses, no more mortgage companies. We'll all be safe.'

She pulled out a sheaf of papers clipped together, gave them to Reynolds, settled back as if all was now explained. With growing astonishment Reynolds read what she apparently had thought fit to introduce. It was an extraordinary document, a signed agreement that all were to adhere to, protecting St Breddaford from the danger of squatters taking over empty properties. He'd been right at least about the squatters, then. But that was only the beginning. Worse was to come.

Her main proposal dealt with the closing of the village. All roads leading to it were to be barricaded at her expense so no one could pass in or out without proof of identity or specific purpose. To ensure which, private guards were to be hired, also at her expense, these to be stationed in strategic towers, as she called them, built in medieval manner where each road entered St Breddaford. That the effect would turn the village into a virtually walled enclosure, such as perhaps it once had been, was something she seemed to take for granted, even welcomed as another return to the past – to say nothing of creating a select ghetto, from which all 'undesirables' were to be barred.

Feeling his working-class hackles rise, John opened his mouth to protest, shut it, read on. The last clause was even more extraordinary. 'And as a final deterrent, no houses to be sold or rented except by common consent, a screening committee for this purpose to be chosen from all legitimate inhabitants.'

Madness, he thought again. He folded the papers up, handed them back. Resisting a temptation to ask if she'd had legal advice on how she could enforce such rules on public roads and private dwelling places, 'And what was the reaction?' he asked in a non-committal voice.

Somewhat acidly she told him that all in all it had been favourable, as she had intended. Except in three instances. And these were the ones she wanted to bring to his attention. For three members had spoken without rhyme or reason, had shown such a selfish disregard for the common good, had caused what she called such a 'slanging match' (the expression Derrymore presumably had picked up from her), that suddenly all her work to bring the meeting together and hold it in line, all her preparatory efforts, were destroyed in an instant. Instead, old arguments were rehashed as people talked out of turn, people who should have had the sense if not the grace to remain quiet. There were even references to the local farmer who had sold off his fields for a housing estate, an old wound whose reopening had caused even more splintering among what should have been her 'devoted adherents', devoted, Reynolds thought ironically, in that she had expected them to be cowed into agreement, more and more like some medieval lord.

She rounded on Reynolds then, sitting straight up, no longer a dryad of the woods, more like an avenging angel, John thought, her face and eyes cold, her chin determined. Did he know what it was like to have a life's work ruined? Did he know how it felt to be forced to listen to idiots? Of course after that she couldn't get anyone to sign her petition; of course no one paid any attention to her warnings; she'd have to start the whole process up again, work even harder to bring them to order and hold them firm . . .

Trying to look sympathetic, Reynolds brought her back to the three rebels she had originally mentioned.

Well, she said, calming down, first there was old Mrs Penlore, did he remember her? Reynolds nodded. Dressed always in widow's weeds, Mrs Penlore was a village relic; with her vacant eyes and her round red cheeks more like a china doll, in her own way a memento from the past. But also, as Lady Rowan now hastened to make clear, a tenant cottager, living in a cottage that belonged to Rowan Manor, beholden in fact to Lady Rowan, and lacking even the decency to show gratitude.

'I don't agree,' Mrs Penlore had piped up. 'I've no fault to find with things as they are, let sleeping dogs lie.'

Why she thought she had the right to say anything, why anything she said should be listened to, she had no idea. But then, Lady Rowan added, rather pettishly, Widow Penlore was known to be somewhat addled; had a reputation in the village for being 'odd'; no doubt in time she could be brought to see the sense of Lady Rowan's proposal, if she had any sense left, that is – undemocratic suggestions in which Lady Rowan appeared to find nothing incongruous, not even blinking when Reynolds himself muttered the word 'coercion'. What bothered Lady Rowan most was that Mrs Penlore had dared resist.

Moreover, since she lived on her own, close to the moors, where she was forever causing trouble, her garden a rubbish heap and her house not much better, she should have been especially grateful for any additional protection. But before the meeting ended she'd again interrupted, saying she liked newcomers in the region, they'd always been that nice to her, she'd no cause for complaint.

Lady Rowan's patience had snapped. 'Trot on home,' Lady Rowan had barked, oblivious to the whispers of sympathy. 'See how you like it when you're attacked by ruffians, see if we care when you're found dead in your bed' –

an expression she now regretted using.

The thought that this elderly villager might commit murder, or even take a hatchet to smash a tub of flowers, was ludicrous, Reynolds thought, trying not to smile. But as a possible victim of attack, that was a different possibility. His smile faded. Although why anyone would kill her, or who might do so, he couldn't imagine, except presumably Lady Rowan herself. And Lady Rowan's offering of herself as the only suspect was equally unlikely.

The second rebel was a different matter, and posed a more serious threat. 'You ought to know him,' Lady Rowan said, 'you're somewhat alike.' An unexpected smile of great brilliance took away the sting to her remark, for except for a mutual interest in literature and art Reynolds couldn't see he and Frank Mathews had much in common. Frank Mathews was a painter (although to be honest no one had ever seen his work), an eccentric painter who thrived on eccentricity more than art. A large-boned man, red-haired, red-bearded, his bad temper was given as the excuse for his keeping to himself. He lived alone in a big house somewhere on the moors close to Bolventor, seldom appeared in the village and rarely spoke to anyone, was spotted every so often on his ancient bicycle, pedalling away to Bodmin, there to play badminton, a game to which he was passionately addicted; in short he was a genuine recluse, the least likely candidate to attend any meeting, let alone have any views to express.

To everyone's amazement he had stood up, positively frothing under his beard, his blue eyes under their thick eyebrows sparkling. 'I for one won't sign any damn petition,' he shouted, 'not to prevent people doing what they like with their own land. And if I had my way, all those who've lost their homes should be invited to take shelter in St Breddaford, or at least be allowed to camp here on the village green as gypsies used to do' – a heresy that had brought condemnation from virtually everyone.

'Then look out,' he'd bellowed above the clamour, 'put your own interests first, cling to self-preservation, you deserve what you get. If that old fool there has her way we'll not only be a laughing stock, we'll be first in line for annihilation. When those poor unfortunates revolt, that is, when those who've been caught by capitalist manipulations rise up against their oppressors. And good luck to 'em.'

'A typical socialist outburst,' Lady Rowan now added to Reynolds, apparently not in the least offended by the insults, only by the unexpectedness of the attack. 'Pitiful. Doesn't know the difference between self-interest and community living. If anyone's a fool he is. A regular old woman. Doesn't understand that if you give an inch they take a mile. And seeing how and where he lives, he's especially vulnerable.'

A maverick then, Frank Mathews, an eccentric. Capable of outbursts of rage, as many people who had had the misfortune to run foul of him would testify, not likely to fit the role of victim. But except for the lady herself, not known to have real enemies. As for murdering, well, a man can't be suspected of murder just because he's eccentric. Reynolds sighed.

The third member of the opposition was as unexpected as the other two: Peter Burns, the neglected chairman, the little village schoolteacher whose meekness was proverbial. Lady Rowan admitted she hadn't expected attack from him either, and had been taken aback by the accuracy of his criticisms.

'I'm a renter here,' Peter Burns had cried, apparently

startling even himself with his outburst. 'I rent a house in that new estate you've all been on about, even though it netted some of you thousands and you shouldn't have reason to mind.'

His voice had surprised her too, firmer than she'd ever heard it, underlined with determination. 'I know I'm an outsider,' he'd gone on, 'someone you've never liked, but I'm not talking about that. My wife and I make our home here in St Breddaford, we're happy here. I work for my living. I pay my rent on time. I shan't agree to a petition that says I have to have permission to rent from some landlord who's no fault to find with me. And if I have to, why, I'll turn squatter myself before I agree to so monstrous a suggestion, and you can have the pleasure of driving me out because I won't go readily.'

And, slamming down his minutes which he'd had no chance of reading, he had stumped off with more dignity – again she admitted it – than she'd thought him capable of. Although all that talk about his wife was sentimental twaddle. A nasty little piece the wife, nouveau riche and vulgar. If there were money to pay the rent, it was Marilyn Burns', not his. Riding on the moors at all hours on a horse she insisted on keeping behind the silly little house, one of the new monstrosities in Farmer Grady's fields; up to no good, they said; not as fond of her husband as he was of her – here a slightly spiteful tone marked Lady Rowan's detached presentation.

She paused as if aware of it, again gave her brilliant smile, allowing Reynolds time to digest what she had told him while packing away her papers, as neatly and precisely as she'd probably done to hide her own discomfort at the end of the meeting. After which, she now explained, the rest of the villagers, confused and angry, had streamed out into the rain and storm, no longer unified as she had hoped, but once more split into many factions.

Most had gone their separate ways on foot. Sou'wester hat firmly pulled down over his ears, Frank Mathews had ridden off on his bike, an upright old Raleigh from a *Wizard of Oz* era, although Reynolds knew he was rumoured to be rich as sin and could have afforded a hundred cars if he'd wanted them. She herself, as a sign of the common cause, had dismissed the Rolls and walked part of the way home too, at least to the outskirts of the village where her chauffeur had waited, while Mrs Penlore, equally stubbornly, had refused a lift and had followed Peter Burns on foot up the hill to her cottage some two miles beyond.

'And there you have it,' Lady Rowan finally concluded. 'Plenty of people abroad last night, all perfectly capable of violence, and at least three who had reason to commit it. And two living alone, either of them possibly open to murderers. But equally capable, with the other, of ruining my village green.'

Reynolds found he had nothing to say. I'm an outsider too, he wanted to tell her, I'm one of those people you want to exclude from St Breddaford, as if we're contaminating its purity. But after all, you're not from an old Cornish family either, although you act as if you are. Perhaps you don't really belong any more than we do, and that's why you put up such a show pretending you do.

He didn't say any of these things. Even if most of the people she'd mentioned were way off-mark, she had just furnished him with a possible list of names, a list where before he had none. For an outsider in the real sense of the professional world, it wasn't much to start with, but it was at least something.

But still that sense remained, although once more he didn't say so, that she was hiding something, that there was some piece of the puzzle she deliberately hadn't given him.

As if she heard his thoughts, as if he had almost asked her what it was, she suddenly leaned forward confessionally and put her hand upon his arm. The hand was long and white, an artist's hand, the nails rounded, the palms soft despite all her gardening. Her eyes, large and intelligent, grew even wider, and her voice became more intent. 'You understand it's me they're really after,' she whispered. 'If someone's murdered, it was by mistake. I stirred them up; it's me they hate.'

For a moment Reynolds was embarrassed. Paranoia always had that effect on him. But he was also startled. She must be a witch, he thought; she seems to know what I'm thinking before I actually think it. And I'm beginning to sound like her – madness, the lot of it. Then, more rationally: damn it, if that's a sop to keep me quiet she can surely do better than that.

Against his will, but aware he must mention it, he said abruptly, 'Chief Inspector Clemow's in charge. Have you spoken to him yet?'

She must have sensed his distaste. At once she was on the defensive. 'Why should I speak to anyone?' she said. 'Except Derrymore, that is,' as if poor Derrymore didn't count, Reynolds thought, half amused that at least in this he had assessed her correctly.

He made no comment. For a moment the thought had come into his head that Chief Inspector Clemow might be more than interested, and he found the idea strangely disturbing. Reason would dictate the opposite, of course, but Clemow could play the ladies' man when it suited him, as he himself knew only too well, to his cost. Lady Rowan's wealth and background – even, Reynolds thought somewhat distractedly, her looks – might soon have Clemow dangling. Clemow can be servile enough if he thinks people important or if he wants something from them. He forced the thought aside. For the first time it occurred to him that if Lady Rowan assumed he himself wasn't easily impressed in the same way, here was really clever flattery.

He put that thought aside as well. Notwithstanding all her nuances, her vague improbabilities, there still might be some glimmer of truth, some ... Stop, he told himself, you're not really investigating anything here. Not yet, at any rate.

'I think you should come forward,' he said, advising her, although she hadn't asked for advice. 'You should tell what you remember, just as you've told me.'

He rose to go. 'It's too important not to tell,' he said, more insistent now when she didn't say anything. 'There won't be any blame attached – how could there be? You weren't to know what the meeting might lead to. If in fact it has. But it may be vital,' he added, as a final sop to her pride. And felt himself completely vindicated when she again declined. Although the decline could have come in a manner more pleasing to himself.

Lady Rowan drew herself up. Her voice changed, became frosty. He imagined she spoke to her chauffeur in this way. 'I've chosen you to tell what I know. Deliberately. I admire your perception. It's evident in everything you write, and I see it now in person, written on your face. So it's up to you to do what you think fit. I shan't do anything. I wipe my hands of it.'

Which is exactly why she's had me there, Reynolds

thought, as he drove away, flattered me in the only way I really care about. Serve me right. And so now I'm hooked for good, and Clemow can bugger off for all I care. If she isn't imagining it all, of course.

Despite his original motives, however personal, even despite his certainty that Lady Rowan had allowed her obsessions to get the better of her, his original judgement still held, that here was a serious woman, who under the frills and trappings of dramatics, was afraid of something real.

Hearing the slam of the car door, and the start of the engine, Lady Rowan relaxed, lay back and closed her eyes. The trembling of her hands suddenly stopped; she held them loosely clasped in her lap, almost as if she were praying. Behind her in the little study which her husband had decorated for her use, sun motes danced against the tall windows, casting shadows on the oak panelling. A sense of calm flowed over her, as if she were willing it to come, a sense of peace whose healing power drove away the fear.

Chapter 4

Unbeknownst to Lady Rowan, or indeed to anyone in St Breddaford, another meeting had taken place on the same evening as her own. It had been held earlier on the moors, by the very people she most disliked, Hal's band, a group who called themselves the New Age Travellers.

Hal wasn't his real name: Meg'd given it him. 'Hal, Prince of Thieves,' she'd said, grinning up at him in the insolent way he liked. 'Get on,' he'd said, but secretly he'd been pleased. Better than the name he'd been stuck with at birth, he'd thought: Joe Bender from Southgate, what's to a name like that?

Her name wasn't Meg, either: it was the name she gave herself. A kind of joke, she'd told him: Meg Merilees, from an old poem, whatever that meant. But then, she was better educated than the rest of them, came from a different class and, sometimes, in spite of her efforts to hide the differences, her past peeped out. Like her feet, he thought.

Her feet were the first things about her that he'd noticed. He couldn't help glancing at them now, thin, delicate, lady's feet, incongruously stuck out under her bedraggled skirts. They were bare. He'd never seen her wearing shoes, although he would have got her some.

'Mortification of the flesh,' she called it, another thing he didn't understand.

She was a small, fragile-looking woman – girl then, she was very young – and, like Lady Rowan, to Hal's dismay, she had taken charge. 'Bloody awful,' she was saying, meaning the weather, her genteel accent contrasting with her language. She made an obscene gesture. 'Stay out in this all summer, if you're bloody stupid. Me, I say, why wait?' Sometimes her language was as coarse as his, Hal thought. He knew without her saying so that vulgarity wasn't natural to her, it was another thing put on to hide her past.

She was seated inside the walls of the old sheep-cote, out of the worst of the wind and wet, her baby asleep on her lap. Wrapped in a piece of sacking she sat close to the fire made from bits of a farm gate, her face turned greedily towards the heat. What she was referring to was their choice of winter quarters; although he'd advised staying where they were for the moment, she wanted to move now, at once, tomorrow. And although he'd asked, well, warned her, to keep quiet, she had openly challenged him.

True, outside the walls the wind was howling like in winter, Hal thought, rattling in gun-shots along the galvanize he'd used for roofing. True, rain dashed in bucketfuls against the walls, threatening the fire. Inside the cote they were dry and warm enough not to grumble, even if all round them the sodden ground was ankle-deep in mud and festering rubbish.

Sparks from the flames flared into the air, then faded out like fireworks; the comforting smell of baking potatoes meant later they'd eat well for once. The camp itself, on the edge of an outlying farm abutting the moors, was perfect for their purposes – away from any road and nicely secluded, the van parked across the only track to keep intruders off.

He'd even made the camp as comfortable as he knew how, to please her. Today, in the storm, he'd brought back the gate, tied to the top of his van, or rather all that was left of the gate after he'd crashed through it to get into the potato field. He hadn't said, 'This will keep you warm,' but that's what he'd meant as he'd hacked the bars apart, then dragged up the sheeting. She hadn't noticed. She should have noticed all his efforts, not started on at him as soon as he'd settled down for the night.

He stared at her. As leader of the Travellers he had the right to stare where and how he liked. She was his woman, he had picked her, they made a pair. Even now when she was so bent on crossing him, her vivacity still attracted him; her thin, eager features, her delicate skin, as always fascinated him. Her skin, for example: he'd never known any so white. Despite her liking for the sun it never darkened or grew rough like other girls', and her hair, long and dark, was always clean. How did she keep it washed, and where, Hal wondered. It was one of the many questions he'd never liked to ask but now felt more and more like asking. Except he knew she'd never tell unless she wanted to – sometimes she was secretive, was Meg. At other times she talked, nonstop, a great outpouring of talk, most of it over his head, yet in its way as fascinating.

She was a creature of extremes, he thought, of opposites. Her liking for sun, for example, it was more than liking, it was a craving, almost as if she were one of those – what did they call them? – Druids, up on Salisbury Plain, worshipping at Stonehenge. Even her likes and dislikes made him uneasy. He knew too by now how clever she was. Too clever by half, he thought, although most

times she hid it just as cleverly. It made him doubly wary
when she argued, never sure what she really meant, never
sure he could answer her if he did. Now, by forcing him to
speak, she was publicly pitting her will against his.

Although the others of the group were pretending not
to listen, they were listening sure enough. These days she
was always challenging him, Hal thought. At first it'd been
in private, a personal contest (or only personal to me, he
searched for words, she's never even acknowledged there
is a struggle, as if it has no consequence. Or as if, here
some emotion stirred, I'm of no importance. As if for
all that self-mortification she's on about, she thinks she
is superior).

'Hold on a moment,' he said, his smile wolfish; he didn't
feel like smiling, not when she baited him. 'It's not that
simple. It's something we should all talk about.'

He turned to his followers, sure of them at least, confident of them. They'd do what he said. He counted arms
and legs, protruding from the huddle of blankets and old
clothing with which they covered themselves, bedded
down like one of those rabbit burrows they dug up for fun.
They were all there, except Ted, and Ted didn't matter.
Ted was a mistake he shouldn't have allowed, and only
had because it had amused Meg.

He leaned his pigtailed head back against the wall and
looked round him nonchalantly. He felt the others looking
back and knew he must be careful. Usually he avoided
confrontation, but now, instinctively, he sensed they'd
despise him if he backed down. 'Nothing in the weather to
be frightened of,' he told them, making fun of her because
she was weak and a woman. 'We'll not melt.' He laughed.
Another woman'd told him once he had a pleasant laugh.
He'd never had trouble with other women. 'Weather isn't

everything,' he said, 'good sense is.'

By good sense he meant team spirit, the loyalty he'd worked so hard to bring about, not expecting then that the one who would try to break it would be Meg herself, not dreaming that she'd not be satisfied ... Although she chose this place, he thought, resentfully, remembering how she'd wheedled him to come here when they'd had to move before, when they were driven out before. But then they had been mates, been bound. It was only when she'd got her way and persuaded him to camp where she wanted that she'd changed, become restless, always wanting to be off on her own, sometimes seeming to brim with excitement, sometimes sunk in depression.

He had always prided himself on fair-mindedness. And he'd been fair with her. He knew enough about women to know that having a baby sometimes changed them. And, 'We work together,' he now told his followers. 'We're a community, see,' a word she'd taught him. 'We wait. Because if we wait we get a better deal. Then, when we go, we go at the right time, and we go together. One for all and all for one.'

He glared around him. 'Like the Cornish,' he added, when they didn't smile and nod agreement as they usually did. 'Their theme song, the one they sing at every bleeding rugger match.'

'The time and place've got to be right.' Once more he found himself explaining. 'No call to rush. We've the summer all before us. Who wants to live cooped up while we've got this?'

His wave went beyond the immediate storm and rain, beyond the immediate litter and mud, out to encompass the surrounding moors. Something in him, too deep for words, was moved by the space and openness; there wasn't much space where he'd come from. As for the mess: we'll clean it up tomorrow, he told himself, as he always did.

Satisfied his explanation would keep them quiet, he looked down at Meg. She was crooning to the child now, rocking it back and forth as if she hadn't heard. 'And that means you too,' he said, more softly, only half in fun. 'No more wandering off on your own, like some bloody queen.'

And, to the others, louder, confidentially, 'This storm's westerly, it won't last.'

'You've said that every day so far in June.'

This last was spoken in a whine, by another man, a short, balding fellow with eyes that should have been bright blue if they hadn't been watery with cold. He coughed to make his point. 'Rain, rain, rain, like a water-spout. So I agrees with Meg.'

He hawked and spat on the fire so that it sizzled. 'Found a place the other day, near the beach, me and Eileen,' he said in an offhand sort of way, looking sideways, slyly. 'The doctor said salt air was good for lungs.'

He didn't add, 'Me and Eileen want to go off on our own,' but Hal could sense it unspoken.

Glad to have a focus for his repressed anger, glad to turn attention away from Meg, 'Trust Merl to think only of hisself,' Hal was sarcastic. 'Trust Merl and Eileen to make it on their own. Well, without the rest of us it won't work.'

Off on his own hobby-horse, he elaborated. 'Go it too soon, go it alone, you'll fail. They'll scent you out, winkle you out like cockles from their bleeding shells. But stick together, it'll be different, we'll be too many for them. Needs organization, see.'

By 'they' and 'them' he meant the police. And by 'organization' (another of her words) he meant, 'You need me to do the organizing.'

He stretched his leather-encased legs, again imitating nonchalance. 'When the time is right, make our decision; when the place is right, move together. Then each gets his own pad, legal, tidy, no fault to that.'

For a moment he thought he had subdued them. Then he saw how Meg had flung her head back, her hair bunched at the nape of her long and swan-curved neck. Her teeth gleamed in the firelight. Suddenly he was afraid. He knew too well how she could make a man look foolish if she wanted to.

'Community.' Again she was baiting him. 'Community is it, all together, one and all. Let's get our terms right, look who's giving orders like a bloody general.'

She was speaking louder now, mimicking him. 'The right time and place, all together, eh, one and all – but only when Hal himself says so. Wait for this, says Hal, wait for that, says Hal, wait for the coppers to drive us out as they did at Taunton, as if we're bleeding cattle. And in the end, even if it's legal, what do we end up with? Some cramped slum, some filthy hovel that's not worth sixpence. I tell you, I for one am sick of it.'

She cocked her head, openly defying him. 'There're plenty of places in St Breddaford this very moment,' she said, 'empty and ready. Big places, room for all. Oh, I don't deny the shit will fly, but what of it? Once we're in, we're in.'

And when he didn't answer, 'Or is it' – and here her eyes grew narrow, she pursed her lips again, whispering mockingly in his ear – 'is it that you have some other reason for waiting, one we don't know about?'

As if, Hal thought, she sensed the wad of bank-notes in his back pocket, as if she almost smelled the bribe.

Her earlier words had caught everyone's notice as she meant. They were all sitting up, paying attention, whispering. She'll have them on the run, Hal thought, conscious of a crisis. He hesitated. He knew she'd thrown down the gauntlet and, had she been a man, he'd have known how to knock her flat. But not how to handle her, her wild wilfulness.

The moment of decision passed, was gone. 'All right,' he said, with his wolfish grin, 'tell us what you have in mind' – calling her bluff, letting her make a fool of herself.

But it was she who called his bluff instead. For when she had told them, when she had spelled out exactly where and how, when she'd left them all struck dumb with the audacity of her plan – 'And now,' she said, 'that's settled, I'll be off to leave the child.'

She stood up with one quick movement, throwing a waterproof cape over her head, covering herself and the baby. 'I'm not afraid of melting either. It's the child I'm thinking of.'

Now she'd got her way she was her old self, smiling to take the hurt out of her words, her wide-mouthed smile that disarmed him. 'I'll leave her where I always do, with friends, then I'll come back. I always do come back. I'm not Bad Ted.'

She smiled a last time. 'That's why everything must be settled now,' she repeated, 'so tomorrow, first thing, we get moving, see.'

Supremely confident, knowing the seed of rebellion well sown, she leaned over him, her long hair close to his pigtailed head. 'But not too early, so we can cuddle first.'

Again her voice was a whisper, for the first time in weeks inviting him, seductive. In spite of himself he felt the lure of it, the promise.

And then, before he could jump up to stop her, before he had the sense to think of it, she was off, openly ignoring him and his orders. He heard her moving through the wet bushes, singing as she went. 'One for all and all for one,' mocking him to the last, defying him to follow.

The others were still watching. Too proud to show resentment, he merely shrugged, stretched out his long legs as if he hadn't a care in the world. There are other women, he was thinking, anger growing, she's not the only one. He could sense the promise, feel the excitement, almost smell it, like scent on her skin. He knew, despite his anger, that there was no other woman for him.

Afterwards, lying sleepless in the dark as the rain and wind abated, he'd puzzled at the unfairness of it. He'd never had to worry like this with other women, although he'd always been easy-going. 'Soft,' his mates called it, but that was the way he was made. The sensation of being bested by a woman was one he'd never had before. And where she went on her own, where she left the child when the weather was wet or cold (or, for that matter, when she wanted to have time off, as she called it, as if he were some sort of burden), she never told him that. Never mentioned former friends, former aquaintances, former encounters; never explained what she had been doing here, never really told him why she'd wanted to come back.

For it was soon obvious that she'd been here before, was familiar with the region to the point of resenting anyone else's knowledge. That's why she kept on at Old Ted, he thought, suddenly aware. She didn't need to worm his hiding places out, she was just testing to see how much he knew. Good job I kept quiet that I'd been here myself. She'd not have accepted that. He hadn't minded in the beginning, he'd been touched, as if she were a child showing off. He'd almost been proud of her stories of the moors in the old days, and her way of retelling them had kept them all amused during this long wet month. But now he sensed there was more to it than that. Her restlessness, for example, he couldn't put a name to it either, like some goad pricking at her. Or excitement, like an undercurrent, like a fever running beneath the skin. Even loving no longer satisfied her – her offer tonight was the first in weeks.

You couldn't blame her for thinking of the child, Hal told himself, turning to lie on his back. She certainly fussed over it. Look at the way she kept it dressed, look how she kept it washed and fed, nothing too much trouble. He didn't like it when she put the child first.

For one thing, although he tolerated it, it wasn't his. He didn't even know who the father was. And she didn't either, at least that's what she said; she wouldn't speak of it; it was another of those things she kept closed away and secret. It hadn't been so in the early days, when he'd seen her first, then she had wanted him – but then, he now told himself, she'd needed him, she hadn't had a choice.

They'd met in a small market town in Somerset, one March morning. She'd been sitting on a bridge, her stomach swollen to twice its size, her feet stretched out so arrogantly that passers-by almost tripped over them. She hadn't looked up when he'd stopped, his own legs straddling hers, but when she did he was startled by her expression, at the same time so aggressive and so defenceless he could have cried.

'Fuck off,' she said, the words doubly obscene because of the accent she spoke them in. 'Go on, fuck off and leave me alone.'

And when he'd refused to move, when he wouldn't go, 'Just like a man,' she'd sneered in a voice jerky with pain, 'knows how to fuck a woman but not its consequence.

Never seen a pregnant woman before, I suppose; just come to gawk. Well stay and gawk for all I care, you'll find plenty to keep you amused.'

For some reason he couldn't explain to himself, he'd chosen to help her, deliberately chosen. He couldn't explain then and he couldn't now what the attraction had been; he wasn't good at explaining, that wasn't his way. He could only feel it. And he'd thought she had too. He'd taken her to hospital, made damn sure they looked after her, brought her out after the baby was born, brought her back to his van. She'd had to rely on him then, she'd had to be grateful.

Suddenly her smile, the scent of her, was a mockery. I've felt you tense beside me, he wanted to shout, stiff as a board you lie, as if you can't bear to have me touch you. He had never said it, he wouldn't dare, he couldn't bear to lose her.

Yet he was the leader, the prince; that should mean something. Again anger stirred. If she's playing fast and loose with me, he thought savagely, if she thinks she can make a fool of me . . . I'll kill her first.

While Reynolds visited Lady Rowan, Sam Trewithin, the estate agent, was sitting in his inner office, sorting properties for sale, thumbing them through like a pack of cards and throwing rejects to the floor. When a commotion outside the door disturbed him – not unusual as the main office faced the green – for a moment he was tempted to join in. Had he been the old Sammy, the office boy with Drew and Pearce, he'd have been outside in a flash, and been welcome. Instead, pretending to arrange photographs in the window (many labelled ominously with words like 'Rock Bottom Offer', or 'Reduced'), he pulled open the purple painted shutters and prepared to eavesdrop.

People were standing outside on the pavement, talking of the murder, how shocked they were. After their reticence of the previous day they seemed to need to come together, to make contact with other living people as if to strengthen their own vulnerability and reconfirm their own sense of being alive. What shocked them was not the murder itself but the unknown victim. The lack of identity grieved them most, as if they had been cheated, as if they had no one to mourn.

Their voices droned on, buzzing like flies trapped on hot glass. Sam caught the words 'Clemow' and 'Incident Room' followed by the name of Hanscastle Farm. He started, dropped a photograph.

Of all the bad luck, he thought, feeling sick. Of all the places on the moor, bloody empty acres of it, miles of it! Head spinning, he bent to retrieve the photograph. And even he himself would never have thought of it, had forgotten it, until those stupid twits of clients put it into his head last year. And then only after he'd shown them everything else, a hundred places at least – simply because they'd insisted.

Clumsily he eased himself back inside the room, and for a moment stood still to stop the trembling. And a complete waste of time, anyhow: a nagging wife and a husband who complained nonstop about cost. Cost, for God's sake, when a year before they'd have been lucky to get anything for twice as much, even if they could have held the sellers to the price, that is. Let them hear the name Hanscastle now, he thought, won't they have something to twitter about? Silly cows. I wished I'd pushed them in while I had the chance.

But once having gone there, what had induced him to return? What madness had persuaded him back as if he were some sort of Heathcliff, reliving *Wuthering Heights*? I'm the fool, he thought even more angrily, and haven't I paid for it?

He picked up his jacket, slung his coat, Italian-style, over his shoulders, and went out, slamming the door. No one turned to look. No one said, 'Hello there, Sam,' or 'What do 'ee think then, boy?' as they once would have done. He was forced to ask, too loudly, and listen to replies that came too hesitatingly slowly. It was the people who didn't answer, the ones at the back who turned away, that he didn't like.

He smiled in the affable way he'd learned, got into his car (new, a sports Jag, red, his mother would have turned in her grave), and drove off fast, too fast. 'Come the good times,' he was thinking, as by instinct he headed up the road towards the open moors, 'come the boom time, didn't you make a fuss of me, invite me into your homes, let me rub shoulders with important folk who wouldn't have looked twice when I was only the local chap with the local firm?'

He slowed to take the cattle grid whose iron bars made a barrier across the tarmac, speeded up as now the narrow road climbed and on either side the unfenced land began to fall away into heather-covered folds. 'Come the recession,' he was thinking even more savagely, 'come the fall, doesn't your true hatred show?'

He drove fast but accurately, following a well-known route. Don't think, he told himself, concentrate. Shut out all that's bad, you've become an expert at what they call compartmentalizing. Remember how you, Sammy Trewithin, tagged a nonentity all your life, learned to talk your way into success, persuading villagers into selling the unsaleable, and buyers into buying the unbuyable? Remember how from the beginning you took risks when Drew and Pearce held back; it was you, not them, who recognized the newcomers' need for luxuries that the local greengrocer and post office shop couldn't satisfy; you who found the perfect spot for the new delicatessen, the new wine bar, the new hair-cuttery, His and Hers, Unisex. And in doing so eventually bought out Drew and Pearce for a mere pittance to start your own agency, making yourself a fortune along the way – now scarcely worth the paper it's written on.

How had it happened so fast, he thought bitterly, the good times, the hail-fellow-well-met camaraderie of the men, the come-hitherness of the women, the easy money flowing like water. Then, within months, all gone, the countryside stripped bare as if a swarm of locusts had settled and then moved on, leaving disaster in their wake.

But not disaster for him, he thought. He had a plan. Didn't he always have plans? This one, however, had to work, his trump card . . . The roughness of the road brought him back to reality. Almost startled, he jerked on the brakes and looked about him. To his right, he caught a distant glint of blue where the sea showed through a gap between the hills, to his left the rocky peak of Bolventor crested against the sky. Ahead of him the road petered off in a circle of grass, what he thought of as a cul-de-sac, beyond which the familiar path wound up through the gorse. And if he had a plan, if he were on the way up again, he thought as he twisted in his seat to back the car, if he was so smart, what in hell was he doing here when he'd sworn to himself it was finished with, when he'd passed the worst moments of his life up here and been lucky to get away intact? Drive off, he told himself, and don't come back. All will be well. Unbidden, the memory of what had happened here last night, the horror of it, rose up to confront him with its mockery.

Chapter 5

Even if she had exaggerated Lady Rowan had served a purpose. She'd given Reynolds a list of names. The obvious leads, like Ted the Tramp and Bestwick, could presumably be left to Clemow and the authorities – that'd be about their speed – but the others, the ones she'd mentioned, Reynolds could visit as he had done her, in an unofficial way, acting only for himself, spurred on by his own self-interest which he found, even in the hard light of reality, more and more compelling. But something else now had also become involved, something he'd almost forgotten – his own professional pride: that too led him on. Once having sensed the lady of the manor had not been open with him, that there were things that she'd hidden, his obtuseness bothered him. And he'd already confessed to curiosity!

His first task therefore, after lunch (a sandwich and a flask of tea in the car), was to find Mrs Penlore's cottage. Widow Penlore, the village's name for her, lived at what she herself would have called a 'fair piece' from St Bredda-ford, as far away from Rowan Court as possible, yet in as old a place. Her house, though, was tumbledown and primitive. Secretive, Reynolds thought, tucked up a side lane where there's just space to squeeze it in, at the end of a narrow track, so overgrown as to daunt most visitors. Here's real antiquity, he thought as he forced his way through a nettle patch. For, although the track was almost buried, underneath it was paved with boulders from the moors, possibly laid centuries ago and rounded with use. On both sides it was surrounded by true Cornish hedges, five foot wide, stone-made, dirt-filled, above which beech trees tunnelled in profusion. Ferns and flowering grasses cascaded between the stones; the sun slanted through the leaves in golden bars; there was the wild rich smell of mould, of rampant grass, of growing things. He had the sudden impression of an anachronistic world cut off from the modern one.

The cottage stood on its own tract of land. Originally there must have been a row of similar small cottages, built for miners perhaps, now knocked into one. Mrs Penlore therefore lived in a house that was surprisingly large, one room wide but four houses long. Granite built, thatch-roofed, vine-covered, it was as picturesque as any cottage in a Beautiful Britain contest. And more genuine than Lady Rowan's recreations, he thought, as he paused to take in its decrepit charm. I'm surprised Lady Rowan hasn't tried to turn the widow out. Or perhaps she has, and failed – there'd be reason for manorial hauteur on one hand and rebellion on the other!

The garden gate was shut but the front door was open. A litter of leaves had collected on the threshold and, as he came towards them, they fluttered. For a moment his heart turned over. Who these days left front doors wide to the world unless they were too careless to shut them? Or were too dead to worry? Hurrying now he went towards the door, called Mrs Penlore's name, softly at first, then louder, peering into a dimness where a jumble of worm-eaten furniture, cracked knick-knacks and tarnished brass meshed in jangled confusion. About to set a cautious foot inside, he was immeasurably relieved to hear a voice in the back garden, presumably the widow's.

As he picked his way past water-butts, stray pipes, up-tipped flower-pots, odd wheels, he saw the truth of Lady Rowan's comment – a rubbish dump. But when he had negotiated passage through a last tangle of lemon-scented bushes, he found Mrs Penlore alone. She was seated on an upturned box in the centre of a small courtyard, and was apparently talking to a tabby cat.

The object of Mrs Penlore's admonishment, a bored look on its face, was curled on a discarded mangle. A bowl of milk, the cause of the dispute, lay upside down, the milk tipped out; under an old ash tree a dog snored lightly in the shade and, on hearing Reynolds, opened a sleepy eye briefly, then slept on. The scent of lilies, white, pollen-covered, was suddenly overpowering – as bucolic a scene, Reynolds thought, trying to introduce himself, as any painted by Constable.

Close up, Mrs Penlore was not quite what he expected either. Ageless rather than old, with her grey hair cut short in frizzled ringlets, she reminded him of a Kerry Blue terrier. Beneath a thick fringe, small black eyes peered, rodent-bright, while the twitching of her nose registering surprise was also mouselike. Here's the true old Cornish, Reynolds thought, a real Victorian, from her black bodice, with its faded lace 'vee' at the neck, to her long black skirts and lace-up boots, muddy with heavy walking.

'Greedy,' Widow Penlore was chirping. She wagged a long fingernail at the tabby. 'Wants more than her fair share. Animals are like children,' she continued, as if Reynolds and she were in the middle of an ongoing conversation. 'Have to be taught good manners. Look at Lou's poor pigs.'

With this astonishing observation she stood up, shook her skirt and added, equally surprisingly, 'It's Lou's fault.'

With difficulty identifying Lou as Bestwick, and presuming she was not accusing him of murder, only complaining about his pigs' lack of manners, Reynolds let the old lady ramble on about a variety of topics, her garrulousness typical of lonely people who talk to themselves. She didn't ask why he'd come, seemed to take his presence for granted, and when she had finished with other animals she'd known, with the medicinal properties of plants (on this she was more precise), with the rising cost of coal, with a dozen different subjects, none connected to the other and none having anything to do with Reynolds' visit, she finally trotted briskly off to make him a cup of herbal tea, leaving him feeling like some Peter Rabbit about to be dosed with camomile.

Any attempt to speak of last night's meeting met with, if not exactly a shying away, a complete lack of interest, as if, he thought, she doesn't even remember it. He drank the tea, a strong infusion of mint and balsam, and bided his time.

When he did finally ask if she'd heard about the 'happenings' at Hanscastle (he used the euphemism deliberately not to frighten her outright), she produced her best non-sequitur. 'Always take Toby there, unkind to tie him up; never leaves my side since Mr Penlore died,' giving the impression that she was on more intimate terms with her dog than her former husband. As for the dog, which hadn't as much as barked, not even raised its head, on hearing its name it suddenly stood up and stretched, and then settled down again in the same somnolent position.

Giving up on warnings or hope of any information, Reynolds stayed a while to enjoy her garden, as he'd suspected an overgrown wilderness packed with treasures. He left with two pots of home-made jam, a recipe against rheumatism, and several cuttings of plants he'd admired, including the unknown lemon bush. And a feeling of freedom, as if he'd emerged from cotton wool. To his surprise he hadn't gone more than a few steps along the lane when she called to him in a clear voice. 'About that meeting, well, it wasn't what I'd call a real meeting, she organized it. Like she always does.'

She had come to her front gate, presumably to see him off, was leaning over it, her eyes still very bright. 'And about closing off the village, well, when Mr Mathews said he preferred the old gypsy days and hoped the gypsies'd come back again I agreed with him.'

She stared at Reynolds over the gate, the cat in her arms. 'Knew a lot, them gypsies,' she said, 'more than they let on. Never does to underestimate them. Could have told the lady of the manor that.'

There was a sudden tinge of venom, a whisper of it. As if she herself became aware of his noticing, she softened her voice back into its usual Cornish burr. 'Myself, I used to like the caravans on the green, the colours was all bright, reminded you of fair days. Mind, they stole the washing if you left it out, but their clothes-pins were always of good pine. And,' pointing to a bunch of leaves that dangled from a pot she'd given him, 'careful of that plant there, its flower's some poisonous.'

Here's a disadvantage I hadn't thought of, Reynolds told himself as he finally extricated himself from her memories. Escape is certainly easier on official calls. Are all the women in this village blessed, or cursed, with the ability to read thoughts? And, like Lady Rowan, is her garrulousness hiding something else? Because if it is, damn me if I can get a feel for what.

Thoughtfully he went back to the car and drove next to Frank Mathews' house. It was on the moors proper, which were close here: he'd scarcely gone a quarter of a mile before the high hedge flattened, gave way to low, heather-covered banks, beyond which rolled an open, treeless plateau rising gently in the distance to the peaks of small rock-studded hillocks. Along the edge of the road sheep grazed, with the perversity of their kind bounding into the road rather than away from it as he tried to pass, and in the distance he could see the dark forms of cattle. This is the backbone of Cornwall, he thought, what people call its secret hinterland. Today, with the wind chasing the clouds, and sun and shadow leaving great purple patches that rippled like the sea, he was aware, as never before, of the beauty that so many people admired.

And you'd have to be an admirer, he thought, or a real hermit, to live up here where Frank Mathews does, in a huge mansion of a place, stuck out in the middle of nowhere, what Sam Trewithin would have called a 'gentleman's private residence', built in the last century for some exiled foreigner (said to be related to deposed European royalty, for whom isolation and loneliness may have proved a godsend).

Originally the house may have been built as an isolated fortress; now it was easily identified. The stone wall surrounding it stood out against the bare landscape like the sides of a box, behind which the triangular shapes of the encircling fir trees looked as if they had been cut from cardboard. True, wall and trees successfully blocked any view of the house itself, while the walls, topped by barbed wire which Reynolds could see glistening as he drove up, made a formidable barrier.

The equally high wooden gates were closed and bolted with a thick metal chain and lock, obviously newly installed – Frank at least must have taken some of Lady Rowan's warnings to heart, Reynolds thought as he rattled the fastenings.

The gate was impossible to force open, and the wall equally impossible to climb, at least not without probable damage to one's person, to say nothing of certain damage to one's clothes. Another drawback to private visits, Reynolds thought ruefully: usually he'd have had a sturdy constable to do his dirty work for him. He went back to his car, took off his jacket, folded it carefully, on second thoughts removed his tie. Then, in shirt-sleeves, feeling rather foolish, he began the lengthy business of circling the outer defences in the hope of finding a weakness.

The walls had been thoroughly constructed, sheer, no gaps, no obvious foot- or handholds. The barbed wire was equally strong, several strands of it, looped above the stones and from them woven back into the branches of the trees. 'Damn,' he thought, wiping blood off his hands, 'there must be some other way in for visitors.' He grinned at himself. And what hermit welcomes visitors, he thought, and who do you think you are, a friend or a snooping cop?

The only possible solution was to scramble over the gate pillars. Some eight feet tall, they at least were free of wire, and were surmounted by stone heraldic beasts, fortunately so well weather-worn that their bases would serve as a handhold. Judging the distance, he made a run, leapt, missed the creature's feet and tore his trousers. A second leap was better. Panting, his heart thudding (he hadn't realized he was so out of shape), he hauled himself up on the top of the gatepost, his arms wrapped round the stone figure, at close quarters possibly a griffin. Feeling even more foolish, as he hung there, planning his next move. He wasn't going any further until he'd made sure of an exit route – easier said than done given the even greater height of the walls on the lower inner side. It was not until he noticed under the trees the scattered logs which would serve for footholds, that he let himself down, still only half convinced he was doing the right thing.

The drive, curling away from the gates, was overgrown, not much more than a bike-track wide, presumably Mathews' bike. Again by instinct he kept to one side, under cover, where laurel thickets gave plenty of hiding places. He saw and heard no one, not even a bird stirred. He glanced at his watch: just after two o'clock. When he came out into the open he hesitated for a moment, scanning the terrace ahead.

What had once been a stretch of gravel was weed-infested, the grass knee-high. Beyond it stood the house, a real Victorian folly, he thought, an Oxford Keble College in miniature, with its turrets and balconies, the whole partially enveloped in straggly ivy writhing in untidy loops. Untrimmed bushes waved in profusion, some almost two storeys high; no tubs of flowers here to soften the harsh, red-brick exterior. For an artist, he thought, Frank Mathews doesn't care much for exterior decoration. And as he crunched towards the front door (an elaborate pointed affair surrounded by what looked like a church porch), where the paint hung in strips and the brass knocker was tarnished green, he wondered what the inside of the house was like: probably worse, he thought, imagining damp wallpaper and rotting floors.

The steps, however, were clean; a pair of boots, mud-covered, was set neatly at one side. He looked at them, they were Frank's boots, he presumed, so presumably also Frank was within. He rang the bell. It jangled with a rusty chime, as if unused for years. No answer. He rang again, thought he heard a sound, he couldn't quite catch what; an unexpected sound, heard once and not repeated, then silence again. If Frank Mathews is home, he thought, he's not home to visitors.

On an impulse he stepped back into the shadow of the arched porch and waited. From where he stood he could not be seen, but could see at least the front half of the house. The windows under their thatch of ivy remained empty, and looking carefully now he could tell that some on the upper storey were hung with what looked like original red velvet curtains. On the ground floor, however, wooden panels had been shoved across the inner sills, a hasty improvisation for shuttering, for in several instances there were gaps where the panels didn't quite meet or had been pushed in askew. But no Frank Mathews showed himself in the cracks, no light appeared in what must have been dim interiors, no curtains twitched.

Giving up on the front of the house, Reynolds wandered round to the rear. The windows here had also been boarded up, equally in haste, he thought: the wood looked new. Standing on tiptoe to peer inside he could see little except stretches of bare floor, streaked with dust. Otherwise nothing; no movement, no one. And beyond again, in the back courtyard, only a rotting series of what must have been stables, grooms' quarters, garden sheds, all the service support necessary for a large household, now empty and uninhabited. Beyond them, an equally overgrown confusion of a back garden, with no signs of any path through more dense undergrowth, no sign of anything alive.

Slowly he returned to the front, listened once more,

then as slowly withdrew, turning every so often to look round. The vacant windows, sleepy now in the afternoon sun, stared back at him. Half convinced, he made his way to the gates, dragged up a stack of wood, scrambled over, again tearing his hands and ruining his shirt. Regaining the comfort of his car he wiped his hands clean on a handkerchief, and combed his hair, which was liberally dusted with cobwebs and leaves. His jacket would hide the shirt, but there was no hiding the tear in the trousers. Then, putting the car in gear, he drove fast towards St Breddaford.

He'd thought of making a last moorland call, but since Derrymore had said the 'others' (he found he was thinking of the whole official investigation team as rivals) had reported the Travellers' disappearance, that could wait. And it was still too early to find Burns, the schoolmaster, returned from school. But when he reached the village, instead of making his 'report' to Derrymore as he had planned, he found himself, almost as if deliberately, circling the green and drawing up in front of the new Incident Room, where the hand-painted sign, 'Tricket's Confectioneries', was still decipherable over the door.

He sat in the car for a while. One doesn't easily go back to the past to confront one's ghosts. Nor is it easy to return to one's former life as a has-been, vulnerably out of place, certainly not with the knowledge that one has already been 'trespassing' – for reasons having nothing to do with crime! Yes these were reservations only he would care about, he thought; probably no one else would. Except perhaps Clemow himself. Although thick-skinned himself, Clemow was unfailingly aware of other people's weaknesses. On the other hand, there was certain information Reynolds would like to have, and only here would he find it. He got out of the car and braced himself.

When he went inside, as he expected, all was sparse efficiency. Clemow had always been efficient, Reynolds had always granted him that. Two girls sat before computers, an innovation these, tapping endlessly. The green symbols flickered, blinked. Several more girls manned a line of phones, a bank of them, established behind what must have been the shop's counter, although none seemed to be ringing at the moment, not a good sign. In the other half of the shop a group of men clustered round what looked like a map. None of them glanced up when Reynolds came in; only the sergeant in charge came forward, young enough not to recognize Reynolds on sight, old enough to have heard of him.

The telling of the name, the passing of it on, caused a little ripple which, in other circumstances, might have been gratifying. The group of men broke apart, one came forward with outstretched hand. 'John, old boy,' Clemow said, 'no idea you'd buried yourself in this neck of the woods. It's a bastard, isn't it?' As if they were still the best of pals, Reynolds thought, the best of friends – on the surface, that is. We might have been meeting regularly, he shows no sign of . . . he buried the word 'shame'.

It was six years since he and Clemow had last met. He hasn't changed much, he thought, although the sandy, over-straggly hair was streaked with white. Clemow was still squarely built, solid, having the snappish temper that goes with that sort of colouring. Today the only sign that Clemow was put out was the way his pale eyes, sandy-lashed, flickered, not looking straight. Reynolds remembered the other's dislike of tall men, always manoeuvring so he wouldn't have to look up to them, never liking to stand close to Reynolds himself, always preferring to speak sitting down. Mollified by that thought, he shook Clemow's hand.

Before coming in, Reynolds had thought out what to say. The past would not be mentioned, of course, although it would dominate every unspoken word. He wasn't certain either how well he could control his own feelings, or Clemow hide his – if the new Chief Inspector had any, that was! Reynolds' excuse, that he was merely passing by and couldn't resist dropping in, was vague enough to be accepted at face value, although whether Clemow would believe him or not was up to Clemow himself. At any rate he had made a first move. First strike to him.

Clemow was in a strange mood which Reynolds fortunately recognized as having nothing to do with his unexpected appearance. 'You've arrived at an appropriate moment,' he was saying, with what was meant to be heavy sarcasm but which sounded merely peevish. 'Our only break.'

He looked at Reynolds with his sideways glance, waiting for Reynolds to ask what. Reynolds didn't give him the satisfaction. Instead he turned towards the map, studying it with deliberate attention. It was an enlargement of the St Breddaford survey map, some of the crucial areas already marked in red, a great red star indicating the yard where the body had been found, a red circle surrounding Hanscastle Farm with its clay-works and fields. Ted's route was also marked in red, the track across the moors one of many similar small dotted lines. And there on the other side of the farm, several miles off, was the main road, with the small line linking it to the farm entrance, this last used by Bestwick. Looking at the map, seeing now how the lines converged, Reynolds was immediately struck by the way Hanscastle seemed to be at its natural centre. For example, here, just to its south, lay St Breddaford itself, and here, westwards, Rowan Manor. Draw a line from Widow Penlore's cottage to Frank Mathews' house, it too would meet at the farm. A coincidence perhaps, but interesting.

'And here's the site of our great new clue,' Clemow was saying even more sarcastically. He pointed to another red star, presumably recently drawn. 'A beauty this. Just what we need. Found by some damned ditcher, I understand, in some damned ditch. Walked to work, he said, and on his way back, there they were. Said they weren't there before, but how do we know that? Perhaps he wasn't looking, perhaps the sun was in his eyes, perhaps he was asleep. All I know for sure is that he was on foot. He was most insistent about that.'

He suddenly gave a harsh laugh, hiding his bad temper under pretence of mirth. 'That's all they do,' he said, 'these damned countryfolk, walk. Like that damned tramp, what's-his-face? Tough as old boots. Live to be a hundred, why not, nothing else to do in this damned countryside. Except rot.'

Despite the comparative mildness of his profanity, his tone was savage, as was the thrust underneath. Again Reynolds said nothing. He knew Clemow's brand of humour well, knew how to twist it if he had a mind to, knew when to watch and wait.

'As for what the ditcher found,' Clemow said, provoked into revealing what he had meant to hide because so far Reynolds had refused to ask, 'what use are they? I mean, rackets, for God's sake, Not one, mind you, but three. Spares, I understand, in case one breaks.'

He reached for a chair, dropped into it heavily, his eyes still not quite making contact. 'A real public danger, a racket, your ultimate murder weapon – if someone could saw off heads with racket strings! As for who left these particular ones in that particular ditch, and why, and what they've got to do with a murder case, your guess is as good as mine. Except I'm bloody tired of chasing bloody red herrings, as cracked as those broken flower-pots.'

He gave an exaggerated shrug. 'But if your average villager is anything to go by, the more red herrings he flushes up the better. I've had twenty people so far identifying the owner: one Frank Mathews, the local badminton champion.'

He gave another shrug. 'And when we asked Frank why he'd left them there, guess what his answer was. "Why not?" As if ditches were dug for depositing unwanted belongings.'

He was beginning to work himself up into a paddy, his face flushing. 'Roll up for the latest St Breddaford craze,' he was continuing, his sarcasm even more ponderous. 'The latest trend, the "in" thing. Rent a ditch for dumping stuff. Better than a pig-sty, less stink.'

Some of his associates laughed uncomfortably: he'd always expected underlings to be attentive. But Reynolds knew the attempt at heavy humour was to hide irritation. Clemow doesn't know much, Reynolds thought, eyeing the man who'd caused him so much pain. He's not found out much, despite all this costly paraphernalia. The thought was pleasing.

'Plays badminton, I understand, does Mathews,' Clemow went on, calming down. 'Every week, regular as clockwork. Strange sort of fellow, my men say, swears like a goddamned trooper.'

'They've been up to see him then?' Reynolds' voice was mild. He noted Clemow's bluster of affirmation. There's a lie, he thought, remembering the barred gates, the wire, the lack of any tyre marks on drive or grounds, the lack of any footprints. You may have phoned, but your men certainly haven't bothered to get up to the house yet.

'He's been seen since? Since the meeting?' he asked.

Clemow stared at him. 'Don't know what you're talking about,' he said. 'Which meeting?' He caught himself with an effort. 'You don't mean the one after which the damn flower-boxes were destroyed?' He laughed. 'You've lost your perspective, John. Good God, we've no time for local pranksters. We've left that to your village bobby. Let him get his thrills from that.'

In the other part of the room a phone rang, was answered, voices rose. Clemow reached over, barked into the mouthpiece, listened, his expression blank. Reynolds watched the way his fingers snapped against each other, like castanets. Always a give-away, those stubby, restless fingers. But whether the news was good or bad, again he wasn't about to ask. He turned away to study the map, waited until Clemow had finished his conversation.

When Clemow rejoined him he looked up in mild interest. The Chief Inspector ran a hand through his hair, an exaggerated gesture of overworked exhaustion which was not lost on Reynolds.

'Holy cow,' Clemow said. 'What a case. Imagine it, up to your knees in pig-shit to find a body, a body that can't be identified because it's in bits. And no one's yet made a move to claim them. Why not, I ask? Even in this god-forsaken hole there must be families, neighbours, friends, who might notice, might possibly have doubts, if one of their nearest and dearest failed to show up next morning. But perhaps it's another country habit to dump them, too, shovel them away as a matter of course.'

He glanced up at Reynolds in the way he had, as if he expected Reynolds to deny or confirm his observation. He's talking too much, Reynolds thought. He's just found out something that's put Frank Mathews and his rackets out of his mind. What would that be, I wonder, to make him drop the one lead he's had like a hot potato?

Clemow went on talking; suddenly he was bubbling with talk. 'So what sort of pervert is this murderer? And why did he murder at all, what's the motive? And where's he slunk back to so that no one has yet noticed he's been out all night, in a storm that dumped two inches of rain and turned your average local lane into a ruddy mud-bath. But there you are, that's the sort of thing your country yokel seems to turn a blind eye to.'

As if his mouth was dry he licked his lips. 'Not a ready source of information, is he, your country yokel, not too bright? And we're stuck here without much hope of getting through his skull that this is serious.

'Take your local policeman,' he went on, continuing to emphasize the word 'your', taking a delight in doing so, 'your local plod, what's his name, Derry something? Thick as a post. Bleating on about those flower-pots as if he were some damned gardener.'

As if a thought had struck him he added, 'You should give him a hand, help him ferret up some clue to keep him quiet. Isn't gardening your new vice these days?'

The attack was vicious, sudden and unexpected. With it he turned away, then turned back as if a final thought had struck him. 'Oh yes,' he said, 'if you've taken to hiking on the moors in your dotage, look out, old son.'

He flicked a look at Reynolds' torn trousers. 'This is a monster, I tell you,' he said. 'Leave it to the experts.'

Reynolds heard the warning, heard the venom. His own

blood boiled. Suddenly all thought of civilized encounter evaporated. He willed Clemow to look at him, forced him to look straight. Damn you for a turncoat, his own glare said, blast you to hell, traitor, blackguard.

He said, his voice still even, 'I've no vices left these days, except the raking in of money, if writing bestsellers can be called a vice. I gave up all others when I left the force. But if you yourself haven't lost the joy of wading through manure heaps, I'd say leave that to country experts. They know more about muck-slinging than you'd dream of.'

But when, honours even, he came outside, he didn't feel so certain. He didn't much like muck-slinging himself when it came to it. And Clemow only snaps like that when he feels cornered, he thought. And he'll know I know he's lying. He hasn't a clue who the murderer is. Nor the victim. But he does know now the sex of the body in the pig-pen. I'll bet my last penny that's the news he's just heard.

A sudden sense of foreboding ran like a trickle of cold water down his spine. Clemow had been right about one thing though: it was a monster of a killing. And even personal feuds would have to give way to that.

Chapter 6

From the Incident Room (what a pretentious name for a former sweet-shop, he thought) only a few steps separated him from the next office. On impulse he decided to pay it a visit, although since the purchase of his house he'd never had reason to do so. Despite all the financial troubles, the lights were on full power and the sign was still in place. Pausing for a moment outside, he eyed it with sudden suspicion. He'd never thought about it before, but somehow now the puce colour didn't look right, nor the glossy painted walls, nor the roof-tiles, copied from some old barn. With new awareness he thought: it's pretentious, too, all sham. No wonder Lady Rowan's horrified. Then, more forgivingly: well, it's to Sam's taste, I suppose, and Sam's done well out of it.

Inside, all was quiet. It was the only time he'd seen Sam without a phone in his hand, or, come to that, been in the office without the phones constantly ringing. But when they had first met, it had still been at the height of the country's prosperity, when everything had been on the go, when everywhere had been bustle and everyone had been busy.

As Reynolds opened the door, Sam jumped up, smiling, hands outstretched, the epitome of a genial host. 'Nice to see you,' he was saying, 'come in, sit down,' speaking in a rather fruity voice where only a trace of Cornish lingered. I suppose he's veneered that as well, Reynolds thought with a moment's nostalgia for the old Sam, who presumably in early days would have still dropped haitches and rounded his vowels with uninhibited gusto.

Yet a good-looking man, Reynolds thought, accepting the offer of a chair, the sort women call handsome. He noted how the clothes emphasized what could be called the vitality within the heavy frame, as if it were straining to break out. The clothes themselves would have changed too, he thought. Now they were 'mod', replacing the shabby suit Sam probably once wore, always navy, the sort that goes shiny along the seams. Like the building, the new Sam seemed made-over, refurbished. And younger too, younger than he really was, healthy, even if slightly overweight. Fitter than I am, I bet, Reynolds thought, not without a touch of envy.

'So what brings you in?' Sam's tone suggested he and Reynolds were the closest of friends in the habit of spending time together. 'Wanting a new residence?'

He laughed, but the laugh was over-eager. And there was an expectant look in his eyes, new lines beside his mouth which Reynolds didn't remember. The strain of the recession, he thought, and was further surprised when Sam added, 'Or is it "our" crime that lures you out? Material for your next book, perhaps?'

He leaned forward earnestly. 'Wish I had your knack,' he said. 'At least books don't lose their value overnight. And I enjoyed your last.'

Reynolds was surprised by this fulsome praise. When he and Trewithin had first met, Sam'd been the soul of tact. It had been one of the things Reynolds had liked about him:

without being asked he'd deliberately suppressed all mention of Reynolds' past as if he had known instinctively that Reynolds wanted it kept private. If details of Reynolds' bookwriting fame had reached him since, presumably he had continued to keep a discreet silence, another thing to like him for, discretion being a rare commodity at the best of times, and virtually unknown in the glass-fishbowl of village life. But if Reynolds had always felt he'd Trewithin to thank for shielding him from unwelcome intrusion, now Trewithin's blatant breaking of the taboo was both out of character and annoying, almost as if Sam had deliberately overstepped the mark.

As if aware he might have offended, Trewithin smiled his easy smile. 'No harm done, I hope,' he said. 'No harm meant. Always liked a village celebrity, you know, but kept under wraps. As for changing houses, a joke these days, not the time or place. Dreadful,' he went on, parodying Lady Rowan if he had but known it. 'Houses for sale sprouting up like bloody weeds, and not a buyer within miles.'

He swivelled in his chair. 'And the one place someone showed interest in – guess which: Hanscastle! Well, she stopped her wanting fast enough when she saw it close.'

'You drove her there?'

Reynolds kept his voice non-committal. Sam laughed for a third time. 'Couldn't get far up that lane,' he said. 'A sea of mud. They'll have found my tracks all right, I told them the Jag'd been there.'

Reynolds jerked his head towards the nearby sweet-shop. 'And what do you make of them?'

Sam made a face, shrugged. 'Were in here first off,' he said. 'Went all along the street yesterday, asking this, asking that. Waste of time, I thought. Followed by

Derrymore. There's a real whodunit sleuth, Derrymore, a real Sherlock, hot on the trail of Lady R's pots. Had I driven over them by mistake? Did I know anyone who might want to rip them out? That sort of thing.

' "Look here, Holmes," I told him. "It's not worth your while, beavering away at me. What I know of flowers wouldn't fit on a fingernail, so go beaver off on someone more deserving." But you've got to say this for him,' he added, 'he's a regular, hardworking chap, nobody's fool, persevering. "You'd not speak so smug," he said, "if you saw what I've seen." '

He gave a shudder that had nothing feigned about it. 'Thank God,' he said fervently, 'I was miles away at the time.'

As if suddenly remembering, his face changed, the full lips turned down. 'Brutal business,' he said, just as Derrymore had done. 'Unthinkable. And could have been any one of us, half the village on the trot after their blasted meeting.'

'If it were a random killing.' Reynolds didn't know why he'd said that, and to his second surprise saw how, for a flicker of a second, Sam's good-natured face darkened. If he hadn't been watching carefully he might have missed it altogether. He hurried on. 'That infamous meeting – you didn't go, I suppose?' And again, although his question was neutral, he noted another flicker, not surprising in the circumstances: Lady Rowan's proposal would put Sam out of business for good.

'Could wring her neck,' Sam said cheerfully. 'Had the gall to send me a note. Always sending everyone notes, could write a novel myself with their contents. But no, I didn't go. Not in the mood to listen while she hectored. I'd plenty of my own homework.'

He winked. 'Had a nicer project,' he said, 'if you get my meaning. A pretty little prospect, shall we say, over Padstow way. Drove from here to meet her just as the meeting let out.'

He winked again. 'A miss who doesn't like being kept waiting,' he said, 'but that night the drive was rough. Windy. Wet. The car got blown about something awful. Got ticked off proper when I did arrive, as if roads and weather were my fault. Never thought to apologize for the times she's kept me dangling.'

He laughed, a man-to-man confidential laugh, a barroom confidence. 'But if you're the one that's late, my God, don't they make you suffer? Women are a bugger, aren't they, whichever way you take them?'

He didn't mention any names, too careful for that, Reynolds thought, not without another twinge of envy. Sam Trewithin was about his age, or only slightly younger, yet Sam Trewithin seemed set on the quest for eternal youth, without a pang of conscience.

'As for Lady Rowan's claque,' Sam reverted smoothly back to the meeting, 'she kept them at it late. I was in the office when it started, and the school lights were still on after ten. Heard them at it, too, hammer and tongs, shouting, banging on tables and such, a real shindig. Then out they came in droves like a swarm of angry bees. First Frank Mathews, shaking his fist, then the little schoolmaster – what's-his-name? – then the others. Made so much noise I couldn't hear myself when I backed over a dustbin lid by mistake.'

He laughed his quick, infectious laugh, showing a row of large white teeth. Something's bothering him, Reynolds thought. No wonder, given the state of his affairs. But he remembered too what the village said of Sam, how he'd changed, matured late, grown up of a sudden. It was only then that it occurred to him that Sam had given himself two alibis for the same occasion, should he need them.

Sam got up to open the door. 'You tell Derrymore what I said of him,' he said. 'Mind you do now, when you see him again, that is.'

The third interview over, John thought, the third to end on a jarring note. As if Sam Trewithin knows, or suspects, that I'm in league with Derrymore. As if everything Sam says could have a double meaning, as if he's toying with words and laughing as he does it. He shook his head. That's paranoia, he thought, I'm just overreacting. Nothing can be that obvious. Nevertheless, he left the village green with some relief and drove to Peter Burns' house, of a design unashamedly modern, of brick and painted wood as incongruous in a granite village as Lady Rowan's state-of-the-art flower-pots.

But when Reynolds had gone, when Sam was sure he was alone and the door was bolted and the shutters closed, the estate agent went back into his inner office. Closing the door there as tightly, he knelt down in front of a safe and carefully removed its contents. Without examining them, without giving them another look, he stuffed them down into what had been an old fireplace, now cunningly concealed behind a decorative fan of silver tinfoil. Pulling out a box of matches from his pocket, he set the papers alight.

They burned with a smouldering flame that filled the room with smoke and left great black marks on the polished wood surround of the fireplace. When they were mainly reduced to ash, he stirred the debris with his foot; then, after waiting for it to cool, scooped it up into a bag which he thrust at the bottom of a waste-paper basket. Only then did he let out a breath as if he had been holding it, as if not until it was finished would he feel secure. The security was only minimal, superficial. Behind it lurked the fear.

Chapter 7

Burns lived on a new estate which lay on the eastern side
of the village. Built despite many local villagers' protests
that it was an eyesore, put up – thrown up, its detractors
said – at the height of the boom, it had been intended for
what Reynolds had been told were 'little folk', as if they
were some sort of elves. In fact the people who live here
are probably quiet, ordinary and hardworking, Reynolds
thought, reassessing them as he slowly wound his way
along identical streets where 'For Rent' signs proliferated.
Here there's no city-dweller excess, no double ownership;
any house here would be a single purchase, made with
agonizing care and forethought, a house bought to live in
until death or divorce broke a couple asunder. Yet, faced
with high mortgage rates and falling prices, the owners
were suffering equally with their more sophisticated
counterparts, perhaps would suffer more by being so eco-
nomically and morally vulnerable to repossession by mortgage companies. No one here would have much sympathy
for Lady Rowan.

Seeking for an excuse to call on the schoolmaster, Reynolds again thought of Lady Rowan. He would ask Peter
Burns what the village thought of her suggestions; he
might very well have asked him that in the normal way of

things. As chairman of the village council, Peter Burns must be used to awkward questions. And as equally used to awkward explanations of the lady of the manor's activities.

Reynolds found Burns' house with difficulty – they all looked alike. Burns lived at number 47, Willow Lane, so named because of the trees that must once have grown along the field. It was a small bungalow, the sort Sam Trewithin would have called split-level, with a wooden carport reached by a short gravel drive. A car, an old Ford, presumably belonging to Peter Burns, was parked haphazardly outside the house and when Reynolds came to the front steps, he heard the sound of running feet.

The front door swung open to reveal a slight tousle-haired man, spectacles askew, whose startled gaze having taken in and rejected his visitor, immediately swivelled beyond Reynolds down the road, as if searching for someone. He seemed so agitated that for the first time Reynolds regretted his impulse to call. To coax a man into confidences you mean to use – without his knowledge, that is – isn't in the best of taste. He was in two minds about withdrawing altogether, with an awkward apology about 'being lost', when something held him back. Burns was still not looking at him directly. Like a nervous horse, the whites of his eyes showing, he was staring over Reynolds' shoulder. Not a jovial type, Reynolds thought, contrasting this lack of welcome with Sam Trewithin's exuberance, not your regular village schoolmaster. He eyed Burns thoughtfully. Nor did Burns have the look of a fighter about him, that was for sure: no wonder Lady Rowan had been taken by surprise at his outburst.

'I'm a neighbour,' Reynolds said into a silence which was beginning to stretch too long. 'We've not met before, but then I've no little brats to off-load on you.'

Continuing silence, not a glimmer of a smile. Damn, Reynolds thought, suddenly disconcerted. Clutching at straws now, uncertain where to begin, he went back to his original idea. 'About that meeting,' he began when Peter Burns broke in sharply. Yet Reynolds' first impression lingered, that the man wasn't really concentrating on what he was saying, wasn't really seeing what was in front of him.

'What meeting?' Burns was asking, sounding more agitated than ever. 'You mean the one two nights ago that Lady Rowan called? What's the problem now?'

For a moment Reynolds himself was silenced. Then his lips twitched. 'As far as I'm concerned it was the usual hot air,' he said, 'but as I wasn't there, I'd like to verify the position.'

This time his attempt at humour succeeded. Gradually Burns relaxed. He wiped his hand slowly over his face, settled his glasses straight in a typical schoolmasterly gesture. 'You'd better come inside,' he said, pushing at the door grudgingly, positioning himself in such a way that he blocked the view, causing Reynolds to hover uneasily in the entrance. All Reynolds could see was a back corridor and one corner of the sitting room, obviously square as a box and painted a dull, pea-soup green. A litter of clothes and books was spread across the floor. Reynolds had the impression that the furniture would be greasily neglected; that probably there were no curtains, at best windows draped with mismatched sheets not quite meeting in the middle. As if they've never really moved in at all, Reynolds thought, as if they're camping out, as if Mrs Burns has no more idea of house decoration than Frank Mathews has.

The thought made him depressed, as if he'd had more than his fair share today of peering in at other people's grimy secrets.

'You've hit the nail on the head,' Burns was saying. 'Meetings, meetings, meetings, enough to make you sick. Always at short notice, so you don't know where you are. "You're the chairman, aren't you?" if you complain.'

He had directed his full attention towards Reynolds now, warming to his theme. 'I'll admit I shouldn't have volunteered for the job,' he said. 'Everyone warned me not to, even the vicar. "Watch out, my boy," Thermond said, "Lady R's a killer." And he ought to know, he had years of her before he retired.'

Once more he wiped his face. 'A proper snob,' he said. 'Thinks she owns the stupid place and has the right to hang you if you trespass. Speaks to you like some nineteenth-century hack politician addressing a bunch of peasants.'

And as Reynolds again assumed a sympathetic air, not all feigned, 'Always had it in for me ever since I took over. Made no bones about it. Thought no one could replace the vicar, Thermond, and complained what was needed was a real country squire – as if I came from some back-street slum and had jumped the queue, as if there were hundreds ahead of me begging for the job.'

He pointed to the doorway. 'Know how we first met? Banged on our door there with a bag of dog turds and tipped them out on the matting. "Proof," she said, "collected by my own hands." '

Startled, Reynolds was drawn to ask, 'Proof of what?' and was rewarded with an even more startling answer.

'That even dogs were conspiring to ruin her precious medieval common,' Burns said. He laughed without mirth. 'Unfortunately,' he said, 'my reaction was not responsive to the glories of the past. But Marilyn gave as good as she got. Never one to mince words, is Marilyn. "A load of dog-shit," she said. "My, someone's been busy!" Lady Rowan's never forgiven her for that.'

He fell silent as suddenly a shadow crossed his face, a look that Reynolds recognized. He'd felt it in himself, many times, when he'd returned home to find the house empty and his wife off with someone else. Remembering what Lady Rowan had said of Marilyn Burns, he thought: if nothing else, her husband deserves a little fellow sympathy, although how to show it without mentioning the wife outright will be tricky.

But Burns continued to do the mentioning for him. Pushing his hands through his hair, making it stand even more on end – another typical schoolmasterly gesture, of frustration perhaps, or desperation – Burns leaned forward confidingly, as if sensing Reynolds' sympathy, as if drawn to confidence. 'Hates my wife as much as me, if that's possible. And all because Marilyn isn't at her beck and call like a lot of the village women and goes out riding and keeps a horse when Madam thinks she shouldn't. "What's a schoolmaster's wife doing with a horse, where's the money coming from?" as if it were any of her business.'

He fell silent until Reynolds ventured a question. Not only out of sympathy, although that was at the back of it. He wanted information too. Or rather, he wanted Burns to keep on talking to get to the heart of things. 'And how does Marilyn take all the hassle?' Reynolds asked, and was rewarded with an answer.

Once more Burns leaned forward confidentially. Reynolds recognized the symptoms. In the past, there had been times when, if anyone had shown him the smallest encouragement, he too would have felt like pouring out his soul as readily, especially to a stranger. It's odd, he thought, I suppose one doesn't feel as ashamed somehow; one doesn't feel as restricted as with a friend. But he had never, in the end, poured out his soul. Now, knowing all this, knowing too how weighted his own interest was, he wanted to warn the younger man, irritated suddenly by a naïvety which made Burns confide so easily in someone he should be suspicious of.

But it was too late. Like the Ancient Mariner, Burns had fixed him with his eye and was determined now to talk, too far gone to heed any warning.

'When we first came here,' Burns said, voice taut with the desperation of one who has been wrestling with a problem that he can no longer keep to himself, 'I swear Marilyn was more keen than I was, planned we'd have the perfect life, settle down to country bliss, the little old schoolhouse in the perfect little old village. She even talked of picking up a second-hand van and camping out wild ourselves. If we hadn't had the money to rent a proper place, that is. Or rather,' he amended, 'if I hadn't found a job. And if Marilyn hadn't had some money: her old man's, to be exact.'

He hesitated for a moment, then hurried on. 'Are you married? Then you know how wives are always right. I'd told her I wouldn't be long that evening, it was only supposed to be a routine thing. We'll go out to dinner afterwards, I promised her, but she laughed. A take-away or fish and chips and a rented video, if I'm lucky, she told me. More like a tray on my lap before the bloody telly, like last night and the night before, while you're off on some fiddle-faddle village twaddle. When that old bitch gets on the war path she'll keep you there for hours. So there I was, caught between the pair of them and no way to satisfy either. It's enough to drive a man to drink.'

Or murder, Reynolds thought, the words leaping into his mind with all the intensity of sound, so that he almost thought he had spoken them aloud.

'Hard lines,' he made himself say, although once again his sympathy wasn't completely feigned. He knew only too well what it was like to come home to rows, to accusations that his work left no time for domestic life.

But Burns was done. He regained his poise. 'Goodness,' he said with an exaggerated look at his watch. 'Time for tea.'

With this fatuous observation, he moved towards the open door where Lady Rowan presumably had deposited her bag of dog-droppings, then stood to one side in so pointed a way that Reynolds had no recourse but to leave. But as Reynolds walked to his car, he was aware that Burns was still standing on the doorstep looking after him. Or rather, perhaps not looking at Reynolds at all, but past him, looking for something, or someone.

And if for a wife who was out, and it her husband's tea-time, where had she gone? And why hide the fact that she was out at all? Unless you wanted to hide something else. Not so much where she was, perhaps, but with whom. Remembering again Lady Rowan's judgement of Marilyn Burns, he guessed that at least in this the lady was right.

Sympathy was one thing. Sensitivity can't blind sensible deduction. At a convenient distance, Reynolds stopped the car and returned part of the distance on foot. At the corner of the estate nearest to Willow Lane, he had spotted a farm gate leading into a field, the remains of the larger field perhaps from which the whole estate had been hacked. He leaned over the gate. As he had thought, it gave on to a stretch of meadow, one side of which backed up to the houses along Willow Lane, where a high new hedge of stone had been built to divide it off.

At the far end of the field was a lean-to shed and, as he waited, he heard a clatter and a horse came round the corner, a straggle of grass in its mouth. Here's a fresh example, he thought, of how there's never any real dividing line between village and county: they slide easily into each other without any obvious break. The horse, a leggy chestnut with a white nose, came trotting up towards the gate, the tuft of grass, or hay perhaps, still dangling from its mouth. It must be Marilyn's horse, he thought, the one she rides all the time, so why isn't she riding it on a day that couldn't be finer if it tried? And if she's somewhere else, somewhere her husband doesn't know, what makes him so anxious about when she's coming home – unless he's frightened she won't return. Or can't.

Puzzling out this conundrum took him part of the way home. It was late by now, and he too was anxious for his tea. But he still had one more call to make, a duty call, so wearily he turned his car one final time and went to find Derrymore, who more and more he was beginning to think of as his accomplice.

Chapter 8

Derrymore had just got back to the local police station, or what passed these days for the local station – actually large for a small village – which was a one-man operation chopped down to size: no banks of telephones, no fancy computers, just one cranky, cast-off typewriter that was always going wrong. The single window was permanently bolted shut – security, Derrymore'd been told – and although the door was open now, the room was stifling after hours of sun.

Behind him was what served as the cell. It was a small, stuffy area sealed off by a steel door, with the required facilities: wooden bedframe, blanket, washbasin and lavatory. Derrymore couldn't remember when it had been last used, and it smelled of mice. For a moment he dreamed of filling it with real criminals as they did in cowboy films; he saw Chief Inspector Clemow, played by John Wayne, clasping him by the hand and saying, 'Well done,' in Wayne's hearty voice.

He'd had a hard day. Resolutely he'd made the necessary inquiries about Lady Rowan's wretched pots. He'd been thorough; after tackling all the obvious suspects (of which there were many: it was no secret for example that the football team were furious at losing their practice ground), he'd concentrated on lesser fry: teenagers, some of the younger children. Even in the best of households, children can slip out at night and get up to mischief. According to the rules then, he'd done his duty, not only because Chief Inspector Clemow had told him to, but because of something John Reynolds had said. 'Is there a link?' Reynolds had asked, and then, 'An axe perhaps.' It had made him think. But before returning to base he'd made an unscheduled visit, one he wished he could forget.

As wearily and for the umpteenth time he'd asked the same routine questions, and met with the same sniggers, on impulse he'd headed towards the moors in search of something different. It was not until he was almost there that he remembered he did not know exactly where the Travellers had been camping, had gleaned their where-abouts more by rumour than actual description. Irritated with himself, he was about to turn round in disgust, when a smell assailed his nostrils through the open window.

He wrinkled his nose. The smell was unique – a revolting mixture of rubbish, charred wood, wet wool, dog-droppings, human ordure, which even in a Belfast slum, under what he came to think of as wartime conditions, he'd found hard to stomach. It had been bad enough in the back streets where some miserable petty quarrel had once more erupted into violence. Here in a peaceful country setting it was doubly obscene.

Of the actual Travellers there was no sign, only the marks of their – van, he supposed; similar to others he'd seen, scarcely fit to be driven, but lavishly plastered with stickers. A litter of broken cardboard, greasy papers, fish-and-chip wrappings, fast-food boxes, bundles of rags, plas-tic tubing, chicken wire, smashed railings, revealed their presence, though, the whole piled liberally round the walls of a sheep-cote. Nearby, the remains of a fire had left a great patch of blackened grass. The half-burnt posts from a farm gate had been dragged to one side, and the farmer, to whom the gate and cote belonged, was mournfully kicking at the charred ends.

He'd looked up when Derrymore stopped, then strode over vengefully. In his hands he held several potatoes with the tops still attached. 'My tatties,' he shouted. 'My land, my gate, my farm. What you going to do about it then?'

Before Derrymore could say anything, he banged the potatoes down on to the car bonnet, splattering rotten pieces across the windscreen. 'You coppers are all the same,' he cried, 'running scared. Can't move them off, you say, until they do something wrong. Well, Mister, here's my list.'

He shook his fist, big as a ham-bone. 'Set their dogs on my sheep, left two mauled dead, and a third of the flock strayed. Broke through the gate so my cattle got out and my best hunter had to be put down. And look what they done to my good hay-field.'

Derrymore looked, took in the fire, the trash, the widening circle beyond of discarded needles, soiled wrappings, human waste. 'Animals,' the farmer said with one last, despairing kick.

For some reason, Derrymore thought of Bestwick's pigs. Less even than animals, he wanted to say, echoing Ted the Tramp: most animals don't foul their own nests. But the farmer had already turned his back and stamped away, leaving Derrymore to get out and sort for clues himself.

He couldn't be sure when the Travellers had left: not long, he thought. Although the embers of their fire were cold and the last two days' sun had dried up some of the worst pools, when he bent to examine the heaps of waste, the stench close to was more nauseating than ever. If he'd come here first, as he should have done, if Clemow hadn't put him off, he might have had a chance to catch them before they fled.

He was suddenly sure they'd done a flit. They'd been here a long while, too long to take off just on a whim. What had driven them off? And where had they gone?

Clemow ought to know about this, he thought. Clemow ought to be keeping tabs on them. Remembering Clemow's lack of interest in Old Ted, he was dubious.

In the course of his work he'd run across plenty of Travellers. After county fairs, pop concerts, even Glastonbury-type festivals, he'd seen them swaggering through St Breddaford, their thin dogs – lurchers, he supposed – snarling at their heels, their women and children trailing behind. But their women followed willingly enough, and the children were rosy-cheeked beneath the dirt. In general he'd not had much time for them, but in principle he'd defended their right to free passage. And although here they'd left more filth than he'd ever seen, and done more damage in real terms, that still didn't add up to trouble of the sort at Hanscastle Farm. Innocence assumed until proof of guilt.

First thing, then, he thought, they must be found, if nothing else to defend their innocence. But how to make Clemow see things in that light? Mention any suspicion to him and he'll pounce on them in a moment as a way to solve the problem – or else ignore them altogether simply because I've dared mention them.

Caught on the horns of a dilemma which was not of his making, Derrymore went back to his car and reversed down the track. His anger was directed against himself. Had I been given leave to make inquiries, he thought, none of this would have happened. But it's out of my hands, it's nothing to do with me. Returning now to base, he had loosened his tie and switched on a kettle. To a visitor, everything would seem normal, low-key and casual. In fact, the very normality made him more depressed.

After all, it was his village, his people; if one of them was killed he ought to be hunting for the killers; if one of them was missing he should join in the search. He was fed up, there's the truth, of being ignored, kept on the outskirts like some poor relative. He stretched his shoulders and pulled his stomach muscles in. Half-way past twenty, coming up to thirty, he was thinking, and nothing yet to show for it. Nothing to be proud of, to give him a sense of fulfilment. And if Chief Inspector Clemow has anything to do with it, I'll be chasing hen thieves until I'm fifty! He caught a glimmer of his reflection in the dusty glass and grimaced. Even his placid looks belied his inner self, he thought. What wouldn't he give for a real piece of action, what wouldn't he do to be part of the real inquiry, make a real 'contribution', as they called it, of some significance. Fat chance of that.

He was just about to heave himself to his feet to turn off the kettle when a shadow darkened the doorway.

'In time to join you?'

It was Reynolds, ex-Inspector Reynolds, that is, who came into the room, sank down in the chair that Derrymore, in a fluster, now vacated, trying at the same time to do up the buttons on his tunic. 'No fuss,' Reynolds was saying with his friendly smile. 'Just an informal visit. Just to keep you up to date.'

He looks rather the worse for wear himself, Derrymore thought, as he went through the ritual of tea pouring, rather as if he's been scrambling through hedges. He noted how the Inspector – all right, that isn't his title now, although he still looks like one – how Mr Reynolds then, clasped his hands round the mug, standard white pottery, and blew appreciatively at the steam. He'd always imagined big-wigs, inspectors and such, only drank hard liquor like they do in films. It's nice to find someone who doesn't put on side, he thought, who acts as if he's one of you, who pays some attention. And, noting the state of the other's clothes: he's been up to something, he thought, suddenly pleased with his own deduction.

He listened attentively while the older man gave him details of Lady Rowan's 'statement', if you could call it that: hysterics was a better word, he thought. Again, secretly he felt pleased that Reynolds had reported back to him direct, a courtesy he much appreciated. In turn he rehashed his own day's work, inadvertently, he realized later, revealing his own frustrations.

Reynolds set down the mug, took out a small pad and studied its contents, making notes with a silver-coloured pen that probably was real silver. For a moment he seemed oblivious to his surroundings, oblivious even to the company he was in, just like my dad working out his football pools, Derrymore thought, and was a second time pleased with his observation.

Reynolds closed the notebook with a snap, secured the pen, picked up the mug. He didn't explain what he had been doing, he didn't have to. 'What do you think, Inspector?' Derrymore broke out, asking what afterwards he realized Mr Reynolds had wanted him to ask. But he didn't think of that at the time. 'Any new leads? Any clues?'

His faith in ex-Inspector Reynolds' skill wasn't disappointed, although Reynolds didn't answer right away. As if, Derrymore thought, he's having some private argument with himself. Or – a third time Derrymore was pleased at his own perspicuity – as if he's engaged in some private vendetta that taxes all his energy. But when at last Reynolds replied, the thoughtful tones suggested only that the ex-Inspector had been concentrating on the workings of his own mind.

'There are a few leads. Some to follow up; some to eliminate.'

He didn't explain how he'd decided which was which, was perhaps deliberately vague about that. Nor did he say if he had come to any conclusions, although Derrymore was hoping he would. While the older man now spoke, Derrymore hastily grabbed a pencil and paper to scribble down what Reynolds passed off as his 'ramblings' – as if those ramblings hadn't solved a hundred cases in the past, as if they didn't form the basis of the ex-Inspector's reputation – or as if they weren't meant to prompt Derrymore's own line of reasoning. And when afterwards, amazed at his own cheek, Derrymore analysed what the Inspector had to say, he sensed that he had been right, that Reynolds had wanted him to make judgements for himself, almost as if he and Reynolds were actually working together as a team.

'We'll start from scratch,' Reynolds said, 'eliminating the obvious. That's Clemow's prerogative. First, where's Mathews?'

When Derrymore stared at him, he repeated the question patiently, although still insistently. Did Derrymore know that Mathews' badminton rackets had been found and Mathews was reputed to have said he didn't want them? At Derrymore's shake of a head, 'Would he have had them strapped to his bike when he left Lady Rowan's meeting?'

When Derrymore looked puzzled, 'Are they dry or wet?' he said.

Patiently Reynolds went on to explain that rackets didn't like wet. If they'd been left out in a ditch, uncovered, since the night of the storm, they'd have been ruined. But it'd been dry since.

He took another sip of tea, scratching at his arm where a long weal was beginning to show red. 'More important, Clemow went out of his way to give the impression that his men had interviewed him, but I'm sure if they did, it can only have been superficially, probably by phone. I'd like to know when the conversation took place, if it did, and what actually was said.'

He didn't explain further, went on reading from his notes. 'Next, there's Peter Burns' wife. What do we know about her, and has anyone talked with her?'

He looked at Derrymore with a look that made Derrymore squirm. Thank God he's not interviewing me, he thought as Reynolds said, 'Can you make an excuse to discover what she did that night? And along the same lines, who's Sam Trewithin's lady friend these days?'

He put down his book with a final tap. 'Last but not least, the Travellers. Well done, by the by, to have made a stab at finding them. Any idea where they've gone?'

At Derrymore's shake of his head, 'I'd like to talk to them. If they've truly moved on, is there some way to put a trace on them?' He fixed his steady look on Derrymore. 'Oh yes, one other thing. Not orthodox, I know, but I'd like to get a squint at the farm where the murder occurred. Undercover, as it were. And is there any way you can get hold of the pathologist's report?'

As Derrymore now openly stared at him, Reynolds explained, 'I'm sure it's come through, but I'm equally sure Chief Inspector Clemow isn't telling what it contains. Until we know we can only guess.'

He suddenly smiled. He's got a good smile, Derrymore thought, makes you want to trust him. 'And just as he's not telling all he knows,' he said, 'suppose we don't? Play our cards close to our chest, why not, makes things more interesting. If you're game for it, that is, if you've no objection.'

Just as if, Derrymore thought later, thumbing through the list, he already's got the jump on Chief Inspector Clemow and isn't especially fond of the great man and knows I don't like him either. As if he and I are in partnership together. As if he's picked me out. All these thoughts were equally exciting, but it was the last that caught his imagination. By gum, he thought, staring out the window: that gives a man a lift, not half. And suddenly full of fresh determination, he rammed on his helmet and strode out of the office, which no longer seemed so hot and cramped.

Later that evening, Mrs Penlore, in her cottage, was mulling over the day's events. The setting sun shone through the kitchen windows, the fire was lit, a vegetable stew simmered on the hob; all was perfectly normal, she thought, humming gently beneath her breath as she chopped the herbs she'd picked that morning.

Mrs Penlore liked everything to be done by rote, she didn't like change, and all her life vegetables were made into stews and herbs plucked at dawn before the night's dew dried. Why habit was so strong in her, she never gave a thought. Why not? she'd have said if asked. To her the natural rhythm of the universe, the swing of seasons, the waxing and waning of the moon, were immutable, beyond argument. It was therefore both natural and right that people's lives should reflect the same unchangeability. But in the past days things had happened that threw her pattern out of kilter.

First the village meeting! She raised the knife, chopped hard. She shouldn't have gone, much less crossed swords with her old enemy. Let her enemy suspect it was deliberate and she'd been in for it. Let any of them suspect that she wasn't as old and helpless as she looked, and her peace would be disturbed, ruining years of careful deception! Long ago she'd adopted the part of village idiot; nothing would force her to give up that role.

And she wouldn't have gone to the meeting, of course, wouldn't have dreamt of it, if she hadn't been persuaded to it, 'For the good of the cause,' they'd said. Much good she'd done the cause. And much good the cause had done her! Better living on your own, she thought, out of sight and out of mind. Once old Penlore was dead, her common-law husband, she'd sunk gratefully back into anonymity. Widow Penlore might be the courtesy name the village gave her, but being a doting old widow was not her true vocation. Leave that to Lady Rowan, she thought with another savage chop: fits the high and mighty figure she thinks she is.

Then there was the murder. Followed by the stranger's visit. Here she paused in her chopping. Normal death she could deal with. She was old and unafraid. For her death was part of the universal round, dust to dust. Not that she was religious, mind, she was no Christian; she preferred the idea of returning naturally to the natural world. But not to die in such a shameful way, not to put shame on Lou's poor pigs. There was something about this death she didn't like, didn't want to think about, wanted to pretend she knew nothing of.

As for the stranger, there was another mystery she couldn't solve. Why he'd come and why he'd questioned her. Because he had been questioning, no doubt of it, although he'd pretended otherwise and she'd pretended not to notice. At first she'd thought he was the police. She was wary of them, as of all officialdom. Go into high gear, she'd told herself, play up a bit. Else they'll be breathing down your neck, prying into every move you make. First the poll tax: whose cottage is this?, if it's yours you have to pay; then, how do you make your living?, how much money do you earn and where do you keep it?, as if money was the only thing worth having and a sack beneath the floor isn't the best place for valuables. And after them, before you can say Jack Robinson, more busybodies at your door, social workers they call them, swarming in to cause more trouble. Benefits! Here she gave another savage chop.

But if the stranger wasn't part of that, was a mere villager as he claimed, that still didn't explain why he'd come. And what he'd wanted of her.

She left the table to give the fire a poke, stirring up the wood-ash. That was the most worrying thing of all, she thought, what his real purpose was. She'd have to think about that. Or pry about a bit herself; ask some questions of her own. But had she put him off the scent? Here her fire-poking became agitated.

Waiting until it was dark, after a while she rose stiffly and put on her coat. Although the evening was warm, she felt the cold. Taking Toby by the lead she sallied out, following the well-known track up to the moors. But whether she would reveal the stranger's visit, or even speak about it, she'd have to think twice about that. And, in any case, she would have to wait until she'd been given leave to speak.

Above her, still in the shelter of the gulley, the others heard the sound of her footsteps and stopped. They'd been walking fast, at times almost running, although they weren't used to haste and the rough track here was difficult. Where they came from there were only flat city streets to walk in, or telegraph posts to climb. It was dark but the sky was clear, like glass, and stars shone brightly as if through frost. Later, if the moon came up, they'd be caught in the open, like sitting ducks. The thought made them hurry on.

They moved slowly, carefully, taking advantage now of every bush and rock to hide their progress, making sure they weren't being followed. And, as they gradually drew away from the shadow of the tor, as at last they saw the metalled road stretching silver in front of them, they began to breathe more easily. They didn't speak of why they'd run, empty-handed, their plastic bags abandoned, nothing but what they stood up in, nothing of all that loot they'd seen, except a new shirt (too big) that Merl had whipped out of its wrappings, and a couple of spoons Eileen had hidden in her coat pocket. Nor why they had to move like this under cover, fearful of being caught and dragged back. They never would.

'Safe,' Merl said fatuously, his blue eyes watering. He didn't add, 'Thank God,' not being a believing man, but his grip on Eileen's hand slackened. It was Eileen who voiced what they both knew. 'Maybe,' she said, 'but only because they let us go.

'Whatever we was wanted for is over and done with,'

she added. 'We'm no use to them now.'

She and Merl looked at each other in sudden under-standing. All that they'd been used for was written in their eyes. And the horror of it wasn't done, would drive them apart in the end.

Chief Inspector Clemow wasn't usually given to heart-searching; it made him uncomfortable, like indigestion. Although his thinking was done in the relative comfort of the former sweet-shop, he couldn't stay still, paced up and down, as if only by moving about could he pick up ideas.

Most of the computer-handlers had long since gone home and, in the semi-darkness, only a few shadowy fig-ures still sat hunched over the consoles, the green lights still flickering. Like Sam, Clemow had sheafs of papers spread over his desk, and had originally meant to settle down, jacket off, to hammer sense out of them. He liked bringing order out of chaos, drawing facts and figures to logical conclusions. But in this case there was nothing logi-cal. Even the facts were nebulous, straws in the wind.

It was the sort of case he had no liking for but Reynolds would. There, he'd admitted it, almost said the words aloud. Reynolds revelled in the strange, the complicated, the unconnected. Always had. Always would. Without Reynolds this case was like trying to take an axe to fog.

And now he'd added the second thing that nagged at him, although he didn't want to admit that either: why, of all the godforsaken villages in the godforsaken country-side, some stupid little murderer had had to choose St Breddaford, the very place where Reynolds had settled. As if deliberately, he thought, wiping his forehead, as if making a fool of me. If it weren't completely preposterous, I'd lay evens that Reynolds cooked it up somehow.

He paced again. Why else, after all these years, after everything that had passed between them might be said to have died a natural death, when at the time Reynolds had done the decent thing and disappeared without a word, had Reynolds suddenly emerged again, large as life and twice as active? And why else had Reynolds hung round today, prying, provoking blunders, forcing revelations that Clemow had meant to keep to himself, if not to show Clemow up as inept and stupid?

Clemow lowered his head, bull-fashion. He knew he was being ridiculous, what he called 'fanciful'. Yet even he couldn't ignore the underlying antagonism beneath Reynolds' supposed mildness. That was only natural of course. After all, he, Clemow, had been the offender. If you could call it an offence, he hastily defended himself. He preferred to consider his revelations to his superiors as an unpleasant duty, an honour-bound duty he owed the Force. It wasn't on his conscience that Reynolds had a drinking problem.

Nor was it his fault that Reynolds' wife was a bitch, whose nymphomania also posed a security risk. Although, looking back, the memory of his hectic weeks with her wasn't exactly all unpleasant. What pissed him off was that afterwards she'd been the one to do the ignoring, had refused his phone calls, proverbially slammed the door in his face and gone off on her own. That certainly rankled. As did the undeniable fact that, after all that struggle between honour and duty, after all that emotional upheaval, he could have had what he wanted without lifting a finger – so that even Reynolds' departure became a triumph of sorts, conversely turning everything he himself had done and said into a bloody waste. If he hated anything it was inefficiency. And now, here again in St

Breddaford, suddenly Reynolds had made him feel especially inefficient.

He shook his head a second time, like a bull facing its tormentors. Take this makeshift office for one thing, these makeshift quarters without decent facilities – one leaky tap and an outdoor privy; add to them makeshift electrics which were always giving trouble, a row of computers which were constantly breaking down, and phone lines that for some reason went dead when it rained. We might as well be back in the Middle Ages, he thought, for all the advantage modern technology's given us, defeated by a climate that's as wet and clinging as a wool blanket.

As for the villagers, closing ranks against us, shutting up like clams, resisting every means of questioning, intimidating my own officers . . . No doubt about it, he felt as lost as if he'd drifted out to sea on one of those north coast Cornish currents. He paced again.

Here, there was no underground city life with its sleaze and guilt and clues; here, you couldn't persuade informers to sell you leads for money or revenge. This was the open countryside, where people's only interests were cows and sheep. You couldn't squeeze information out of such people; they didn't even know when they were being squeezed. Take that maniac badminton player, he thought. In any reasonable place a witness who refused to co-operate like that would be bounced off to clink so fast he'd scarcely know what had hit him. And that other maniac was no better, Lady Whatnot, thrusting herself and her bloody flower-pots into the limelight. To say nothing of her designs for – no, demented visions of – a fortified St Breddaford!

You can keep your medieval village and stuff it, he thought angrily, just get me back to civilization quick. Give me a decent clue, that's all I ask, something to bite into, and I'll be off and running so fast you won't see me for dust. But while I wait for that, to show I'm still in charge, to prove to Reynolds I'm better than he thinks, I'll haul that Mathews fellow in for questioning, red beard and all; I'll teach him to make a fool of me with his flaming rackets and his flaming cheek and his flaming flaunting of the law.

Chapter 9

Next morning, before seven, the first phone call came – Derrymore, bumbling with excitement. He'd penetrated the Incident Room, he said, broken through the barricades, wormed their secrets out . . . or words to that effect. As if, Reynolds thought, jolting fully awake, he's so fired up he wants to make this 'his' case as much as I do. And if we better Clemow in the process – more power to us.

It seemed that after Reynolds had left last night, on impulse Derrymore'd driven round to the nearest pub (in the next village since the closing of St Breddaford's). He'd found half of St Breddaford there, relaxing in the evening sun, enjoying their beer in the open air, although it was not so pleasant, he'd hastened to add, as the old Fox and Goose. Naturally enough talk had centred round the murder, and naturally enough he'd 'come into conversation' with a young female person, one Sue Henderson by name. 'Very nice, too,' Derrymore said. Reynolds imagined him figuratively licking his lips.

They'd talked for a while, then as both were leaving at the same time, had continued the conversation in Derrymore's battered car. For hours, he said. Again, naturally enough, talk veered round to work: what Derrymore did, what she did. It turned out she was a typist for the inquiry team. What a coincidence, she kept exclaiming, we're in the same field, almost. (Actually, as Derrymore made a delicate aside to explain, at this point in time they were still seated in his car outside his mother's cottage, and Miss Henderson, possibly due to the beer she had imbibed, was becoming amorous.)

'She made attempts to place her arms around my neck,' was Derrymore's official description of this scene of potential seduction, which, although he did not say so, might presumably have eventually taken place had she, Miss Henderson, not introduced the story of the murder and the mutilated body. 'It makes your flesh creep,' she'd said. 'Especially because it was a woman.'

'I double-checked,' Derrymore said, professional pride just showing. 'Didn't pick up on it right away, asked about other things, gradually led back to it. Don't think she even realized what she'd said. You were right, sir, the pathologists have identified the remains, at least to sex.'

'No other clues as to who it was?'

'Miss Henderson said no, and I'm sure she wasn't lying. Said Clemow's having fits over it. Said he's never known a case like it.'

'Anything new on Mathews?'

'Miss Henderson said there'd been a row about that too.' Derrymore chortled at the thought. 'You were right on that. Clemow's men hadn't interviewed in the flesh, only by phone. Complained the house was barricaded off like a prison and that they couldn't get in. So then and there, after you'd gone, Clemow sent them off again – ye gods, didn't he just send them! Told them to scale the fence, a barbed-wire fence and all, and when they came back with their tunics ripped he fined them for tearing their uniforms ... But they swore they'd seen the man himself, no doubt of it. He refused to let them in but spoke to them from an upstairs window. Told them to bugger off good and proper. Stuff his rackets and that sort of thing, just as he had on the phone.'

At Reynolds' non-committal grunt, 'Well, that's what they said. But it adds up to another red herring, doesn't it, sir? I mean,' he hesitated, 'if Mr Mathews is safe at home, what do his rackets count?'

'*If* he's safe at home.' Reynolds picked up on the word. 'Remember we live by "ifs". Actually, I was at his house earlier yesterday, Constable. Certainly someone was inside.' He fell silent, trying again to analyse what it was exactly that he'd heard when he'd come upon that stark, ugly house, trying to recall in detail what he'd felt when the noise startled him. And what the noise itself had been to make him so sure Mathews had no part in it, that sudden, unexpected sound that had betrayed the presence of someone, some human person, inside.

He put Mathews aside for the moment and said, 'I think we need to make a new list of priorities. Can a chat with the tramp be arranged?'

Derrymore brightened considerably. 'I can go up first thing to talk to him, he's still camping out with Bestwick. At the same time we could talk to the ditcher who found the rackets, a friend of his. Then, on the way, we can swing past Hanscastle Farm.'

He sounded relieved that Reynolds did not demur about accompanying him. Reynolds imagined him wiping his forehead before continuing. 'Thought old Ted might tell us more about the Travellers. Because there's still no news of them, and since it appears Clemow's no longer interested in them, they're low on the list of priorities.' There was a choke in his voice like suppressed laughter.

Reynolds could imagine the satisfied grin. 'But I'm sure, given time, we can trace their whereabouts.'

Reynolds noted the 'we' and 'us' that Derrymore used with such relish. But all he said was, 'Well done, Constable.' And, having made plans to set off within the hour, in Derrymore's car, itself a dicey prospect, Reynolds put down the phone, pleased with his protégé's progress. If he'd been in charge he'd have had old Ted in for further questioning straight off. And certainly in Clemow's place he'd have more than torn a strip off the men who'd made such a cock-up of interviewing a vital witness. But then Clemow wouldn't classify Mathews as vital either. In Clemow's mind, Mathews was linked to a village meeting which Clemow had already decided was unimportant. And when Clemow made up his mind, nothing could change him, not even murder if it stared him in the face. Again Reynolds brooded. One thing was certain. If the body in the sty was a woman, perforce it couldn't be Mathews. But neither was Mathews in his house.

He grimaced. I'm like an old woman too, he thought, relying on instinct. But that sense of what was right or wrong had always come instinctively to him. Suddenly excited, he hurried to get dressed.

These plans ground to a halt when the second phone call came. It was equally unexpected and contained less pleasant news. 'Marilyn's disappeared.' Peter Burns' voice was anguished. 'She hasn't come back.'

Out the misery poured, like a tap unstopped, the misery of a man whose wife is hell-bent on leaving him, the familiar cry, 'How was I to know it'd all go sour?' How indeed, Reynolds thought, making consoling noises; those with most to lose are always the last to know.

'I know we only m-m-met yesterday,' Burns was stuttering, the words tumbling over themselves. 'But I've found out since who you are. Or rather, I always knew who you were, but didn't put you and your name together, if you know what I m-m-mean. And I thought, why not ask your advice first? You seemed, well, you s-s-seemed...' Here his voice faltered, as if even mentioning ideas like 'kind' or 'sympathetic' would break him down altogether.

In such cases, Reynolds always found crisp questioning effective, like a bucket of cold water. After a second attempt, 'Can't be staying with friends,' Burns said, calming down, the effort of answering making him coherent. 'Her best friend is off somewhere, Majorca I think, lapping up the sun. Always trying to get Marilyn to come with her, hang the expense, make him cough up, she says. That's me they're talking about, cough up, as if I've got a fortune stashed away. How often can you go abroad on a teacher's pay?'

'Could Marilyn have joined this friend somehow?'

'No.' Burns was adamant. 'She'd have had to pack. None of her things are gone and she's left her passport. She just wasn't there when I got back, as if she'd gone for a walk or something.'

'And when was that?'

In the ensuing silence, Reynolds felt the hairs on the back of his neck rise as they always did. He repeated even more gently, 'Exactly what time are we speaking of?'

He didn't have to add, 'Was it the night of the meeting, Mr Burns? Was it the night of the murder at Hanscastle Farm?' The continuing silence answered him.

But when he suggested, as he knew he should have done in the beginning, that Burns immediately get in touch with Constable Derrymore, Burns dug in his heels. 'It's you I want to speak to,' he said obstinately, like a spoilt child,

121

just as Lady Rowan had done. In the end he agreed to see both Derrymore and Reynolds. Which was why the visit to old Ted and the trip to Hanscastle were delayed, and even the Travellers' and Mathews' whereabouts took second place, as concentration fixed on what had become of Marilyn Burns.

Since this was official business, Reynolds was spared the ordeal of being driven by Derrymore. To his relief, when Derrymore arrived shortly afterwards, he accepted that it would be more correct for Reynolds to follow in his own car. But he made no objection to Reynolds' coming.

They found Peter Burns in his sitting room, the room he'd half concealed from Reynolds on the previous visit. It was not quite as bad a jumble as before, as if someone had made an effort to tidy up, although it still had an unlived-in look: no flowers, no plants, none of the trinkets with which some women surround themselves. And Reynolds'd been right about the curtains, or rather lack of them. The walls however were dominated by one large photograph. In black and white, it was a picture of the moors, a dramatic view of a wild and lonely landscape, stretching up to what looked like a rock-studded tor. Reynolds made a mental note to examine it when he had a chance.

Burns didn't look up when they came in through the unlocked front door. ('As if,' Derrymore said afterwards, 'he didn't care who we were.') He was slumped on the sofa, head in hands. Contrasting Burns' lack of interest now with his previous expectancy, Reynolds thought, 'Here's a man without hope.' Whether without hope of his wife's return, or hope of maintaining his own innocence, it was impossible at this stage to tell, but certainly from his expression, Burns was a man in torment.

Burns accepted Reynolds' presence as a matter of

course, and addressed most of his answers to him, although Derrymore did the actual questioning. Much of the time the schoolteacher spoke rather to himself, elaborating on the theme he had revealed to Reynolds, namely his misfortune in loving a wife who no longer loved him back.

Gradually, by skilful questioning on Derrymore's part, the story began to unfold. Apparently on the night in question, the night of the meeting and the murder, Peter Burns had had a bitter quarrel with his wife – one, he now admitted, of many such quarrels in recent months, each more acrimonious than the last. He had already hinted at one cause: his chairmanship of the village council and his commitment to village life. Now he revealed a second: what Marilyn herself did when she was left alone. Because she didn't stay indoors, waiting patiently for him. Oh no. When he had to go out in the evening on school matters, to parents' meetings, council affairs, things of that sort, she was off on her own. 'What's sauce for the goose,' she'd said. True the evening in question had been terrible, no fit night for man or beast, but storms had never bothered her before. 'She likes them,' he said. And when he had returned, she had gone.

Leaving the next obvious questions dangling, Derrymore returned to details of what had happened before Burns himself had left. He'd lit the fire, Burns said, to make amends for the quarrel, to patch things up. And she must have spent part of the evening in front of it on this very sofa, watching TV; he'd found the set on when he'd returned, as were the lights. Nothing odd about that. With careless disregard for cost, Marilyn Burns never turned appliances off. But this time, before she'd gone, she'd also found something else to keep her amused.

He pointed mutely to a pile of children's exercise books, still strewn in the corner where they'd been left, presumably brought home for correction. Now the covers were smeared red, and when Derrymore tried to pick one up he found the pages were stuck together with the same red nail polish – Reynolds had a sudden image of Marilyn Burns sitting on the worn sofa, her feet bare, carefully painting each toe and smiling. Better red polish than red ink, she might have giggled as she let the drips fall.

When Peter had seen her last, she had been wearing a fleecy housecoat with little underneath, not from any thoughts of allurement, he hastened to point out, but from inertia. 'She used to sleep until noon,' he said. 'Said it wasn't worth the trouble of getting up.' Again Reynolds had the impression he was telling the truth when he added, 'Said, come evening, what was there to look forward to, what was there to anticipate in a house she'd come to loathe?' Reynolds sighed. It was such an old, old story; he'd heard it so often before.

Burns was continuing. Before their marriage she'd had a job, friends, an existence of her own which, when they'd decided to come here, she'd apparently been willing to leave behind. But once here, once village life had closed its grip, she'd changed her mind. Marilyn Burns, née Cartwright, was born and bred to expect more out of life, she taunted; she should have set her sights higher than a country teacher. With the sadness that comes from recognition, Reynolds thought that Marilyn wouldn't have meant things to go sour either, would have had high hopes at first. She couldn't have imagined the monotony of time, from dreary morning to drearier evening, suddenly reduced to the humdrum round of cooking and housework – occupations she obviously despised. And, without children – well, they hadn't thought of children yet, Burns said, suddenly blushing furiously; without a family there wasn't much for her to do.

As Burns spoke, Reynolds imagined Marilyn herself looking round in frustrated fury, just as his own wife had done, while Peter Burns himself, tickled with the monotony, as if he had invented it, settled down complacently to village life. Again he heard his own wife rail. Whose fault was it that wives were left alone at night? Whose fault that they looked elsewhere for fun?

So here's the crux of it, Reynolds thought, a bored young woman, a long evening to get through, barely eight o'clock, yet dark as midwinter. No local friend to visit, no one to exchange girlish confidences with – at twenty-six she would still feel girlish – no one in the whole damn place worth talking to. Staying here like this, she'd think, she'd as soon be dead, boxed in a coffin. Just as Reynolds' wife had thought.

The decision to go out must have been sudden, although Peter Burns could only guess at what happened next. He'd found her slippers lying on the stairs, as if she'd kicked them off, and had found the bedroom in disarray. Not as if there'd been an intruder, he hastened to say, rather as if she'd torn clothes out of the wardrobe at random, leaving garments dangling.

What clothes had she put on? Trousers, he thought, a cream-coloured jersey. 'One I gave her,' he said, focusing for a moment, 'she looked good in pale colours, set off her dark hair.'

Here, overcome, he had to stop, leaving them to imagine the rest: a last quick glance in the mirror, eyeshadow added to enhance the hazel eyes, a rapid smear of lipstick, scarlet to match the nail polish, then out through the door which she'd left ajar with the same careless abandon.

What would have caused such a decision – a telephone call, a visitor? Burns shrugged. No one came to the house, he said. Yes, she might have heard from someone, but she also did things on impulse. In fine weather, as soon as not she'd be off at all hours on her horse. 'At first I thought she'd taken Rufus,' he added, 'but she wouldn't risk him in such weather. She's a good rider: Daddy gave her her first horse when she was ten.' The way he said 'Daddy' showed what he thought of Mr Cartwright.

'Did she take the car then?'

No answer, just a shake of the head.

'Taxi?'

Again a shake. 'I checked,' he said.

Derrymore put his pencil down, pretended to study his notes. Now comes the crucial bit, Reynolds thought. He caught Derrymore's glance, gave a small signal that only Derrymore could see, indicating the photograph on the wall. Derrymore leaned forward. His voice was still even, did not lose its soothing effect. A shrewd interviewer, Reynolds thought, doesn't miss a chance, yet doesn't scare the quarry off, talks him into the palm of his hand.

'Where do you think she went? Would she have told you where?'

Again no answer.

'Did she go on the moors that night?' And then, 'What would she do there after dark?'

To Reynolds' surprise, Burns turned on Derrymore with a look that could only be called hate. 'You know,' he shouted, his voice trembling with suppressed rage. 'The whole damn village knows! Some man, of course, goddamnit. There, are you satisfied?'

While Derrymore in turn made sympathetic noises, 'Oh,

I don't know who, she'd never admit who, would never even admit there was anyone. But when I pressed her she said she'd prefer anyone to . . .' He swallowed hard. '. . . me.'

'And she's been gone three days?' Derrymore's voice was still bland, not a trace of what he must be thinking. 'Isn't that rather long to wait? Didn't you think of contacting the police before, Mr Burns, under the circumstances?'

He paused again. And when Burns still sat hunched in misery, 'You've heard of what's happened at Hanscastle Farm?' he said.

Burns' face, already pale, had whitened visibly at these last questions. Now Reynolds thought he was about to faint. When he spoke again, a nerve jumped beside his mouth; he had to cover it with his hand. 'I kept expecting her,' he stuttered. 'She'd never been gone so long before. I thought any moment she'd be back. I never imagined . . .'

He bit his lip. 'Someone's done it.' The words jerked out of him like sobs. 'But why? Why would anyone do that to my wife?'

Why indeed, Reynolds thought? He exchanged another glance with Derrymore over Burns' head. 'We'll file a missing person report right away,' Derrymore said, briskly, getting to his feet. 'If you'll just come with us, sir.'

'To the station?' Burns' sobs suddenly dried up. He too jumped up, almost wringing his hands. 'The police station,' he repeated. 'My God, it'll ruin me. Think what the village'll say. Or the children. I've told you all I know. What more do you want? I've done nothing wrong.'

'Just routine, a formality.' Derrymore remained sympathetic but firm. And so he continued while Burns, still protesting, was led to Derrymore's car and, equally protesting, was driven off to Clemow's less tender mercy.

Tactfully Reynolds waited in the background until they were gone, giving himself time to look again at the photograph. Under a lowering sky, a handful of rocks surrounded what looked like a mound of earth, the whole encircled by gorse bushes – the moors at their most sinister, he thought; not the scene to inspire a woman who hated country life.

Later, Reynolds waited in his car round the corner from the Incident Room, feeling almost furtive, like some bank robber. ('No, I'll not come in,' he said, to Derrymore's inquiring look, 'you carry on.') He pulled out a pen and began to rewrite his notes. The victim was probably Marilyn Burns; the chief suspect, obviously, her estranged husband, Peter Burns – if you discounted some unknown lover that is, who might or might not exist, might be Burns' own invention or might be Burns' reason for attacking his wife. But if he didn't exist, then what cause did Burns have to murder his wife with such brutality? And why, as if following Lady R's example, in God's name has Burns deliberately brought attention on himself? That made even less sense.

And Burns himself was as unlikely a wife-murderer, Reynolds thought, as any he'd met; surely not capable of murder of this type – although, come to think of it, most murderers seemed unlikely when you first met them. And even Lady Rowan had been surprised at Burns' outburst. There's more to Peter Burns than meets the eye, he thought, but I still don't see him as a fully fledged monster.

He drew a line across the book, wrote a new heading: Suspects. Who else beside Burns? Well, to start with, who else had been on the moors at the time of the murder? Probably dozens, he thought gloomily – farmers, shepherds, even hikers, all going about their normal lives.

Although, given the state of the weather that night, fewer than usual. And since he had no way as yet of knowing who these unknown multitudes were, nor any clues to trace them, for the moment he'd stick with his known list.

It included all those whose names had already come forward: Ted the Tramp, Bestwick the pig-owner, the Travellers (in their entirety, however many of them there were), followed by other individuals such as Widow Penlore, Sam Trewithin the estate agent, and Frank Mathews, the recluse. All of these by their own admission had been in the vicinity of Hanscastle at some time on or about that night, almost all of them on 'legitimate business', to coin a phrase. For example, Ted and Lou Bestwick had gone there to clean a sty and butcher pigs, while Sam was surely within his rights to try to sell property if he could. Mathews presumably must have cycled close to the farm to leave, or lose, his rackets in a ditch for a ditcher to find, and Widow Penlore, if she could be relied upon, walked there regularly with her dog. As for the Travellers, since they had been squatting on farmland adjoining the moors and had been in the vicinity for several weeks, presumably they too might have come across Hanscastle, although until they had been traced, their movements could not fully be known.

He stared at his list. It looked formidably long. All people who had access to the moors at night, all with grudges of some sort, but none, as far as he knew, against Marilyn Burns. Nor was there any obvious link to her. What their knowledge of, or possible relationship to Marilyn Burns was, it was impossible as yet to guess. Several men might fit the role of her supposed lover (although he didn't see Mathews in that part, for example, nor for that matter Old Ted!). As for any relationship linking this unlikely group, again it was impossible to imagine at this stage, except, he supposed, for the obvious point that all in some way had had dealings with the lady who had set the whole case rolling – Lady Rowan herself – and that seemed even more far-fetched. Whichever way you look, he thought, at the moment the only person with a motive for killing is Peter Burns, especially if it's true there's a lover in the background.

'The chief's pleased,' Derrymore broke in on Reynolds' reverie. He leaned on his open window. 'Even thanked me himself. Smiled as if fit to bust.'

Reynolds, who knew Clemow's sharklike grin when he closed in for a kill, refrained from asking questions and let Derrymore continue. 'Slammed his fist upon the desk, fingers twitching, said that closed the case up nicely, and they could all get the hell out of this godforsaken hole.'

He gave a shrug. 'That's all he seemed to think about,' he added thoughtfully. 'Sewing it up and getting out.'

'And what do you think?'

'Well,' said Derrymore, hesitantly at first then warming to his theme, 'the Chief Inspector seemed so sure, it was hard to think up counter-arguments. Not that he asked me, you understand. But I wouldn't like to bet on it. To begin with, someone still has to make a proper identification of the remains before we really know it's Mrs Burns. And I got to thinking. Why has Burns come forward now, when there was no need to? I mean, the body might not be identified, although I suppose there might be some clue somewhere, but we don't know how much's . . .' He paused delicately to swallow the word 'left'.

'And until the body's identified, he could have sat tight and hoped to get away with it.' Reynolds nodded.

'Quite,' Derrymore said eagerly. 'On the other hand, he

might have come forward because he's afraid she'd be identified without him, and then where would he be, not even having reported her missing?'

'But suppose people start asking questions – where's she gone, sort of thing?'

'He could lie, couldn't he, could say she'd run on home to Daddy or gone off suddenly on holiday, could in fact invent any number of yarns that would be hard to prove or disprove and would let him off the hook even if she were found later. Except no one else might bother to make inquiries anyway, at least not in the village. She doesn't seem popular.'

He paused for breath. 'One thing's certain,' he said more soberly, 'identification won't be a pretty job, and if the poor bugger did it to her, serve him right.'

As Reynolds again made a non-committal grunt, 'So what's your impression, sir?'

'My impression?' For once Reynolds was unusually hesitant. 'I think it's all too pat,' he said at last. 'I suspect Burns told the truth that he'd been expecting her back. And that there is a boy-friend somewhere whom he doesn't know but thinks the rest of the world does. On the other hand, like all truths, he's told only part of it. When you mentioned the station, making statements and so on, suddenly it was his own image as schoolmaster that mattered. That wasn't feigned either. Funny for a murderer to be worried about something so petty, when murder itself doesn't seem to bother him.'

He snapped his notebook shut. 'Like you, I think the man is traumatized. He's only now put two and two together and found they've added up to six. To sum up, I think he protests too much about the wrong thing in order to hide something else. But what, that's for us to find out.'

'And the body in the sty?'

'My guess,' Reynolds said, 'for what it's worth, is that poor Marilyn Burns ran from what she thought of as a horror of a life and in doing so met an even more horrible death.'

Both men were silent for a while. 'What about the Travellers?' Reynolds then asked, as at Derrymore's insistence he now prepared to clamber into Derrymore's car, and Derrymore prepared to start it, struggling to retrieve the keys from a too tight trouser pocket. 'Have they turned up yet?'

'I've put a search out for them myself,' Derrymore said. 'Within my province that. For the damage they did the farmer. But so far no luck.'

He turned the ignition, swore under his breath as the engine failed to catch. 'They'll show up soon enough. They always do. Your proverbial bad penny.'

He turned the ignition again, waited, let the clutch out. With a shudder his ancient vehicle coughed into action and began to inch slowly and jerkily away from the kerb.

'Now where to, sir?' he asked happily.

Before Reynolds could answer, the decision was made for them. A girl, one of the typists he presumed, came out of the Incident Room and stood for a moment under the sweet-shop sign. She was a pretty girl, Reynolds thought, with a mass of fair hair tied up in ribbons, and smoky grey eyes. Then, seeing the car about to go off, she waved furiously to catch Derrymore's attention and came running after him.

'There you are,' Miss Henderson (he presumed it was Miss Henderson) panted in a breathy voice made more breathless by haste. 'The Chief's got a job for you – just come in. Damn it, he said, where's he gone? So I said I'd see if I could catch you outside.'

She smiled, showing all her pretty teeth, leaning one shapely elbow on the open window. 'A Lady Rowan,' she said. 'The lady with the flower-boxes. Wanting to make a statement. Very important, she said. So the Chief's passed it on to you. Since you'd handled Burns so well.'

And with this last (in Reynolds' opinion) condescending compliment, she gave a flashing smile and floated back indoors on a waft of perfume, leaving a flustered Derrymore and an intrigued Reynolds to deal with this third and, as it was to turn out, most crucial telephone call.

Chapter 10

'It started with a letter,' Lady Rowan said, in a voice that could only be called subdued. 'A year ago. Last summer.'

She received Reynolds and Derrymore in the main hall, not the intimate little study where she had ensconced Reynolds last time. There was no coffee prepared today, no elaborate staging. If anything she seemed to have rung the Incident Room on the spur of the moment, seemed to accept Derrymore's and Reynolds' joint arrival without question.

'I didn't save that one, or the others, but I remember the first one came from nearby,' she was saying, in the same quiet voice. 'Wadebridge, I think it was. Well done, it said. Saving the village green makes you one of us.'

She herself looked unexpectedly vulnerable, fragile almost, under the high domed ceiling with its bands of wooden rafters; the large, overstuffed chairs served to separate rather than draw her closer to the two men.

She was wearing her familiar floating garments, like Bedouin robes, Reynolds thought, unadorned except for a heavy gold cross. He noted how her hands reached for it almost without her knowing. And how again she smoothed down the layers of material, making her fingers do something to stop the trembling. As before he had the sensation, today even more overpowering, that she was afraid – afraid, he realized, of letting fear show.

Other letters had followed, she now explained, anonymous letters, all in the same style, put together by cutting out and crudely pasting words on rough brown paper, the sort used for wrapping parcels. All purported to praise what she was doing, yet in such a fulsome way she felt they meant the opposite. It wasn't exactly what they said, she repeated, her high white forehead knotting with effort, but the ambiguity. Each had a double meaning that made her uncomfortable. She'd tried to ignore them, tried to laugh them off, even tried to convince herself they came from villagers who secretly supported her. She had begun to dread their arrival. And yet, if a day passed without one, she missed it, as if it had become essential to her: 'Almost,' she said, 'as if someone was guessing my thoughts.'

The final one was different from the rest, although composed in the same way. It was what she called an invitation, asking her to 'join us' in some – party, reception, meeting – she'd never been sure what.

'Midsummer's Night,' she said. 'On the moors. Close to Bolventor. No, I didn't accept, of course. No, I don't know why.'

She had gone very pale. Even her lips were pale, and her hands crept again towards the cross. Reynolds felt a sudden surge of awareness. Her voice was unnaturally stiff, her body stiff; he sensed the effort to hold herself upright. Suddenly he was reminded of the war – his war as a volunteer officer in Aden in the sixties – when he'd helped in the rescue of a friend. It was something he didn't think about much, had tried, like other unpleasantness, to eradicate from his thoughts. Now it came back, the suddenness of the explosion, the paleness – like her the poor chap had gone almost white, as if all life had been leached out of him. Yet there was no trace of wound, until someone had unbuttoned the shirt. Then blood had suddenly come flooding out in a secret, horrific gush.

'And you never told anyone, showed anyone, these letters before you destroyed them?' Derrymore, at his most formal, sat forward on the chair, his back straight, his feet in line upon the rug, ready to jump to attention.

She closed her eyes as if she found the question unnecessary. 'I'm not stupid,' was all she said. 'Although what I did, some time afterwards, was stupid.' Refraining heroically from looking at Reynolds, Derrymore continued to take notes while she went on in the same dull monotone. 'A few days later, I found myself near the actual site. Of the invitation. I'd gone for a drive, and, quite by chance, there it was. The name. Scrawled on a piece of board like a signpost. So I told Masters, he's the chauffeur, to go on towards it.'

She's lying, Reynolds thought again. She meant to find it. Curious perhaps. Or something else. But certainly not by chance.

'I'd presumed it was a farm,' she was saying, 'but there weren't any farms up that lane. It ended on the open moor, with hills all round, with no way forward and only a little turning space cut into the grass.'

Again she fingered her cross. 'It may surprise you, but I like walking,' she said. 'It was a fine day. I told Masters to wait while I gave the dogs a run. I thought perhaps the farm was over the first hill, but when I'd climbed it I found only more open land, a vast expanse. You couldn't judge how far, there seemed to be no horizon, nothing but heather and rocks and, away at the furthest point, the shadow of Bolventor.

'The car looked very small down below,' she continued. 'I could see Masters smoking beside it, although he's not supposed to. I wanted to turn back, but instead walked on and presently came to a kind of gulley with a sheep-track running beside it. And where the gulley opened up, I saw we'd looped round in a circle and were under the tor again but on its other side. Below us, sheltered by the slope of the land, was a ruined building – the farm, I suppose – about a quarter of a mile ahead, but hemmed round by what looked like hills of sand. And, closer to where I was, between me and the farm if you like, running down from the crest of another hill, was a stand of trees.'

She closed her eyes. As if she's trying to remember, Reynolds thought. Or to block out memory.

'Before I could come to the trees,' she said, 'there was a broken-down wall with rusty barbed wire on top. In one place the wire'd been cut, so I climbed over and found myself in a patch of scrub, brambles, gorse and such, grass waist-high, that sort of thing. Wild land.'

She did shudder then. 'Wild land,' she repeated, 'old land. You felt its oldness. There were even traces of stone circles in the undergrowth, ancient hut circles, you could see them clearly, several of them, grouped along the inside of the wall, like bee-hives.'

She stopped as if she could not continue; her hand went to her throat, her face was drawn. While they waited for her to go on, Reynolds was struck again by how beautiful she looked in repose, without any of the false animation that had so irritated him the first time they met. This was the lady herself, pared to the bone. He felt a sudden spurt of desire that was new to him, a wanting to shelter her from whatever must come next. Take your time, he wanted to tell her, as he had so often in more formal terms cautioned other reluctant witnesses. Reflect. Try, for your own sake, to get it straight. Her fragility seemed to break through his own defence. Suddenly he wanted to have the right to defend her from herself.

Perhaps she sensed this, just as before she had sensed his other change of mood. Making a brave effort, she began to describe what else lay inside the wall. Beyond the hut circles which made a kind of inner barricade – a second, ancient wall within the more modern outer one – she noticed a faint track in the grass. The track was barely discernible, recently made and then allowed to grow over again. It wound the last few yards towards the trees and yet seemed somehow to stretch for miles.

The trees themselves were firs, their low-lying branches making a third dense wall. There was a gap, however, on the right-hand side, to which the track led. But where it entered the wood, a hawthorn branch had been stuck into the ground like an archway. It had been put there deliberately. She had seen where the top had been looped and tied to a separate piece of wood. You wouldn't notice unless you got up close: it was so cleverly done, it almost looked natural.

'The dogs saw it when I did,' she said. 'They had been running on ahead but now they stopped and wouldn't go under it. One actually sat down and whined. I thought at first it must be electrically wired, which didn't make sense: why wire an arch in the middle of a patch of grass? But of course it wasn't that. Dogs sense things, too,' she said.

'I didn't force them,' she went on. 'I left them and ducked under the hawthorn branch. Although I didn't really want to.'

She leaned forward, clutching her cross openly now. 'I don't know if you can understand,' she said. 'I both wanted yet didn't want. It was the strangest feeling. I remember also how warm I felt, suddenly hot, as if the heat of the day were trapped there. Yet on the moors, despite the sun, it had been cold. And it was very quiet. Still. On the moors there's always wind. It was only when I got right under the first branches that I heard the noise.

'A buzzing,' she said, 'a humming of thousands and thousands of flies. And there, in a clearing, was a stake. With a head on it.

'I'm sure it was an animal,' she said, 'what was left of it. I saw horns, ram's horns, perhaps, I didn't stay to look. I ran. But I remember the place, and the name of the farm. Hanscastle,' she said.

Her hands had stopped trembling. She sat up. 'I ran all the way back to the car, at least wherever I could run,' she said. 'I got in and told Masters to drive away. I've never been back there since. And I've never spoken about it to anyone, not even to him, although I'm sure he'd remember going there. He'd have seen how out of breath I was. And at the time he mentioned how frightened the dogs were.'

And how frightened you were, Reynolds thought. Unable to restrain himself, he said in a voice made harsh by tension, 'You didn't tell me all this when I came before.'

It was a statement, not a question, and she made no attempt to apologize or explain; just stared ahead with her dark, intelligent eyes. When she did answer, her voice had become impersonal, frosty. She'd speak to Masters in exactly the same way. 'What do you expect me to tell, Inspector? That I was involved with Satanic worship?

'That's what it is, isn't it?' she cried, and now both men could sense the fear, and more than fear, in her voice. 'Some witches' coven. Do you think I want to be connected with that? I've told you what I know, and that's enough. But that body in the pig-pen, they say now it didn't have a head. And it'll soon be Midsummer again.'

It's strange, Reynolds thought, as he had so often in the past, you sit in some peaceful room like this, and listen to horror. Or you walk into some ordinary place and horror jumps out at you, as if it's always been waiting.

'I'm glad you've come forward,' Derrymore said, taking up the slack, speaking soothingly, although she hadn't asked for soothing. 'You've done the right thing. I'll pass the information on. You should have spoken up before, of course, but you mustn't blame yourself. Have you any idea who sent the first letter? Was it the same person who sent the . . . invitation I think you called it?'

If she felt Reynolds' unspoken reproof, she didn't show remorse. 'I've said I didn't keep the letters,' she said, her voice cold. 'And after that they stopped. I thought it was because I hadn't gone at their request. More recently, however, after the events of these past days, I've begun to wonder if it was rather because I did go when I shouldn't have. It's possible someone was watching. Someone could have reported it.'

The thought seemed both to frighten yet animate her. 'For one thing, there's the man who owns the pigs: he might have been hiding there. And wasn't there a tramp with him?'

Reynolds didn't comment. Personally he doubted it. It was her way of putting them off some scent. Besides, Bestwick was too lazy, and Ted too much a vagrant to be a good spy. But all that could be checked, of course. When, on their way to the village to retrieve Reynolds' car, Derrymore asked him again what he thought, Reynolds said, 'She's keeping something back.' Even saying so aloud made him angry. 'First pulled the wool over my eyes, all that waffle about her bloody meeting. Now, throwing Bestwick's name as a bait, pretending she doesn't know who the letters are from. Look how many times she twisted to avoid answering straight. She may not know for sure, Constable, but she guesses. And ten to one it's that which frightens her.'

He calmed down. 'But the rest of it: letters she has or hasn't kept, invitations to some witches' Sabbath, sacrifice, animal or human – it all sounds far-fetched. As if the lady doth protest too much. On the other hand, I think she believes in what she saw. So what do you know about witches and their doings here on Bodmin Moor? And I don't mean the children's book variety.'

To his surprise, Derrymore took the question seriously. 'There's always been talk,' he began, 'but only talk, nothing positive. When I was a boy, people whispered about these things. And, as you know, sir, there are some very old and weird places up on the moors, ancient places. They used to say the Druids worshipped there and held human sacrifices. There was a case several years ago, before I was on the force; you may remember it. Some pre-Christian holy well that had been taken over and desecrated, the well itself decked with streamers, votive flags, bits of dead animals, you name it. But never anything like that here in St Breddaford. Not that I'm aware of.'

And he would know, Reynolds thought; that was the sort of thing a good local policeman would know. 'Having said that,' Derrymore now continued, more slowly than ever, as if trying to put thoughts in order, 'Midsummer's Day always brings out the strange in people, as if it's some sort of licence to do odd things. Rock concerts, raves, folk festivals, notice how they all favour June – to say nothing of those so-called sun-worshippers at Stonehenge. And something else. Ever notice the number of little shops that opened everywhere – proliferated's the word, suddenly every village had to have one – the sort that sold posters, incense, candles, funny little statues of dragons and monsters and such? Even masks. Devil's masks,' he said.

'Myself I thought they came in with the newcomers,' he added, 'were part of city life that the newcomers brought with them. Probably were connected with drugs, although that's harder to prove. The girls who worked in them were always local girls, fresh out of school. Simple country girls. Didn't know anything, not even who their employers were. Someone "up-country", they'd say. Well, it was a job, and I suppose better than selling soap in the local Boots.'

They had come to the village green again, he pulled up with a jerk, sounding aggrieved. 'You won't find many of those shops left now,' he said. 'With the recession, when the newcomers left, they collapsed, were among the first places to go under. Good riddance. You've seen the empty one in St Breddaford?'

Reynolds remembered it, a slightly furtive little place with a dust-streaked window, like so many others abandoned now. But he'd never been inside. 'They sold posters too,' Derrymore said suddenly. 'Special ones, the ones they hid. Buried behind the more harmless sort of wild-life or mountain scenery. Great staring faces, monstrous gargoyles. "You get rid of these," I told the girl in St Breddaford. "Scare people half to death." '

He was silent, as if only then aware of what he'd said. After a while he added, 'She's still about, on the dole I think if I can get hold of her. And now what next, sir? Because if you've no objection I think Hanscastle Farm's our first stop before we tackle anything else.'

And without waiting for reply, without waiting for

Reynolds to get out, retrieve his own vehicle and follow him, to the other's amusement he jerked his own car into gear and drove them both off, chin sticking out determinedly.

The lane leading to Hanscastle Farm was still rutted with thick oily puddles that made the wheels spin. Today there were no police, no frantic press, no spectators, only the stillness of an old ruin smouldering in the sun, the empty pig-pen scraped clean but its stench unmistakable. Tags of red tape fluttered where Bestwick's van had been parked, his driving certainly erratic, as the zigzag marks on the dried mud at the verge showed. Red tape also marked the criss-crossings of various boots and shoes, dried footprints whose patterns dipped in and out of the festering pools. Nothing much new to be found here, Reynolds thought, although he followed all these tracks as far as he was able. In any case, they would already all have been examined closely and their duplicates recorded on file. Clemow was too well-trained not to be thorough here, and it was the sort of work he liked.

Stepping gingerly across the drained courtyard, the two men next peered through the splattered windows, straining to see the inside of the house. It was a shell. Floors and doors had long been removed and the walls were cracked and broken, the remaining plaster splattered with dirt. Once it may have been a home for a genial God-fearing farmer; now, in spite of the sun, it felt cold, the cold of ancient indifference to modern tragedy.

Glad to move away, Reynolds let Derrymore lead him round the back, following roughly the track which Ted had used. They climbed steadily. Sand heaps, like little pyramids, rose on their left; on their right, clumps of trees shimmered in the heat. Soon they were sweating in the sun, glad of their boots as they waded through patches of bog or stumbled over heather roots twisting snakelike between the bracken. When at last they reached the top, they soon found where Ted had made his first turn from the open moor, then, moving sideways, began the search for Lady Rowan's route.

They were above the sand piles now, on what seemed an open plateau, just as she had depicted it, without horizon or limit. High up like this there was a breeze which dried the sweat; underfoot crickets jumped; overhead skylarks spun away into the blue, small dark specks too small to create such a volume of sound. Again, despite the seriousness of their quest, Reynolds felt a flicker of appreciation, when abruptly Derrymore stopped.

Ahead of them, looking closer than it was, a jagged line of rocks marked the crest of Bolventor; nearer, another track circled from the tor back towards the farm, a thin sheep-track this, running into a stand of trees that stood dark green and dense, a fir wood, just as Lady Rowan had described.

'That's it,' Derrymore panted. He consulted a map pulled from an inner pocket. 'If she followed round Bolventor as she claimed, the car would have been left here.' He jabbed with his thumb. 'We'll check on that later. But if she came this way, those must be the trees.'

'Has anyone else been up here yet?' Reynolds asked, meaning Clemow's men and grinned, amused at the thought.

'Not bloody likely,' Derrymore grinned back. 'You won't catch them getting their feet wet.'

As they approached the fir trees, they began to recognize where they were. They could see the farm below; from this angle it looked quite different, the shape of the building settled comfortably into the hill, as if it had grown there. They found the wall, climbed over, passed the bramble-covered hut circles. There was no hawthorn arch today, but there was still a path, very faint, like a badger's track, leading towards the trees. And for a moment, unconsciously perhaps, both men paused to listen.

Then Derrymore went resolutely forward, brushing aside the branches so Reynolds could follow. Side by side both men began to search, never separated by much more than a trunk's width, yet suddenly both feeling very much on their own – unconsciously they found themselves tiptoeing. It was very still within the trees, no wind, no sound except the stir of their own feet through the thick scattering of pine needles. The light was dim, deep green, like an underwater cavern. But although they found what might have been Lady Rowan's clearing, it was empty. And although they traversed the plantation from end to end, crossing and recrossing within its secret depths, they saw nothing, heard nothing, found nothing. It was only when they emerged into the open for the last time that Reynolds looked up.

At first he did not recognize what he saw: the bracken-studded bank above them, crowned with its concentric circle of thorns: the photograph that had been hanging in Marilyn Burns' sitting room. He opened his mouth to shout, found he couldn't speak, probably the smell of fir sap had dried his throat. Or perhaps it was anticipation that set his heart pounding. Derrymore, who had long ago removed his helmet and was bent over, swiping at the bits of fir clinging in brown patches to his serge trousers, actually jumped when Reynolds tugged at his arm and pointed.

Not waiting to explain, Reynolds started up the bank, its

sides as steep and fiercely defended now by gorse as it ever had been in its two thousand yards of history. Here there was no track. Both men had to scrabble for footing, their nails broken by the stony ground, their faces scratched by thorns. When they reached the outer bank, they plunged down into a ditch through a mass of brambles thick as a man's arm, then scrambled up the other side through a blackthorn thicket to the top of the inner bank. And then, suddenly, there they were, within Hans Castle itself, the old Bronze Age fort for which the farm had been named, with its rings of encircling banks and ditches leading to the flat central enclosure.

The enclosure was a perfect circle, not large, at best meant to give security to only a small group of people. But it was not its size or shape that overwhelmed, it was its colour, a deep, unexpected purple where bluebells had formed a dense mat. The mass and shimmer of colour was almost blinding as if a circle of the sky had been cut out and pasted there. It took a moment or two to focus on what should have been immediately apparent, the grey slab of granite with the wooden stakes set at its east and western ends, two freshly sharpened stakes, jutting nakedly above the rich carpet of flowers.

'Two,' Derrymore said later, when they had had time to examine the stakes, when they had paced out the distance between them and the granite slab, when they had forced their way round the rim of the enclosure and taken measurements; when, after careful searching, they found another path, an easier one this, coming up from the opposite side, probably the one used by whoever had hammered the stakes in place.

Derrymore was not just stating the obvious; the thought had leapt into both men's minds. Two stakes – for a Midsummer's ritual, two days hence. And if the headless body in the pig-pen was the first, who would be the second victim? Had this second victim already been singled out and sacrificed? Or was there time to prevent a second murder as hideous as the first?

Chapter 11

This terrifying prospect changed everything. A host of new conjectures and new possibilities immediately sprang to mind, then gave way to haste. For if they were right, then on Midsummer's Night the old fort would see a second murder as barbaric as the first. Against that thought, all rivalries paled into insignificance.

'Clemow's got to be told.' Not without a pang, Reynolds overruled Derrymore. 'It's too big for us. He's got to handle it, we can't.'

But when, back at the Incident Room, Reynolds tried to persuade Clemow of the urgency, the Chief Inspector scarcely bothered to listen; Reynolds might as soon talk to a barn door. At first Clemow had been in a good mood. He admitted that several new clues had been found – scraps of clothes, cream-coloured wool – to make identification of the body certain. Burns himself had already been charged with the murder of his wife; the case was solved. 'I've got Burns safe,' Clemow said, with a wink to his staff who were trying to eavesdrop. 'Give me a few more hours, he'll break.'

When he confesses to murdering Marilyn Burns, was what Clemow meant. But when Reynolds tried to argue, when, for once, Reynolds urged caution, Clemow turned nasty, taking pleasure in exercising his superiority, flaunting it. You haven't caught me off-guard today, his behaviour said.

Any suggestion of fresh evidence was met with open laughter, as was any request for further investigation. As for keeping watch at Hanscastle Farm, or issuing a public warning, 'You can't be serious,' Clemow said, at his most sarcastic. 'If you're suggesting diverting a routine domestic crime into some witch-hunt; if you're telling us Burns is also leader of a witches' coven,' here he gave another wink, 'you need your head examined. What proof do you have? And who would believe you if you did?'

Taking advantage of Reynolds' discomfiture, he gloated. 'It's you I'm thinking of, old chap,' he said, his condescension worse than sarcasm. 'You don't want to be caught barking up the wrong tree.' He smirked. 'Or rather, barking up the wrong broomstick.'

Making it clear that Reynolds' very presence was an added insult, Clemow went on to suggest, with a contemptuous snort, that if Reynolds were besotted with witches and – what were they called? – with Cornish 'piskies' and such, he, Clemow had more pressing matters well in hand. As for sharpened stakes, Midsummer rituals, sacrificial rites – once more he gave his contemptuous laugh – surely Hanscastle was already enough in the news to keep all would-be witches and drunkards at home. And that's where Reynolds ought to be, snug by the fire, slippers on, glass in hand.

'Stick to your writings, old son,' Clemow said, smiling patronizingly. 'Keep your imagination for books. As for that blithering idiot you've seduced, trotting at your heels,' here Clemow's voice became icy cold, 'that Derrydance or whatever his name is, I'll have him dancing to a new tune when I get hold of him. I'll have him off the Force. Aiding and abetting a has-been, addled with booze.'

This last was said sotto voce, but Reynolds heard it clearly enough. He wheeled round. Suddenly, all the things that he should have said six years ago and hadn't, rose up like bile. 'Say that again,' he gritted, 'utter one more ruddy lie, it's you'll be off the Force, if there's anything left of you, that is, after I've pushed your lies down your throat.'

His outburst terrified Clemow. He could see the man's fear in the way Clemow's jaw opened and his mouth worked. Like a fish, Reynolds thought, like a goddamn fish caught hook, line and sinker. He stared at Clemow, taking in the white hair, the petulant mouth, the arrogance, thin as paper. Whatever did my wife see in him, he thought?

As rapidly as it had come, his anger evaporated. 'She used you, you know,' he said, conversationally. 'You were just the means to an end. You were no more than the others, just the last of a long line in a game she was growing tired of. In fact, if anything I owe you thanks for getting her to let me go. Your having each other was more than worth my freedom.'

And, having said this aloud to the man whom he had once cursed for trying to cause his ruin, he did feel free, jubilant.

He looked long and hard at Clemow. 'But if your conscience won't let you listen to reason,' he said, 'at least send someone to take a look for themselves. You've nothing to lose by agreeing. And certainly nothing to gain by refusal.'

But when once more Reynolds found himself outside the Incident Room, his own sense of impotence still remained. No matter how deeply he and Clemow mauled each other, what was more important was preventing another death – if a second murder were planned, that is, and finding the murderer – if in fact there was another murderer.

Too many 'ifs', Reynolds thought, standing under the faded sweet-shop sign. Too many imponderables. Suppose I've let my dislike of the man cloud *my* reason; suppose for once Clemow's right and – what had Clemow's telling phrase been? – I've 'barked up the wrong tree'. Suppose after all we're dealing here with nothing worse than childish games, country lads playing with wood, cowboys and Indians. And suppose, like Burns himself, I've added two and two together and come up with six. But if I'm wrong, then Burns is worse than any witch or warlock and, under the schoolmasterly disguise, he really is a monster.

Round and round his thoughts raced. Perhaps he had lost touch. Always before he'd followed his instincts, and never before had they let him down. Suppose now his old sense of the rightness of things, the sense that Lady Rowan had commented on, had deserted him? He might have allowed Lady Rowan's disclosures to influence him too strongly, he might have been misled by her. But surely she believed what she'd last told them, surely she wasn't lying then?

Remembering how he'd felt when he'd entered the enclosure – the creeping of the flesh, the sense of what Lady Rowan had called 'old evil' – he was sure he was on the right track. But how to convince the world, and Chief Inspector Clemow, of that? It was at this point that fate intervened and gave him the first real lead he'd had. Or rather, Derrymore did.

Diplomatically, Derrymore had waited outside the Incident Room while Reynolds made his appeal. He now reappeared, beaming with delight, wiping his forehead with a ragged handkerchief, red-faced and hot, looking as if he'd gone back to reclimb Hanscastle.

'I've found her,' he cried. 'The girl in the St Breddaford shop. Remember I said it'd been shut down. While you were bearding the lion in his den, I took a stroll down Becket's Lane, and there she was, just coming out. Says she was told to keep the key and go in from time to time to check on things. Been out of work since, and not over-bright, but she's conscientious. Remembers all the regulars. And guess who came in every week, like clockwork, she says, buying this and buying that, and what she didn't buy fingering, as if she'd like to pocket it. Little Widow Penlore, that's who. A real village witch, or so she claims. Never went to see her herself, she said, but all the other kids did, to cure warts and things. And probably worse,' Derrymore added, with unexpected modern practicality. 'Unwanted pregnancies high on the list. Why else would she stay in business? But there you have her, your professional witch, if ever you want one.'

As for Reynolds' warnings of Clemow's threats, 'The Chief Inspector can go jump in a lake.' Derrymore was firm about that. 'If you'll see to Penlore, I'll tackle the ditcher. And round up old Ted. And if you want someone to watch up at the farm, count me in. On or off the Force.'

Reynolds caught up with Mrs Penlore just as she and her dog were starting out through the gate, presumably heading towards the moors. On seeing him, or perhaps hearing his car, with a surprising show of speed she turned into a gap in the hedge and scurried off, like a frightened rabbit.

Abandoning all pretence of a 'neighbourly visit', Reynolds ran after her, down an even narrower track almost obscured with nettles and briars. He was convinced he'd lost her when he came upon her crouching under a hawthorn tree like some genuine hobgoblin. By then he was so out of breath he abandoned any attempt at friendly courtesies.

'We have to talk,' he said, his voice abrupt. He caught her arm so she couldn't escape. 'Back at your house. There's things I need to look at and ask about.'

She didn't answer. He hazarded a guess. 'Such as where you got those pieces in your sitting room,' he said, 'and what you use them for.'

Sulky silence.

'And who comes to you for medical help,' he added, 'and what sort of medicines you sell.'

She stared at him, her mouth turned down, her feet, in the too-large boots, firmly planted among the tree roots. He took a final chance.

'I'd like to know about those medicines,' he said. 'And what garbage you put in them.'

At that deliberate insult she positively bristled. 'Only the freshest,' she cried, 'nothing wrong to them. But there, you city-dwellers think yourself so smart. You don't understand.'

'Then you show me,' he said. He gave her arm a tug. 'Lay on, Macduff.'

If she understood the reference or not, she certainly understood that he was serious. The dog, which had been sitting at her feet, stood up and began to plod forward. She followed it; Reynolds was close behind them both. And sure enough, in a little while, the track wound round and brought them back to her garden. All the while she kept up a running commentary of grievances, all pretence of senile rambling put aside: the moors were free, who was he to stop her going there, a stranger, poking in his nose where he wasn't wanted? And how were poor women to live if they were forbidden to use the fruits of the earth that the Lord provided? These days it was always the same. Don't do this, don't do that, made you sick. Not like the old times, more's the pity, when the young showed respect for old customs and people in general had the sense to listen to their betters. What was the point of growing old if you weren't treated right? All were arguments Reynolds agreed with in principle but now ignored, refusing to be drawn into discussion.

Once in her garden, he made his way round the house as he had done the first time, pushing through the assorted debris. Her kitchen at the back was as disordered as her garden: a jumble pile. But in a kind of lean-to scullery, tacked on to one side, he struck gold: glass demijohns full of dubious-coloured liquids, row upon careful row of bottles, jars, bunches of sweet-smelling herbs – he made a quick but thorough search while she looked on apparently without interest.

Under insistent questioning, she reluctantly answered him. Yes, of course she'd found the herbs, and yes, of course she knew where they grew: that was her secret. She kept them in reserve, she said, for when they were needed.

Here her eyes grew crafty. She shot Reynolds the malicious glance he remembered. 'I don't make people ill,' she said, 'I try to cure them.'

But when she saw him choosing several of her jars and potions, she grew angry again. 'Here, leave them alone,' she screeched, 'you've no call to rob me.'

'I have if they're clues in a murder case,' Reynolds said. Let her stew in that, he thought as, abandoning any hope of getting through the rubbish inside the house, he headed outside again, round to the front.

She grew agitated now, trying to pull him back, screaming that the door was locked. When, discovering she was right, he prepared to force his way in, she again tried to block him, clawing at his back, teeth and nails like a wild cat. Finally he tore her off and rammed his shoulder against the wood. As the rotten panels splintered and she screeched again in protest, 'I'll pay for the repairs,' he said.

The lock gave way, he stepped inside, into that darkened room with its cluttered tables and shelves, its scatterings of objects like votive offerings, its odd gleams and glitters. The broken door let in some light; when he pulled the curtains the material ripped. He was looking at a room crammed with knick-knacks – what had Derrymore called them? gargoyles – statues in brass and copper, carvings in stone. He picked one up, a male figure with a grotesque head, its body contorted into an obscene pose. He dropped it in disgust

'You've no right.' She was whining now, tremulous. Suddenly giving up on stopping him, she had retreated to the back corner where she now leaned against the wall, arms crossed on her breast, more than ever like some gnarled gnome. 'Where's your search warrant? Where's your card?'

He presumed she meant a policeman's badge. 'And where's yours?' he countered. 'Where's your pass, or invitation, to Midsummer's Night? Who sent it? And last year, when Lady Rowan received one, did it come from you?'

'That bitch,' she cried, 'not likely. She's not fit to walk this earth.'

I was right about them then, Reynolds thought, but he felt no pleasure in their hatred. 'Did you send it?' he persisted.

Her mouth worked, her eyes grew sly. 'That'd be telling,'

she said. She leaned towards him, her anger at her broken door seemingly forgotten. 'Isn't just everyone who's invited,' she told him, 'isn't just a walk-in, help-yourself affair, open to the public. You're chosen, see. Special. Mind you, some of us have worked for it.'

Like I have. The words lingered on the air, an unspoken boast. Curiosity got the better of him. 'And what do you do when you get there?'

'Talk,' she said promptly, 'you'd be surprised how lonely you get. Meet up with friends. Exchange ideas.'

She smiled as if savouring the memory. A coffee circle, Reynolds thought, almost smiling back, a Women's Institute exchange: my recipe for transforming frogs in return for yours. Except transforming frogs and other such magic tricks weren't what they met for.

'Last year,' he said, 'you chose Hanscastle woods. A fir wood to be exact. This year it's Hanscastle Fort. Why Hanscastle?'

When again she didn't answer, 'Because it's off the beaten track? Because you're afraid of people finding out? Or is it something worse than that?'

She began to say, 'Nothing to be afraid of,' when he turned on her. 'Unless you're selected for the sacrifice,' he said.

He leaned towards her, raising his voice. 'Who was the sacrifice last year? Who is it this?'

'Don't know anything about that.' Now Widow Penlore did sound frightened, and a fearful look came into her eyes. If she could have, she would have backed even further into the corner. 'That's not what I'm talking about,' she said. 'Nothing about that. I'm remembering the past, the good days, when we were young, before it all went wrong and cold.'

She began to shiver, holding her arms even tighter across her skinny chest. 'The good times,' she crooned, 'when the world was fresh, when I danced the night through under the stars. When Di Rowan was eager enough to be one of us, before wealth ruined her and made her hard.'

'And what do you know about Di Rowan?' he said. 'Her real name, for example, the one she had before she married. And how do you come to know so much about her? You do, don't you? A lot.'

He was pressing her now, his own curiosity as urgent as his need for information. Whether she would have answered him, he never knew. A sudden sound startled him.

It startled her too. She put out a hand to ward him off. 'We was only doing our usual walk when you pounced on us,' she whined, 'past the garden wall, and round the back, Toby and me, never out of earshot. I wouldn't have run and left it, never, never, unless you made me to.'

'Left what?' he said. Breaking in upon her excuses, again seizing her arm and dragging her aside, he leaned across her to find what she was trying to hide.

Behind her in the corner was another curtain, draped across an inner door. When he pushed it open, for a moment he was rendered speechless, although he should have guessed what lay behind it from the sound.

He was looking down the hallway, or rather passage, the long thin corridor like the ones on old-fashioned trains. Presumably it gave access to each of the former cottages, an addition made when they were changed into one dwelling. He'd seen the corridor from the other end where it was jammed with stuff. Here it was more open, blocked only by a pram. And in the pram was a baby, freshly awake and bawling, as babies tend to do.

But it wasn't its yells, or its red and wrinkled face, or even its presence that was so surprising. It was the way it was dressed, in a frock of fine white lace, long and frilled, like a Christmas cracker, from which its feet stuck out, pale pink and arching, like rabbits' paws. When he looked at them carefully he noticed that even the minute nails were coloured pink. On its downy head was a small lace cap, copied surely from a Holbein painting, a dainty cap, stiff as starch could make it.

Although he knew nothing about infants, he recognized something unusual here. 'Like a princess,' was the thought that came into his mind. He was to remember it.

Mrs Penlore snatched the child up, wrapping it in one swift movement in a long shawl – white too, he noted, as finely made. 'There, there, my lover,' she cried, 'did the naughty man startle her? Did she wake up sudden and want her mither? Old Granny's here.'

She turned on Reynolds, like a tiger, he thought, actually snarling, for the moment the triumphant female poised against the crestfallen male. 'Don't you know what babies are? And don't you know they can't be left, not even for a moment? And don't you ask who her mither is, 'cos I don't have to tell you nothing. Except I looks after her proper else her mither wouldn't leave her to me so often, would she now?'

Under the barrage of righteous indignation, Reynolds beat a retreat, unable to shake her from her crooning over the child, as before he was unable to shake her from her protestations of innocence. Both preoccupations were deliberate, he thought, easy ways of protecting herself from the unpleasantness of truth. Certain of only two things – that this was never any ordinary village child, not dressed in that fashion; and that whoever had left it with

Widow Penlore was no ordinary village mother using the widow's babysitting services while she went out shopping – he retired to the garden to retrieve the jars he'd chosen. He was just about to slam the front gate shut, when inside the house he heard the child cry out again and then stop short, as if someone had tried to smother the noise.

The cut-off cry seemed to echo like the wailing of wind, or the cry of a bird. When it ebbed away, it was the image of Frank Mathews' house that rose up before him, with its bare blank walls, its bare blank windows, and its torment-ing hint of unsolved mystery. His heart jumped painfully. And the meaning of the sound he'd heard there, the sound which had previously escaped him, became apparent: the stifled cry of a child in the house of a recluse who had no love for man or woman, and who was on record as saying all brats should be drowned at birth. Suddenly the whole question of Frank Mathews leapt to the forefront: who else was in Frank's house, and where was Frank? Cursing himself for an idiot, he picked up the jars, ran to his car and spun down the path, heading for the moors and discovery.

But when he reached Mathews' house, he was too late. The gates were open, as was the front door, the lights were on. Whoever had been in the house had gone. And if Frank Mathews had been there on Reynolds' first visit and had wanted to answer, if later he had heard the knocking of Clemow's men and again had wanted to cry out, he could not have done. He had been blindfolded and gagged, left naked in the cellar, among the litter and rubble he himself had tossed there.

Nor could he talk now. He was already dead, strangled with an old piece of rope, the body still warm when Reyn-olds found it.

Later, looking down again at the crumpled remains which Clemow's men, summoned by telephone, had cut free and then covered with a piece of frayed matting in an apparent gesture of respect, Reynolds was overcome with the futility of his profession. Always too late, he thought savagely, always a jump behind. For the first time in days he felt tired, his own body sagged. He felt the old craving. It was at moments like this, after defeat, that drink most promised salvation.

He straightened up and went slowly up the cellar stairs, pushing his way past the photographers, the forensic specialists, the fingerprint analysts. All around him the house was full of bustle, the usual hum of activity that he recognized from long experience, the avid air of expectancy that accompanies policemen about their work. But we detectives are always crime-solvers, he thought sadly, almost never crime-preventers, like doctors only called in when disease has taken hold.

Clemow was standing in the hall. When he saw Reynolds he came towards him quickly, ready to do battle.

'My men talked to him, Mathews; they swear it. Actually saw him standing at that window up there. There didn't seem any reason to doubt he'd chucked those rackets out himself. And they never were much of a clue.'

His manner was eager; too eager, Reynolds thought, forcing himself to listen. 'Of course I wasn't satisfied,' Clemow was continuing, his voice more under control at Reynolds' lack of response. 'Had in fact planned to send someone back with a search warrant.'

He paused, eyeing Reynolds obliquely, in the way he had, to see if his arguments were working. If that's true, Reynolds guessed; more likely Clemow felt insulted that Mathews hadn't responded in the way he should have done. Petty lie or petty truth, it didn't seem to matter. He nodded as if in agreement.

'I wasn't satisfied,' Clemow was repeating, still intent on excuses, elaborating now and no doubt partially mollified by that nod of seeming approval. 'I smelt something wrong. I intended sending two of my best men, if you hadn't got here first.'

He eyed Reynolds, as if debating asking what Reynolds was doing in Mathews' house anyway, then thought better of it. 'And what do you make of it?' he said offhandedly, as if he weren't fishing for information. When Reynolds, refusing to be drawn, remained silent, off on another track he gestured at the dilapidated walls. 'I meant the house,' he said. He stared round at the damp and dirty floor, the litter of neglect with which Frank had surrounded himself for years, as if only then noticing. 'Imagine inheriting all this,' he said with a touch of wonder. 'Never did a thing with it, I'm told, just camped out in a couple of rooms like a squatter. And the whole house loaded with stuff, my men tell me; I mean antiques, silver, jewellery, you name it, drawerfuls of clothes still in their original packages, a bloody wardrobe of suits, all moth-eaten.' He sounded personally affronted.

'Frank Mathews was a socialist,' Reynolds interrupted. 'Frank wanted to share his goods with the world. So whom did he choose to share them with?'

Clemow looked plaintive. 'I don't follow,' he began as he used to do so often in the past, when Reynolds, away on some train of thought, had left him far behind. 'There's no one here now. We're going over the place with a fine-tooth comb.'

'But there was.' Reynolds was terse. 'Someone with a child. Someone who cared as little as Frank did for the goods of the world.'

At Clemow's start, Reynolds continued. 'For God's sake, man, they left those valuables behind. So what sort of people are we dealing with, to ignore the riches of the world and live in a man's house and kill him for the fun of it?' He added, 'Because when you find out you'll find Marilyn Burns' killer as well.

'Burns couldn't have done this,' Reynolds added when Clemow didn't reply.

Clemow's shoulders sagged. He felt for a dust-grimed chair and sat down heavily, legs apart, hands on his knees. 'My God,' he said, 'been fooled proper, made right idiots of.'

He seemed shaken by this admission, more than by the actual proof of it. He caught hold of Reynolds' arm and drew him down beside him in the way he used to do, the expression on his round face suddenly defeated, almost deflated. If anything, Reynolds thought, he seems relieved I'm here. But he didn't feel any triumph in that thought.

'So what do you advise?' Clemow had given up his posturing, had relinquised pride, was actually begging. 'You must have had some reason for being here before us. What was it?' And again when Reynolds remained silent, 'For God's sake, don't clam up. Where does that leave us now? What shall we do next?'

Reynolds thought quickly. Here was revenge complete, if he wanted to claim it, if he in turn wanted to gloat. But his desire for triumph seemed, like Clemow's, to have withered. Well, there was no need to rehash the wherefores and whys of his presence – they could wait; nor did he have to rub salt in the wound by pointing out that Clemow should have taken him seriously when he had the chance.

He stared down at Clemow's dropping shoulders. Suddenly he couldn't stand the sight of them, nor listen for another moment to Clemow's whingeing.

'All right,' he said, 'I'll help. First, free Burns. Because he's got no more to do with it than I have. Second, round up all the other suspects and grill them for clues. Third, use Derrymore. He's good with the locals, better than we'll be.'

As if that wasn't what he'd been aiming for since Derrymore originally told him about the body in the sty.

And leaving Clemow mulling things over, he drove away – in search of the other woman who had conned him with her lies.

At first Reynolds thought Lady Rowan was expecting him. He couldn't be sure, though, for she was in the garden, kneeling by a flowerbed to pull at weeds, and had time to adjust to his presence before she met his gaze. The air was heavy with the scent of lavender and roses, the great heads of delphiniums swayed under their own weight, underfoot the grass was deep like moss. He had the sudden image of a medieval lady seated in her bower, receiving homage from her courtly knight.

She didn't get up immediately, rested on her heels looking at him with her large, grave eyes. He had the sudden wish, a stupid one, to be here as her friend, much as he had pretended to himself the first time. He imagined himself kneeling beside her there in the grass and helping her tie up her plants, their hands meeting, their fingers entwined.

She gave her brilliant smile, said, 'You like gardening. I'm thinning out here if there's anything you'd like.'

Caught again off-balance by her strange ability to guess his thoughts, he blurted out, 'How do you know that?' and did not know whether to be relieved or disappointed when she said prosaically, 'From one of your books, *The Make*

Peace House, I think. You describe a garden so accurately, your knowledge shows.'

She rose to her feet in one graceful movement, waving aside his proffered hand. 'You've something you want to talk about,' she said, 'but I've told you all I know. I've nothing more to add.'

'Except who wrote those letters,' he said. 'Did Widow Penlore?'

'Icky Penlore,' she interrupted, 'that trash? She's illiterate.'

He ignored the contempt in her voice. 'Icky,' he said thoughtfully, 'that's a funny name. I've never heard her called that.'

'It's what she was called at school,' she said impatiently, 'but that's nothing to do with it.'

'At school,' he repeated, 'a childhood name. And she calls you Di. The names you knew each other by when you were children together. But she's much older than you.'

There was no question, a statement. She twirled on him. 'So?' she cried. 'I never said otherwise. Yes, I knew her. In fact I once admired her, as children do an older girl. All right, I've admitted I was poor, a poor girl who married rich. Does it matter who I knew in those days?

'We didn't come from St Breddaford,' after a while she went on, 'only a small, insignificant village in Devon. Miles away. No one knows me here.'

'Except Icky.' And that's why you paid her off with a house, he thought, that's really why you both hate each other. And is that why you want to become Queen of St Breddaford, to make up for all the humiliation of your youth when you were poor and insignificant?

'Icky kept your secret,' he said. He felt he owed the widow that. He gazed about him. All this, he thought, looking at the smooth long lawns, somnolent in the sun, the clipped hedges, the vivid flowers, contrasting the exquisite order with Icky Penlore's tattered wilderness. Yet apparently it was not enough. Could poverty give one such a burning desire for luxury, he thought, could a deprived childhood engender such ambition to succeed? And what was to become of all this wealth; who would get it when the rich, the successful, Lady Rowan was no more?

'It's a big place, this,' he said. 'Too big. What's to become of it?'

'That question is impertinent,' she said. Her eyes flashed. 'Go back to your gardening, Inspector, where you belong. You've been neglecting it.'

Another rebuff, he thought, not without a rueful smile; the second person in so many hours to tell me I'm past my prime.

'Gardens can stand neglect,' he said, 'better than wives. Or husbands, for that matter.' He thought of Marilyn and Peter Burns. 'And did your parents know you were living here?' he asked.

She shook her head again. At his look, 'What's so wrong with that?' she cried again. 'I never went back to my home myself, never saw my parents, cut myself off. I had to, going back would have smothered me.'

'And did they mind that you'd—'

'Outgrown them?' She finished the sentence for him. 'Of course not. I'd already done that before I left.'

She leaned towards him, wanting suddenly to explain. 'You can't imagine it, can you, a village child with a burning desire for all things artistic? An unusual child: gifted, sensitive, clever, longing to see the world. I was expected to stay at home and work, marry a labourer like my father, my cravings satisfied as Icky's were, with little bits of rough-made pottery and wild flowers and fairy trinkets and such. That's what they called it in those days, fairy stuff. For my parents, going off to art school was as mad as flying to the moon. They never even imagined that I'd have it in me to break free. But after the war there were scholarships for people like me. And I've told you I had talent.'

'And met a rich man who became your husband.'

It was his turn to finish her story and bring her back on track. 'You said once,' he said, 'that it was you they wanted. Why was that?'

The sweat was beading on her face, her long hair was drenched with it. Again he sensed her fear, the same fear he thought that he had felt in Widow Penlore. 'It's hate,' she said.

But why choose Burns' wife instead, he thought, what had she done? Why choose Frank Mathews?

The answer sprang into his mind as if he had shouted it. 'To punish them.'

Urgency came back to him in waves. He forced himself to speak softly – stroking, they called it, probing to scrape out the last remnants of truth. 'If you had told me all this, if you had told me what I now know about Icky Penlore, a second murder might have been prevented.'

'A second murder.' She was stammering. She caught hold of him, her hand shaking. 'Who's the second?'

When he told her she let go and sat down on the grass, sank down like a doll with its stuffing gone. 'I didn't know,' she said.

'I've only just found out myself,' he said. He looked down at her thoughtfully. 'Have you anything to say, anything to add, that might tell us who the murderer is? Or what you know about devil worship here in St Breddaford?'

To his surprise she laughed. 'Devil worship, witches'

covens,' she mocked him much as Clemow had done. 'I told you, Inspector, I have no part in children's games.'

'Then what is it?' he cried. 'For God's sake what? You owe me that.'

He meant only that, as she had asked of her own free will to see him, had herself drawn him into the whole business, she should at least play fair. And perhaps she saw it as meaning that too, although afterwards he couldn't be sure if she hadn't taken it in another, more personal sense. When she spoke again her voice was low, almost a murmur, then growing in strength as if she were bringing herself to repeat what must have been a formula.

'They say the worship is the oldest in the world, before men destroyed it. And of itself it takes the threefold guise, the essential woman. Maid, harlot, crone.'

He looked at her, completely bemused. For a moment he thought she had gone quite mad. Then he saw she was in fact completely calm, although she was breathing hard. And as they stared at each other, she seated on the grass, he bent over her, comprehension struck. Once more he felt the hairs rise on the back of his neck.

'The old worship,' he repeated, 'the old mystery that flourished before Greece and Rome. The mother goddess cult, dead these thousands of years and yet still alive.'

She didn't say yes, she didn't say no, just sat and looked at him. And gradually things she'd said began to fit into place. Why she and Icky had quarrelled, for example, had been friends and parted, their marriages tearing them apart – not because of wealth and position as he'd thought, but because whereas Icky would have married for convenience, a nonentity of a man – he'd been right that she'd cared more for her dog than Mr Penlore – Diana Rowan had had the misfortune, in Icky's eyes, to have loved her husband.

'You know who the harlot is,' Lady Rowan was intoning. 'The village whore, who else? And I was to have played the part of crone.'

She suddenly stiffened. 'And to think I walked home alone that night,' she said, 'the night of the first murder. Poor Frank. He took my place.'

He remembered suddenly what she'd said of Mathews. 'A regular old woman.'

Perhaps she remembered too. She laughed in a hard, almost purposeful way. 'Well, he deserved it,' she said. 'As for maids, I doubt if there are any left these days.'

As he stared at her, mystified, 'There must be a maid,' she insisted. 'The third sacrifice.'

He heard himself whisper, 'There were only two stakes,' and her whispered reply, 'For the dead only.' And the image of that blue-flowered clearing rose up before him with its two white sharpened posts and the flat granite stone between, the altar stone, where the victim must be offered up, alive. How many times, long centuries ago, had human sacrifice taken place on that very spot; how often in the far past had the stone been stained and the priest splattered with the sacrificial blood? And it seemed to him he heard the sigh of the watching throng, like the soughing of the wind, as some white-gowned figure raised the sacred knife and plunged it into the living victim's heart. It equally seemed an age of time before he came back to himself with a start and found himself still in Lady Rowan's garden. His mouth was dry, his chest heaved as if he had been running.

'And is that all you can tell me,' he said, 'is that really all?'

At her nod, he told her, 'It'll have to be reported, it's no use trying to hide. I'll have to tell Chief Inspector Clemow and he'll want to see you. You may be held for questioning. Clemow may—'

'Suspect?'

Her smile was sweet, almost forgiving. 'Do I look like a murderess, Inspector. Do you think I could do that to anyone?'

For the first time he let himself wonder. 'Possibly,' he said soberly. 'Perhaps.'

And was rewarded by another brilliant smile that mocked him as it forgave. Later, at home, he was to remember that smile, he was never to forget it; much later, when he sat alone in his empty house, staring at the empty future. The cupboard door was open, the bottle top ripped off. He held up the brimming glass and drank, to the loss of trust, to the end of innocence.

Chapter 12

The news of Frank Mathews' death spread fresh fear through the village. This time, as if hardened by repetition, the inhabitants of St Breddaford huddled immediately outside the former sweet-shop, waiting for news. But the door remained firmly closed and no one from the inquiry team appeared to issue a statement (although according to connoisseurs of TV crime, they should have done). Instead the villagers were forced to listen to their own experts, whose explanations formed a running commentary on village gossip.

'Always knew it wasn't Burns,' one matron was declaring, smug with gratification. 'If another murder's taken place while he's inside, stands to reason he didn't do it. Of course can't say I liked his wife, stuck up, she was, but he'd not hurt a fly.'

'All very well,' another woman cried, pushing forward eagerly, 'I didn't like Frank Mathews no better. But neither did he deserve murdering.' While a third speaker added to the tension by asking, 'If Burns didn't kill Mathews, who did?'

There was a murmur, a rustle. 'So who's the other murderer in St Breddaford?' The third speaker, having captured attention, was warming to his theme. 'Someone we all know; perhaps one of us.' And for a moment everyone in the group shrank, as if the finger of suspicion rested on their individual shoulders.

The sense of gloom, of growing anxiety, was heightened when police cars drew up, each disgorging a cargo of passengers – what was the official term, those 'helping' with inquiries? – as if no one was bright enough to replace the word 'helping' with 'suspected'. People surged forward, drew back, repelled. 'One of us.' Here was the proof of it.

First to arrive was John Reynolds (who most knew only as the owner of Old Forge Cottage). He drove his own car and unloaded what looked like a crate of jam-jars. Without a word, without even looking up, he disappeared inside, leaving a wave of speculation in his wake. Behind him came an official car carrying Mrs Penlore. The widow's protests could be heard even before she was helped out, dragging her dog with her. Once on the pavement she began to limp, so pathetically she seemed to be in need of carrying, and for one ludicrous moment it seemed that Clemow's officers would stuff her in the pram that also accompanied her – a baby's pram, empty now but clean and neat, obviously used recently. God knows what an old woman was doing with a pram, and why it had been brought in as evidence. When she and it had been manoeuvred up the steps, the whispers broke out again. Where was the baby, whose was it, where had it come from, where gone? The women in the crowd were already fast dividing into factions over the importance of these suspects and clues.

Following her came Derrymore with Old Ted, equally protesting. However, when the old man saw the mass of people, swelling by the moment, he straightened up and tipped his hat, trotting up to the door, spry as a peacock.

And God knows what he was there for, either; everyone within miles knew what he'd found; he'd drowned himself in a hundred barrels full of beer by the rehashing of his discovery. With him came an old countryman, freshly shaved and dressed in his Sunday suit, the ditcher who had uncovered Frank's rackets, and whose discovery now overshadowed Ted's.

But the climax of the 'round-up', the real cliff-hanger, was the last arrival. At the sight of the Rolls the crowd drew back; the chauffeur held the door open; out stepped Lady Rowan, dressed in black, with a sort of veil drawn over her face. Lady Rowan as a suspect caused a palpable ripple, only partially dispelled when the Chief Inspector was seen to greet her as she sailed in, like some fully rigged galleon. And then the Incident Room door slammed shut again and the show was over. The spectators were left to their own theories. All except Sam Trewithin.

For Sam this flurry of activity came as a climax to a frustrating afternoon. Following his own advice to himself, he'd been concentrating on business, still trying desperately to keep himself and his agency afloat. But this afternoon his meeting with the local council had been postponed again for the umpteenth time, and his main ally among them had as suddenly turned coy (a defection which of itself was an unexpected blow; the man, one of his former clients, was tottering on the edge of financial ruin like Sam himself). The continuing disappearance of Hal and the Travellers (Sam's last trump card) was equally frustrating, and had caused Sam all kinds of problems. All-in-all the afternoon had been hellish, although no trace of preoccupation showed when he'd joined the throng. It was seeing Reynolds, guessing why Reynolds had been called in, that sent a cold shiver down Sam's spine.

He backed against the wall, as out of breath as if someone had rammed a bar against his ribs. The on-going arguments, by now mostly acrimonious, passed over his head; he scarcely heard them. Or if he did he wanted to shout at the perpetrators for being stupid fools. 'Wake up,' he wanted to bawl. 'Don't you see what's going on? Don't you know who Reynolds is?'

Ever since the ex-Inspector had come into his office, Sam too had been afraid – afraid Reynolds would become involved, sure if he did that Reynolds would discover his secret. Now he was certain that Reynolds lay behind this extraordinary gathering of suspects, had caused all these witnesses to be brought in so that information could be wrung out of them. Equally he was certain that Reynolds was biding his time to pounce on him.

True, he had his excuses ready, could swear he was also a victim, was as ignorant as the next man about what had really happened, in fact knew nothing. But he had decided it would be better not to be here when the questioning started. As unobtrusively as he'd arrived, he slipped away and hurried to his office where, with his usual thoroughness, he'd already made preparations. Without his meaning too, once more he was accompanied by the memory of what had really happened the night of Lady Rowan's meeting, and what it had done to him.

Inside the sweet-shop, officers bustled about importantly, glad to have something positive on hand after three days of inactivity. At the back of the shop several smaller rooms, once used for storage and still smelling damply of chocolate and toffee, were commandeered for interviews, and here the new arrivals were ushered, one to a room. Meanwhile a team prepared to do the interviewing, under

Reynolds' expert guidance. Sam Trewithin's guess had been shrewd. Clemow was actually allowing Reynolds to take charge.

In public, Reynolds deferred to him; in private he was already arranging the order in which he wished to see the various detainees, according to his idea of their importance.

In spite of his own disappointment and, more than that, feeling of new betrayal (if that word wasn't too strong; after all, what he felt for Lady Rowan had been unsaid, existed only in his own mind), once back on the job, Reynolds was totally professional. If he had had a drink or two, he had not got completely drunk; despite an aching head and furrowed tongue he had no problem in spelling out exactly how the interviews should be conducted, and by whom, had coached the interviewers on methods and procedures, even to a prepared list of questions, so thorough in all things that hopes of 'cracking' the mystery surrounding the case now ran high – providing Clemow stuck to his part of the bargain.

Reynolds knew Clemow well enough to have fears that he might interfere. After initial gloom, Clemow easily bounced back. It was to avoid the possibility of interference, therefore, that reluctantly Reynolds allowed the Chief Inspector to lay claim to Lady Rowan as the chief prize, not meaning exactly to throw the lady to the wolves as he'd threatened, but rather obliged to offer her up to keep Clemow quiet. If he also hoped that Clemow's thoroughness might break the lady down, if he banked on Clemow's famed efficiency, he was, alas, quite mistaken. Meeting Clemow for the first time, the lady proved more than capable of holding her own. Instead of the probing she doubtless deserved, she made another convert, shamelessly twisting the Chief Inspector round her fingers as easily as she'd twisted Reynolds.

'Charming,' Clemow was afterwards to confide, when in his heavy fashion he'd guided her through her abortive meeting and the subsequent attack on her flower-pots. As Reynolds had hoped, he concentrated on material clues – for example, who else was at her meeting, and why had it ended the way it did; what had she done to annoy those present; why had she waited so long to confide in the police? But instead of exploring these questions as he ought to have done and, almost paranoid, by shying away from the darker, more nebulous side, he avoided any mention of the happenings of the previous year, and ignored completely the threatening letters. In short, by rehashing accurately all that already had been told but uncovering nothing new, Clemow failed completely to break down the lady's resistance, and fared as badly as Reynolds had done. Despite Reynolds' hopes for him, he yielded the field to Lady Rowan without firing a shot.

When finally she broke in impatiently, 'I've explained all this,' her imperious manner so unnerved the Chief Inspector (as did her constant repetition that St Breddaford was under attack) that all he could bleat was, 'Quite,' although his tone was anything but certain. He rose. 'And who's to blame for that?'

His query was meant to be jocular. He didn't expect her reply. For the first time he was jarred out of complacency. 'You are,' she said, 'and all the thousands like you. All of you who forget the past and replace its beauty with ugliness.'

Meanwhile, relying on Derrymore to keep Icky Penlore quiet (for at the sight of Lady Rowan she had stiffened and Toby had growled), Reynolds concentrated first on

Burns. A few hours' detention, even one in an old sweet-store, had not defeated Burns; if anything it had made him even more defiant. When he saw Reynolds, he broke out into loud protestations, still seemingly more upset by the actual accusation than the nature of the crime. Grief at his wife's death, grief for the loss of what he called 'my own reputation' jarred with each other in blatant contradiction. Goad a mild man too far, Reynolds thought, and he'll turn to violence. Burns as a violent man still seemed unlikely, yet now, if given the chance, he attacked anyone who questioned his innocence.

When news of a second murder was broached, obliquely, without naming the victim, Burns jumped up, banging his hand on the table so fiercely that the obligatory recording device crackled. 'There you are,' he shouted, his unshaven face suddenly mottling purple, 'I told you a killer was roaming loose.' It was only after he'd calmed down that he appeared to realize this second murder, happening as it did while he was locked up, lessened the suspicion cast on him.

Only lessened; did not entirely exonerate him. As far as Clemow was concerned, Burns wasn't ripe for releasing yet. 'We may still be dealing with two crimes,' Clemow had said, 'and a bird in the hand is better than none.' So while Burns was still in custody Reynolds drew him back again and again from his grievances to the night of the murder. What had he and his wife really quarrelled about, what had actually been said when they parted that he had felt the need 'to make amends'?

And gradually, as Burns began to listen to reason, those qualities which had once made him a good teacher started to reveal themselves. Finally, his resistance over, he allowed himself to co-operate, sometimes showing himself

177

capable of subtlety, sometimes even anticipating Reynolds' line of questioning.

First he admitted that the quarrel, like many others, had been mainly about Marilyn's 'friends'. Or man friend, to be exact. What Marilyn saw in him, why did she persist, why was she so bent on ruining herself and her marriage, and so forth? Questions which Marilyn stoutly refused to answer, denying any implicit accusation. 'You're inventing things,' she'd laughed at him. But also, in a way, this last quarrel had had an extra edge to it; for once Marilyn hadn't had things all her own way, he'd stood up to her.

'If you leave this house tonight,' he'd threatened her, 'you don't come back. If you're not here when I return, we're finished' – threats that now he regretted as having a double meaning he hadn't intended.

Of course he hadn't meant them, they'd been uttered in the heat of the moment. And perhaps in turn his unusual outburst had given him courage to stand up to Lady Rowan. Although in his personal affairs it hadn't been wise – Marilyn didn't take kindly to his speaking out. Challenged, she'd do exactly what she shouldn't, out of obstinate perversity.

Of course, he'd been devastated when he returned from the meeting to find the house empty, his notebooks ruined, everywhere the signs of impetuous departure – he'd sat down and wept. And of course the quarrel had also been the reason for his own silence when she didn't return. He didn't want to believe that she'd accepted his challenge and thrown him over for what he called her 'fancy man'. He wanted her to come back, he willed it. It was only after hours of waiting that he'd reluctantly faced the fact that she'd left him. And more hours still before the awful thought occurred that there might be another cause for her disappearance.

'That's where I do blame myself,' he now admitted, 'that I drove her to it.'

As to the lover, the man she'd run to find, so fast she'd not bothered to turn off the television or close the front door, not a clue, not a hint, not even in the village where gossip thrived and where he knew she wasn't liked. 'The husband's always the last to know,' Burns said with unconscious irony, as if it were a newly discovered maxim.

He'd said before that Marilyn herself always denied that there was a secret man friend. But if there wasn't a lover, what was she doing, off on her own at all hours, immersed in some private project that seemed to sap her concentration and leave nothing for him?

It was then, changing the subject abruptly, Reynolds asked about the photograph in the sitting room. Where had it come from? Why was it kept there? Had Burns himself ever been to the place?

Burns seemed surprised at the questions. The photograph was Marilyn's, he said. She'd bought it – found it, she said, in one of the small shops that was closing down – he didn't remember when, perhaps a few months ago, but he knew where the shop was. In Becket's Lane, close to the village green. As for hanging it on the wall, she'd done so partly to annoy him because, although they owned other pictures, she hadn't even bothered to sort them out. He had no idea what the picture was, hadn't even known it was a real place. 'I thought it was, well, an artistic composition,' he said lamely, 'something that caught her fancy.' When Reynolds, as if in an aside, mentioned an old fort above Hanscastle Farm, Burns looked askance. 'Never heard of it before,' he said.

Leaving Burns for the moment, but more than ever convinced he had nothing to do with his wife's death, Reynolds moved on to the ditcher and Old Ted – not because he thought either was involved with murder, but because they might give him other clues.

Old Ted didn't like sharing attention, and the old ditcher didn't know how to handle it. Neither was a good witness. Patiently, Reynolds steered them beyond their actual discovery, to where and what they had been doing prior to it. The ditcher he let go early after ascertaining that the rackets had truly been in a ditch and had been found mid-morning; they must have been dumped after the storm because they were not wet. To Reynolds' regret, and despite assurances to the contrary, the poor man left in a fret, sure he was accused of stealing. As for Old Ted, when he realized that it wasn't himself and his find that were of interest, only what he knew of the Travellers, like a spoilt child he sulkily refused to talk. Reynolds had to summon up all his skill to coax out replies, and only after prodding did Ted grumpily admit he didn't 'know' the Travellers at all, had no idea how long they'd been together or who they really were. He'd scarcely ever spoken to them as individuals, and had escaped from them without becoming intimate with their customs. (Here he gave Reynolds a sharp glance which said, 'So much for stupid questions.') As for the relationship between them, he wasn't the sort to pry into people's lives. (Again a sharp look.) No, he didn't like the one called Meg, and yes, he didn't much care for Hal, for reasons previously given. But, having said that, he also admitted that if Hal had been brought up right, if he, Ted, had had the training of him, Hal wouldn't be all bad ... Like Bestwick's pigs, Reynolds thought, half amused.

He listened as Ted elaborated with surprising fluency, fiddling with his hat where the flowers were beginning to wilt. 'Hal had this thing too about freedom, see. He loved the countryside. He could be loving. The rest were full of hate.'

And to Reynolds' inquiring look, he shook his head. 'Got to get rid of all that hate,' he said. 'Hate's no good.'

Which shows there's more to common sense, Reynolds thought, than all the textbooks on psychology.

He leaned forward. 'If they left their campsite, where would they go? Did you share your other routes with them, did you show them other haunts?'

'I'm not a complete idiot.' Ted was succinct. 'And I've already explained they'd have liked to get at my secrets, but I was too sharp for them.'

Reynolds persisted. 'You spoke of escape just now,' he said. 'Were you frightened by them, frightened of what they might do?'

Ted considered. 'Perhaps,' he said.

'And if they hadn't anywhere to hide, could they have broken into someone's house?' he asked. 'Could Hal have killed for it?'

To his surprise Ted laughed, a laugh which turned into a cough. 'Why would he do that?' he cackled. 'There'd be no need.'

He laughed and coughed at the same time. 'They was always talking of it,' he said. 'Squatting, they called it. But Hal said wait. They was each going to be given a house. During the winter months. Out of the weather. That's what Hal meant by community, see. All at one time.'

At Reynolds' stare he cackled again. 'I told young Derrymore the first morning,' he said. 'That's why I'd left. What would I want with living in a house?'

When Reynolds, cursing himself for an idiot, asked who was going to give them this house, Ted laughed a last time. 'Sammy Trewithin, of course,' he said, 'who else?'

Which is why Icky Penlore was left until Sammy Trewithin was found. And why Sam could no longer escape from what he had been trying to hide.

It took but a moment to send two of Clemow's officers along the main street to Sam's office. It was already late but they found him there, along with his packed suitcase, passport and French francs on the desk in front of him, his car outside loaded, everything in readiness for a speedy getaway – except he hadn't gone. As if at the last moment, they said, he had waited for them, mesmerized, like a rabbit confronted by a fox. Guilt takes some people that way, Reynolds thought when they told him, when he saw how Sam now slumped heavily in a chair; some people can't stand guilt.

Like Clemow, Sam had a deflated look, suddenly shrunk into his clothes. The fair hair had thinned, as if before it'd been padded by a wig; the ruddy cheeks had paled, the worry lines deepened: he looked twice his age.

Presently, however, when the immediate shock wore off, he was all eagerness to talk, as if a weight was being lifted from his shoulders. The police as confessional box, an old story. And gradually, as he spoke, he recovered something of his former ebullience. Again Reynolds listened patiently. It was an old trick, confess to something small to hide something large. They would come to the large in time.

With many a self-deprecating smile, with many a self-deprecating shrug, Sam now admitted to his plan for saving his business. And, incidentally, his dealing with the Travellers. At best it was a shabby little trick, scarcely worth the trouble it had caused. Reynolds stared impassively ahead as Sam defended his policy of housing the homeless at government expense, presumably keeping the rents thus gained for himself, although that wasn't mentioned. At least not mentioned until Reynolds put the actual question: what did Sam himself gain from this tortuous financial juggling? Sam stared at him. 'I'd have thought it obvious,' he said, in the tone he must once have used to his old employers when he was in the process of buying them out. 'I get tenants, the council pays the bill, I pocket the cash.'

He jabbed with his finger, suddenly serious. 'I've properties of my own, too, you know,' he boasted. 'Bought 'em up when the going was good. I'm not squeamish who lives in those. As long as the pounds keep flowing, I don't care where they come from.'

Most likely from my taxes, Reynolds thought, irritated. He let Sam waffle on about the numbers of homeless, the numbers of empty properties, the need for putting one in the other, on the one hand echoing what Lady Rowan had said, and on the other advocating the very procedures whose dangers she had, apparently now, not exaggerated at her meeting. Amazing, Reynolds thought. Here's a so-called professional man, a successful man, as full of codswallop as Lady Rowan. They deserve each other. He couldn't restrain his sarcasm.

'Why select the Travellers as the recipients of so much munificence?' he asked.

Sam ignored the sarcasm, but he grew more cagey. Well, he said, he'd seen their camp on the moors, had Reynolds? If Reynolds had, he'd know that if anyone was in need of housing, they were. 'They are the homeless,' he said.

'And when did you see them last?'

Here Sam hesitated, an almost indiscernible pause. 'The night of Lady Rowan's meeting,' he said.

'Why?'

Again Sam looked embarrassed, mumbled that money had passed between them, which Reynolds took to mean he'd offered a bribe. 'Their leader and I,' Sam now hastened to excuse himself, 'Hal and I, made an agreement. He would hold the band together, I'd get them places to live.'

Under questioning, he admitted freely the Travellers weren't his usual type of 'clients', the sort he'd become used to, and he certainly didn't have much confidence in their keeping their word. But he needed a group to start with, and Hal had seemed a decent sort, happy to have his 'band', his 'followers' looked after. 'In winter,' Sam now explained, 'social conscience works overtime. A few cases of pneumonia causes miracles with Social Services; the council's bound to give support. And it'll be the saving of the housing trade, see if it won't, better than empty buildings.' Here he had the audacity to wink.

Again Reynolds let him waffle on, saving his most important questions to the end.

'So if you met this Hal to discuss business matters,' he said, 'where and when did you meet? And how did you fit him in with the girl you told me about, the "poppet" that didn't like being kept waiting?'

Sam didn't seem put off by these questions, handled them with surprising ease. Well, said Sam again, his tone confidential, as for explaining where he met the Travellers, it was his own suggestion that they meet at Hanscastle Farm or, to be exact, in the lane leading to the farm. It was convenient for him and for the Travellers, enabling them to take a short cut across the moor. And although it was true he'd never have thought of going to Hanscastle Farm except for the clients who'd jogged his memory, he'd not been there with them as recently as he might have suggested. His records would show when – last year, he thought. At that he sat up straighter, as if proud of his confession.

It was a bitch of a lane, he added; in wet weather a bloody bog. He'd pointed that out already to the inquiry officers; they'd have seen his tyre marks, the Jag's tyres were obvious.

Refraining from asking if he'd also lied to the inquiry officers, Reynolds continued to listen to Sam's answers to his patient questions. Yes, Sam knew about the ancient fort, he'd been there as a boy. And yes, of course he knew about the pigs. 'Get a cut of bacon when there's a killing,' he said with another wink.

As for the girl, here Sam turned shy, admitting he'd been stupid. He'd made a first mistake, broken his own rule about keeping personal pleasure and business apart. He'd seen the girl at the campsite, she'd caught his attention then; no, he didn't call her 'poppet' in her hearing.

'St Breddaford knew nothing about this girl-friend?' Reynolds asked.

Sam laughed and tapped the side of his nose, as if to suggest cleverness. They might gossip about his 'poppets', he said, but that's all they could ever do. He'd always been discreet before. Found it wiser to pick girls up by chance, far from home base, as it were, 'gather them'; a sudden look in a pub, a sudden smile, an idle chat when he felt like it. And then to part as casually, usually as friends; there was an end to it, nothing permanent or complicated. And that's what he'd done with this girl.

So St Breddaford had no idea who the girl was, or where she came from? No, Sam explained, sometimes he didn't know himself. 'St Breddaford can only envy,' he said, with something like smugness in his voice, as if suggesting envy sprang from the fact that, after forty years of frightened abstinence, he'd had the guts to break free from their inhibitions, lust running like gorse-fire.

And had she lusted, this last little 'poppet'? At that, Sam openly grinned. He didn't know her name or anything about her, he went on to explain. He'd taken her as lightly as he had other girls. He thought he'd found a bargain.

'And you didn't? Something went wrong?'

For the first time Sam grew quiet.

'And you didn't know Marilyn Burns? You never met her, you were never involved with her? You didn't see her that same night?'

Here Sam was overtaken by a fit of coughing. He had to stop, ask for a drink, complained of the cold. He needed a smoke to stop his hands shaking, he said. Reynolds waited for the performance to end. He'd seen hands shake like that before, and it wasn't from cold.

The tape machine running again, the room quiet, Reynolds bore down. A first mistake; Trewithin had spoke of his 'first mistake'. What then was the second?

Here once more Sam began to falter, to stutter, to repeat himself. It wasn't until Reynolds threw him the answer that he could bring himself to admit that Marilyn Burns had been the other mistake. He knew who she was, of course, but he hadn't had anything to do with her, hadn't wanted to become entangled with her in any way. It was only that she'd come into his office, asking to look at his property list. She and her husband wanted to move, she said, buy a place of their own with land; she kept a horse.

At first he'd believed her, she dressed well, spoke authoritatively. He knew who Burns was too, and the sort of place she was speaking about wasn't what you bought on a schoolteacher's salary. On the other hand, the rumour was that she had the money. It wasn't until he'd offered to take her out to look places over that she began to come on strong. 'All over me,' he said.

Well, he had some principles, he said, almost proudly. It went against his other rule to have a local woman whom he knew and who, worse luck, would know him. Yet her interest had been flattering. He hadn't resisted long.

But only the one time. He'd swear to it. Afterwards he'd told her straight that he didn't want to see her again, said he didn't think it fair on her husband. He hadn't told the truth, that it wasn't safe for him, but if she were sensible she'd see it that way too. As far as he was concerned, it was over with as soon as it had begun. Months ago now, it was, more than a year. Again his records would show the day he'd driven her out. Where had they gone? Nowhere special, certainly not up on the moors. And he hadn't seen her since. Here again he stopped.

Reynolds tried another tack. If Sam met Hal at the farm, then where did he meet the girl?

After a while, Sam reluctantly explained. It was the girl, he said, who'd reminded him about the fort, showed him where to park so he came up on it from the moorland side. 'You'd think it was exposed up there,' he said, with a little flash of the old Sam, touting dubious property. 'Open to the elements. And it is. But just below the western bank, under the ditch, is a cave cut into the rock face; probably an entrance to a mine, but dry and surprisingly large. You could hunt ten years and you'd never find it, unless someone showed you where. I went there often as a boy but didn't know it existed. And I don't know how she found it, but she did.'

So that was his undoing, Reynolds said. He folded his

notebook shut with a decisive bang. 'You met Marilyn Burns again, and she agreed to come to this cave with you that night of storm and rain?'

And when Sam did not reply but again sagged in his chair, 'Marilyn knew about Hanscastle; she had a photograph of the fort in her living room.'

That dry fact set Sam back. Reynolds could see the shock of it in his eyes. But again he recovered. Nothing to do with him, he hastened to defend himself. She hadn't learned anything about it from him. And if she went up there regularly, it was news to him. And if she were at Hanscastle that night of the storm – again he hesitated – it certainly wasn't with him.

He'd not seen her for over a year, he repeated; he'd never taken her to the cave, never showed it to her for the simple reason he didn't know about it himself then, hadn't he just explained that? As for what Marilyn had been doing in the meanwhile since their (presumably) last and only encounter, well, if he'd thought about it, which he hadn't, he'd have supposed that whatever itch had got into her she'd got over it. All nice and tidy. She hadn't seemed the kind of woman to hold a grudge.

So what had actually happened, the night of the village meeting? Well, he'd explained, hadn't he, that after talking with Hal earlier in the evening, he'd gone back to his office, waiting to see what would be the outcome of Lady Rowan's plans, fat chance she had of success. He was still sufficiently in control of himself to give the impression he'd enjoyed the prospect of spoiling her little schemes.

Then, much later, after Lady Rowan and the others had dispersed, he'd returned via the moorland route to meet the new 'poppet', just as he'd explained. He'd lied about driving to Padstow, but he *had* backed over the dustbin as he left. Someone should have heard the noise, they'd verify the time. He'd left his car as usual at the end of what he thought of as the cul-de-sac, where the road petered out and the moors began. It was a bad night, but the wind had gone round to the north which often means better weather, and he'd had no trouble getting up the banks, he knew the way in the dark.

So he'd climbed up to the cave, gone inside, settled down to wait? Yes, he'd lied too about keeping her waiting, he'd always had to wait for her, she told him she had difficulty getting away. There was a lantern in the cave, he'd lit that, there was food, drink; he'd poured himself a whisky, spread out blankets – 'All very cosy!' Reynolds had to bite the sarcasm back.

'Look,' Sam said suddenly, 'I didn't trust her. I never trust any woman and I suppose they don't trust me. But they didn't have to set me up the way they did.' He mused for a while, as if on the unfairness of the world.

'They set you up?' Reynolds pounced. What did Sam mean by that? Who were the 'they'? What else did Sam know about that night?

At first Sam only shook his head. He'd told what he knew. But under constant prodding he continued at last. It seemed the girl at the camp wasn't so new after all. He had met her first last spring, 'A pick-up in a pub. Near Padstow,' he said, somewhat self-righteously, as if at least he'd told the truth for once. He'd had what he called 'a good time', a series of one-night stands with her, before she'd upped and left. Nothing odd in that, modern girls were like that. Listening to this self-satisfied recital of amorous success, Reynolds was seized with sudden revulsion. Whatever do women see in him, he thought, and how can creeps like Trewithin get away with so much?

Sam was saying he was surprised to find the girl at the Travellers' camp. Why? Well, he didn't know, she hadn't seemed the type. (That means money, Reynolds thought. He made a note.) Anyway, obviously Sam hadn't expected to see her again. He didn't let on he knew her, she made signs for him not to, but later, as he was leaving, she waited for him, made it clear she was glad of the meeting, suggested they start up again. So they began their rendezvous, when she could get away. She'd always been flighty, but now kept saying how difficult it was. Did the difficulties include having other lovers? That question made Sam uncomfortable, as if his own masculinity was being challenged. He shied away from an answer, didn't know, when pressed said he supposed so. All he did know was that one night she'd surprised him by asking if she were his one and only, did he love her true, that sort of mush, rather out of character, he'd thought at the time. And did he think he could play fast and loose with all the women that he met? She'd cut out the heart of any rival, that she would; things that he'd taken with a pinch of salt. He'd actually laughed. Sitting up naked in the back of the Jag, with her curling round him like a snake, he'd laughed at her ferocity, her kitten-like ferocity that made her comically young and vulnerable.

Emotional blackmail would get nowhere with him, he'd told her, paternally severe. So she'd better forget blackmail. He didn't mean to be caught. 'But I was,' he said.

Suddenly Sam's manner changed. His little moments of defiance, his little attempts at jokes were cut off short, once more he sagged into his clothes, reluctant now, words so squeezed out of him, drop by painful drop, that Reynolds almost felt sorry for him, On the night in question, then, the night of the murder, Sam explained, he had waited inside the cave. By now it was very late but he wasn't tired. He was, well, excited, full of anticipation, that sort of thing.

'And then?'

Sam had expected the girl. She was odd about a lot of things, secretive, but when she said she'd come, she usually did. Yes, she always came alone, except this one time. And this time, yes, she'd come with someone. Yes, someone he knew, but hadn't expected ever to see again. His whisper was so low it could scarcely be heard.

'Marilyn Burns,' Reynolds said, finishing the tale for him.

Under severe questioning, Sam never changed his story. He'd expected the girl alone. He'd never dreamed of seeing Marilyn. Yes, the pair of them together; no, not separate, not one by one, but together, arm in arm and laughing, appearing out of nowhere like some monstrous apparition. Standing just inside the cave where the light cast enormous shadows, they blocked the entrance, then step by step advanced on him, forcing him to retreat, their voices booming out at him, their accusations echoing and re-echoing like some nightmare.

'What did they say?'

Here Sam's voice dropped, he whispered, suggesting that they'd dragged up every private detail of his love-making, wantonly rehashed every shameful intimacy, making a mock of it.

'Couldn't you stop them? Didn't you try? A big man like you?' Reynolds couldn't quite keep the incredulity out of his voice.

'She had a knife,' Sam said.

And in the end she'd used it. 'Look,' he said. Suddenly unzipping his trousers, he showed the unhealed scar, the thin red cut along the groin that, luckily for him, had not gone in too far, the painful flick of a knife-blade, made as if in fun, that doesn't go too deep the first time.

He was on his hands and knees by then, grovelling, he said. They made him grovel. As he spoke now, sweat ran down his face. He looked as if he might faint.

'I thought I was done for,' he said simply, 'and so I would have been, had Marilyn not suddenly drawn back. "Oh, let the old fart go," Marilyn said, as if bored, "enough is enough." '

It wasn't enough for the other one, the one with the knife. But by drawing back, Marilyn had broken the tension. He'd seen his chance. Lowering his head like a battering ram, he had barged through them, taking another cut on the arm that again wasn't serious. Down the rain-drenched banks in a flurry of stone and mud, back to his car. Off home to nurse his wounds and try to forget the laughter. He'd hear their laughter until the day he died.

Exhausted, as if he'd run that race again, he leaned his head upon the table – might even have slept – while Reynolds had the tape rewound so he could listen again to this improbably story. But was it improbable?

There were flaws all over it, all the marks of self-protection and deceit, all the sleaze, all the posturing of a man whose life revolves around posturing. But that could wait. 'What was Marilyn wearing?' he asked, and listened while Sam haltingly described the last clothes she had put on, incidentally verifying her husband's description. 'And the girl with the knife,' he asked. 'What was her name? Can you tell me anything about her?'

'She had no name that I know of.' Sam was insistent about that. 'I never saw her around other people, and she never wanted me to know anything about her. I wanted to ask Hal, but she warned me off.'

He seemed surprised when Reynolds asked, with another touch of sarcasm that couldn't be suppressed, why, given the obvious amorous entanglements, he had persisted with his housing schemes? 'I'm a dead duck if I don't,' Sam said, as if that explained it all. 'Besides, I'm sure Hal'll be back, although to tell the truth I was glad to hear they'd all cleared off for the moment. Gave me time to breathe. But I wouldn't be found dead near Hanscastle again.' It was typical of the man, Reynolds thought, that he didn't see the bad taste of that last remark.

'It doesn't make sense,' Reynolds said. And to Sam's indignant splutter, to Sam's insistence on his records, on his wounds as evidence, 'They aren't proof, you could have altered your records or stabbed yourself. But we can check up on all that. Your torn trousers, for example, there'd be stains on them. But the rest you've told us, what does it actually consist of?: that you have a hideout on Hanscastle Fort where you go regularly, that you were there on the night of the murder with the murdered woman and afterwards didn't say a word. And that you lie readily when it pleases you; more lies than truth!'

'Who would have believed me if I'd told the truth?' Sam said, unconsciously echoing Clemow. 'You don't even now.'

Having told the worst that he could tell, his natural instinct for survival was beginning to re-emerge. 'Why should I murder her?' Sam was continuing. 'I told you I scarcely knew her.'

'What about Mathews? He had a big empty house.'

'As for empty houses,' Sam said, with a touch of spirit, 'I've no need for them. I've got empty houses coming out of my ears. And I scarcely knew Mathews either.'

'But Mathews knew of you,' Reynolds said. 'He's on record as saying he'd turn St Breddaford Green over to the homeless; not quite what you had in mind. Suppose you were trying to stop him?'

Sam leaned forward confidentially. 'I'll tell you what I do think,' he said earnestly. 'I didn't have anything to do with him, but I bet my last penny that that she-devil did. And want to know something else? I think now if Marilyn hadn't intervened I'd be the one in the pig-sty. Whether she'd have helped put me there I don't know, but if she ended there herself it's because she saved my life. And that's why I'm glad,' he said, 'that it's all come out at last. So you can find the truth.' And again it was typical of the man that he believed his own extravagance.

'It's flimsy,' Reynolds said when, leaving Sam, he went to confer outside with Derrymore. 'A pack of cards. Pull out one piece and the whole falls down. A girl he doesn't expect, but admits to having had an affair with, a girl he does expect who is jealous; the two of them together, in cahoots as it were, not over him but out to get revenge, in some mutual bond of womanish sympathy.'

He suddenly stopped, repeated the last words under his breath. They seemed to stand out as if outlined in black, like a piece of a jigsaw, like a piece of a vast jigsaw puzzle that was suddenly beginning to fall into place. 'By God,' he said, 'that's it.'

He sprang up from the chair where he'd been sitting and slapped the startled Derrymore across the back. 'That's it!' he repeated. 'Marilyn Burns wasn't lying. And nor was Peter Burns. Marilyn didn't have a man friend, but she was obsessed – obsessed with this other girl of Sam's, although anything less like a poppet I can't imagine. With the girl herself, or with her feminist trappings, as perhaps she saw them. That's what Marilyn's up to when she goes off on her own, that's why she's got a picture of Hanscastle

Fort in her living room. And when perhaps one or the other of the two women lets drop her dealings with Sam, Marilyn goes up there that night to have it out with him, a substitute for the husband she's perhaps come to despise.

'But Marilyn only wants to frighten Sam, she doesn't want to hurt him like the other one does, she doesn't intend to kill. Probably killing has never been mentioned, if it had she'd have been shocked. She stops the game. And when she does, when she won't play any more, she becomes the victim instead.'

The extent of his reasoning, the distance and place where it had brought him threatened to overwhelm. 'For if that's so,' he said slowly, 'we're talking of a woman killing another woman, of a girl with strength enough to lug a headless body back down the hill after she's chopped off the head. What'd give a young woman the idea of doing that, or the super strength to do it?'

Again he and Derrymore looked at each other; the puzzle steadied, the last piece slid into place. 'Someone obsessed by the old cult,' Derrymore said as slowly, 'someone Penlore and Lady R both know.'

'And someone who visits Penlore and takes her drugs.'

With that last remark, Reynolds turned, leaving Sam to Derrymore, and went into the last room where Widow Penlore had been put. Icky had been difficult, and Derrymore had got nowhere with her. She'd had Toby taken out and brought in with maddening regularity, she'd kept up a commentary of grievances that would have taxed the patience of a saint, all the while refusing to give away any information. To all of Derrymore's prodding – who was the child's mother?, how often had she cared for it?, surely not only while its mother went shopping as had been suggested?, what else did she know of the mother and her habits? – she pretended she didn't hear the questions, cupping her hand round her ear and asking Derrymore to shout.

'Sweet little thing it was,' was all she said when he persisted about the baby, himself coming to the conclusion that the baby was a vital clue. She shook her head, as if already the child should be spoken of in the past tense. Either she really did not know, Derrymore said – not the names of mother and baby, not the baby's age, no details – or she refused to give the information. As for the father, in the way of her cult she didn't even care who he was, had no curiosity about him.

But even her formidable use of the non sequitur was fading. When Sue Henderson brought in cups of tea (incidentally taking the chance to smile at Derrymore), instead of grumbling about the taste, the old woman started to gulp hers down, a first pandering to her own comfort, a first relaxation of her fierce guard.

Now, on seeing Reynolds, she started off on another track. 'Might have known it was your fault,' she cried, wiping her hand across her mouth. She positively spat, at her most venomous. 'Might have known you'd take her part. Just like a man. I'm still here but she's off, scot-free.'

Without difficulty identifying the 'she', but until later not understanding that Icky was angry because Lady Rowan had been allowed to drive away, Reynolds tried to interrupt but she plunged on. 'I've told you plenty of times I've nothing to do with it. It's what Di Rowan found in the great outside world.'

The spite was full throttle now, unrepentant. 'That's what she called it, the great outside world, as if those she left behind – me, for example – were nothing but dross.'

There was a curious note of grief beneath the malice,

that even the years hadn't healed, a sense of loss, abandonment. It didn't need Icky's admission, 'I loved her, of course, but she didn't me, not enough to keep her where she belonged,' to suggest how deep that sense of grief was.

'Listen, Icky,' Reynolds said. He signalled to an officer to turn off the recording machine, stood in front of her, hands clasped behind his back, his legs brushing against hers so close she couldn't move. His voice was low so no one else could hear. 'This isn't one of your bloody games, you against Di Rowan. I've told you once and say again, it's murder. I've got to know who the mother of the baby is. I think you know her well. I think she's been coming to see you all summer, not just to leave the baby, but to get help in other ways. Haven't you been giving her some of your remedies?'

She ignored the reference to her herbals, stared at him as intently as Lady Rowan had done. Suddenly, under the wrinkled skin and frizzled hair, he saw what the younger Icky must have looked like, a hint of her, an impression. But her mouth remained obstinately closed.

'I think she's one of the Travellers,' he said, ad-libbing, trying to break through her defences. 'Perhaps she came back here with them because the father of her child is a local man.' He hazarded a guess.

'Is it Sam Trewithin's child? Because I think it might be.'

'Sam Trewithin's.' Her voice was scornful but he caught a flicker of fear in her eyes. 'Not old Sammy's. Sammy'd be too careful, he'd be afraid. And you're doing a lot of thinking for a police officer.'

'You'll get protection,' he told her, when she still didn't say anything more. 'I'll see to that, I'll get Chief Inspector Clemow to authorize it.'

'Chief Inspector Clemow's an idiot.' Her unexpected

assessment caught him off-guard. 'But you aren't.' This grudging admission was immediately suppressed. 'Your protection can't save me if I tell you what I know.'

She stared at him. 'It's not only for myself,' she cried, 'I don't matter. But I promised. And the faithful don't break their word.'

Across the green behind them, the church clock boomed twelve. Midnight. A new day. June the twenty-third. Another thought struck him with terror. When did actual Midsummer's Eve begin, now or tonight?

'She's already committed two murders,' he was shouting at her now, oblivious of the use of intimidation, snatching at ideas to break her down. 'She may plan a third. If you don't help us catch her first, then you're as guilty as she is. More so, because you know what you're doing, and she must be mad, or drugged.

'You'll be put in prison,' he went on. 'Shut up, behind bars, never allowed out. Imagine that, Icky, you'd not stand that long. And what about Toby? How'd he manage? He'd have to be put down.'

He didn't know what made him say that, but a change came over her face. Her mouth dropped open, she gaped at him.

He pressed home his advantage. 'That woman whose child you care for, where does she come from, who is she?'

She muttered something, he couldn't believe what he'd heard.

'What?' he said. He bent over her. 'Who?'

And when she finally told him, when she admitted what she knew, he felt it like a body blow.

Chapter 13

'You didn't.' Reynolds, furious with the world, furious with himself for allowing Clemow to botch things, had just discovered that Clemow had allowed Lady Rowan to leave. 'Wanted to spare her,' was Clemow's excuse when Reynolds angrily confronted him. 'Besides, I still don't hold much with your theories. As far as I'm concerned,' here Clemow ventured to smile, his initial disappointment over Burns beginning to be supplanted by the prospect of Trewithin, 'a "real" estate agent is better than some unreal witches' coven.'

'The devil it is,' Reynolds said angrily, 'you'd be surprised.' And with that uncharacteristically weak reply he beckoned to one of Clemow's men, commandeered an official car, turned on his heel and left. Which is why Lady Rowan, perhaps beginning to celebrate her release, was startled to see him again so soon.

She hadn't taken off her cape, was standing with a decanter in her hand when he strode into her little sitting room. She looked pointedly at the clock, then at her dressing-gowned butler who had tried to keep him out and was still hovering anxiously. At last, reluctantly, she waved the man away. She and Reynolds faced each other, two opponents at last on equal ground, no holds barred. She didn't invite him to sit down, didn't offer him a drink, continued to pour one for herself. And he didn't apologize for his intrusion.

He looked around him, like someone looking at a favourite place for the last time, at the drawn draperies in the windows hiding the rose garden beyond; at the silk-covered chairs – rose-coloured too, he noticed; at the silver, the porcelain, the books, all the trappings of wealth. Overpoweringly, the scent of roses filled the air. One side of him was tempted. Here's beauty, he thought almost longingly, here's opulence to drown a man. Arabian Nights. The genie with the golden lamp. The bird of para-dise. And in thinking that felt the other side of him rise up against the waste, the wantonness, the treachery.

He didn't know that he was going to burst out with it straight away, direct, unambiguously, what he had almost asked before but hadn't quite. He only knew that, when he had, at last he'd come to the very heart. 'So who's to inherit this?' he said.

She stiffened as for a blow, the decanter clasped between her hands, a prisoner tied to the rack, in that melodramatic pose he intuitively disliked and yet for once was so completely genuine that he felt himself to be a real executioner.

'Sons?' He was testing, taunting her. 'Or daughters? One or many?'

His thoughts ran in tune with hers. Not many, not children, no superfluity for her, no sons. Only one. One child. A female child to rear in her own image, a second self, a girl to lavish all the wealth and luxury on, that would be her style. Exclusive, unique.

'Where is she now?'

'I don't know.'

The whisper was full of pain, of guilt.

The guilt took him aback. He'd expected denial, refusal, silence. But not to know where that daughter was, to have lost touch, was as cruel as, in retrospect, his mocking repetition of her, '*Don't know?*'

'I *don't*.' She almost screamed the words. 'I left my parents, why shouldn't she?'

He thought, left them to go up in the world, but that's not what your daughter did. 'There's no way she could go up from this,' he said.

He made a gesture that took in their surroundings. 'So if she didn't go up,' he said softly, 'she must have gone down. What did she go down to?'

She stared at him. In her eyes he saw all the answers she couldn't give. 'A run-away,' he said, hating himself now for saying it, his anger suddenly gone. 'A drop-out. Fashionable, isn't it, these days? The more they've got, the less they value it. No good at school, I suppose, hated that posh school you sent her to. Broke out as soon as she was old enough.'

Took to the streets, drink, drugs, he finished to himself, hating what her family was, hating her parents most of all. Or perhaps now her father's dead, concentrating that hate on the surviving mother. A wanderer, an exile from society. A Traveller, returning to the hated home to display that hate like an open wound.

'Why didn't you speak about her?' To me, he meant. 'You made sure no one knew about her, kept her identity hidden.' As if she had some deformity, he thought, something that marred your sense of perfection.

'She wasn't always like that.' The cry burst out. 'At school it was books she loved. We thought she'd study literature. Her father planned Oxford. He planned

201

everything for her. She was his favourite.'

'Was it you who first showed dislike? When she was little did you make her feel unwanted? Did you resent the bond with your husband?' The questions gathered force but he didn't have to ask them. She was telling him herself.

'Always his favourite, just the two of them, as if I didn't exist. Little things like bedtime. He had to be home to put her to bed; never me, never the nanny, only him. And later, whenever I tried to talk to her, up went a barrier. That's why I insisted she be sent away to school, of course, and she hated me for it. And when he died she couldn't stand it. Never really came home afterwards. Always wanted to spend holidays with friends, and when she was expelled, drug-taking they said, just went off to London and disappeared. I only knew she was alive when the bank statements came. He'd left her money in her own right, the only stupid mistake he made.'

She looked down. 'Blamed me, of course, for his death. "Wish you'd died instead," she said.'

'And she wrote you the letters, she sent the invitation? You knew that at the time?' He ignored her last remarks almost as if she hadn't spoken them; he couldn't deal with them at the moment, he couldn't spare the time for pity or understanding. 'You must have known she was somewhere in the neighbourhood and made no attempt to find her?'

'I suppose so,' she said. 'I wasn't thinking clearly. I was too upset.'

'But that's the real reason why you went to Hanscastle, to see for yourself what she was up to? And you did attend the Midsummer festivities last year, although you said not?'

'No,' she said, with a flash of spirit. 'I've told you, I discovered where it was later.'

'But you went there deliberately. And you knew what she planned.'

His statements, not questions now, hit at her like blows. He saw her flinch.

'I guessed,' she said at last. 'I suspected. I didn't know for sure until this year. Not until after the village meeting when I first asked for you.'

He waited.

'Next morning,' she said. She was staring at the decanter which she still held, her hands now were twisting and twisting its stopper, as if to break it apart. 'Before the news of the murder. Another letter. The same style but different.'

He waited for her to get a hold of herself. After a while, 'More vicious,' she said, 'immediate. No longer suggesting I was one of them (never meant anyway), but showing all the pent-up despair. They're full of despair,' she cried, 'the young these days. Nothing seems to work for them, all's turned to emptiness.'

'What did the letter say?'

For answer she delved into the depths of her skirt, produced a crumpled piece of paper. 'It's all I have left,' she said, and he didn't know if she meant that even an expression of hate was better than silence.

He unfolded the paper. On it, crudely drawn, was a caricature of a head stuck on a spike. The face was distorted, but recognizable: Lady Rowan herself, as she might be twenty years on. Underneath, in letters cut from a newspaper, were the words, 'Join us if you dare.'

He looked at it dispassionately. Nothing artistic here, he thought, only ugliness.

'And did you know what it meant?'

'Only when I heard about the body in the sty,' she cried.

She shuddered. Her hands made grasping motions. 'I thought she meant it for me.'

'But she spared you, did she?' he said softly. 'Any reason why?'

'I don't know, I don't know,' she said, starting to weep. 'Perhaps there was no reason. Perhaps she just did things on whim. Perhaps she's not all evil, it was all a mistake.'

'It's murder,' he said brutally. 'And she means to murder again.'

That shocked her back. 'You can't be sure, you can only guess, you—'

'Yes,' he said. 'But when we do find out, or rather,' he corrected himself, '*if* we do, before she commits another crime, that'll be the third she's charged with. And the third the worst.'

And as she had originally quoted at him now, he quoted back, 'Maid, harlot, crone.'

For once she did not understand him. Slowly she put the decanter down, releasing it as if her fingers were glued to it. Her nails made a clinking sound on the polished wood. He repeated himself, then repeated what else she'd said. 'Marilyn Burns, the harlot; Mathews, the old woman. As for maids, who're left, except children or babes in arms?

'She has had a baby,' he went on. 'Your daughter has a child, your granddaughter. Perhaps she thinks killing your granddaughter will hurt you more than killing you.'

At that her reserve broke. She leapt towards him and began to flail out, sending china and bottles flying. They crashed to the floor, breaking, splintering, splashing great stains across the rose-coloured silk. 'I don't believe you, you're inventing it. You're saying it to get even.' Her eyes widened, her nails spread. He was reminded suddenly, horribly, of an Indian idol he'd once seen: the Goddess of

Wrath, in all her staring rage. He held his ground.

After a while she grew quiet, almost calm. She smiled at him, a travesty of her former smile. 'You'll have to stop her then, won't you?' she said sweetly, at her most appealing. 'You'll have to deal with it. It can be hushed up, can't it, if it's handled right?'

If you handle it, she meant. *You can cover things up, you're good at that.*

The sweetness was the worst thing of all.

He thought of the child he'd glimpsed in Widow Penlore's cottage, its christening robes and wrappings fit for a princess. How long can a child live deprived of food and warmth? How long exposed and naked? How easy is it to smash the fragile skull under the lacy cap, to crush the tiny skeleton, to tear out the tiny heart?

He said, 'Each time we've talked you've tricked me with your lies, made me believe your half-truths as if truth's something to gamble with, like cards. But if your grandchild's murdered, then it will be your fault for gambling with its life. Unless you tell me where your daughter is.'

And so it was after all this while, after all her half-truths, half-lies, she told him what she really knew, what he'd already half guessed, but couldn't be sure about.

'I don't know where the Travellers are,' she said. 'But I warned you of the danger from them, didn't I? I warned everyone. You can't say I didn't do that. We called her Belle, the beautiful, the beloved. And so she was. But she'd have no part of it when her father was gone. I don't know where she is, any more than you do. I've not seen her since. She ran away, she changed her name . . .'

He waited. 'It was a poem that she used to love,' she said. She had continued to weep, tears flowing steadily. 'She learned it as a child. "I'll be a gypsy too, one day," she used to say. "A gypsy called Meg." '

Meg sat outside the van, waiting for the dawn. The night had been warm and short, barely dark; soon the sun would come up in a ball of crimson fire. The day of days was approaching, when there would be barely any night.

She'd not slept at all, she rarely slept now, her need for sleep repressed by the drugs she sniffed or – in the case of Widow Penlore's concoctions – drank, the mixture like wine, but with its leaves and petals unstrained, the bottles tied with grasses and flowers like votive offerings. She sat upright in her usual fashion, back to the wheel, her child in its usual place in her lap.

She gazed at it almost tenderly as the growing light allowed her to pick out its features, its long-lashed eyes, its snub nose, its rose-red mouth. When it stirred she wrapped it in the shawl again and rocked it against her, her own face contorted with some mixture of emotions.

She had already let Hal out, like a dog, she thought, to be walked and watered at intervals, although ostensibly he was supposed to be keeping guard on the other side of the quarry where the van was hidden. She looked at him now with barely veiled contempt where he squatted down in the undergrowth, like some boy scout, a bloody boy scout, doing his bloody duty.

The van itself was empty; there were no others left. One by one, following Merl and Eileen's example, they'd drifted off, Hal's band that he'd been so proud of. Better that they went. She and Hal could manage, more would be too many. But she'd needed Hal. That's why she had to stay awake, and why, even now, she had to watch him like a hawk to make sure he didn't run as the others had. She felt for the revolver beside her, the only thing she'd taken from Frank's house. It was loaded and she knew how to shoot. Father had taught her how.

She'd let the others go when she was finished with them, not before. And she might let Hal go then too, she wasn't sure yet. The others had been frightened of her, had ended up doing everything she asked. They certainly hadn't belonged to Hal any more. His loyal band, as he'd thought of them, was finished with. If he'd tried to rebel, as on a couple of occasions she'd thought he would, they certainly wouldn't have supported him. But Hal wouldn't rebel now. What he'd seen and done would keep him nicely subdued. She picked the gun up and squinted down the barrel.

The morning was growing out of the east, spreading its light and heat, drying off the coolness of the dew. Away under the lip of the quarry, a bird began to sing. Only today to get through. She could hold Hal for that long.

The van was carefully hidden, in the disused quarry he'd found last year. Together they'd pushed the van far in against the cliff, then covered it with branches and leaves torn from the bushes that grew along the edge, camouflaging it so well that, if anyone did make his way into the clearing or scrambled up to the quarry top, there'd be nothing to be seen. That was something else she'd needed Hal's help for, that and for the driving. But she hadn't told him she knew how to drive. If she had to she could drive the van, although it was bigger than she'd been used to.

She'd praised him when he'd finished, always gave praise where it was due, but he'd grumbled just loudly enough for her to hear, his return to the open air giving him a short-lived spurt of courage. 'All I'm good for now, I suppose,' he'd said, not so much angry as despondent. She hadn't bothered to reply.

She smiled to herself, remembering how he'd finally confessed his little secret, what she already knew, what he and Sam Trewithin had devised. She almost laughed as she remembered how he'd paced nervously up and down beside the sheep-cote on the morning they were to leave, running a nervous finger under the collar of his tattered shirt as if it were too small for him. 'What do I want with a place as big as Buckingham Palace?' he'd said. 'That wasn't what Sam had in mind for us.'

She'd let him talk, pretending sympathy. What she knew of Sam Trewithin would turn any plan to ash.

'What would Sam call this?' she'd said later, when she made him take her that night, alone in the dark. 'Would Sam call this treason? Would you?' But by then he was too frightened to say what he really thought.

Fear's the trap I've made for him, she thought; that's why he won't run.

Yet nevertheless she mistrusted him, watching him through eyes slitted against the sun. Mistrusted the moments, rarer now than at first, when he got through her guard, the moments when they had first met when she had sensed what she supposed could be called the decency of him, the unexpected niceness. She didn't want his niceness, she didn't need it. She was Meg the gypsy who lived on her own. 'And shall Trelawney die?' she crooned. 'There's twenty thousand Cornish men will know the reason why!' The Cornish anthem, loudly enough for Hal to hear. So that Hal, in the long damp grass opposite, would hear her and remember. And be truly afraid.

Across the quarry, within sight and easy range of her, Hal crouched, fingering almost superstitiously the mat of coarse red hair that he kept in his pocket. How had she thought of it? he wondered. How had she thought of and planned everything so carefully, even down to the very moment they'd caught Frank Mathews on the road as he'd cycled past, that fragile-looking girl whom part of him still wanted to protect? And who he now knew wasn't fragile at all, was as strong as he was, perhaps in some ways stronger.

She'd made sure they'd all played a part in the catching, although she'd done the actual work, shoving Hal aside when he'd tried to stop her and standing up in front of Frank, holding out her hand like a beggar, with a garland of flowers round her head like some silly crown. 'Just fifty for a cup of tea,' she'd said, meaning fifty pence, and when Frank had scowled, had ignored her and cycled on, only then, at her command, had they all come streaming out from behind the hedge to knock him down. And when Frank'd been tied up and led back to the van, and his gear had been scattered (including the rackets, which common sense had told Hal they'd do better to keep), she'd been the one to encourage them to trip him up and then, when he stumbled, jerk him upright as if he were some sort of animal, jeering when he'd tried to shout that he was on their side – hadn't he said so the night before? – on and on until they got tired and gagged him quiet.

Why had they picked on Frank at all, he wondered? It wasn't just for his house. 'Old queen,' she'd cried, her face suddenly distorted with hate. 'Stinking old thing.'

What's she got against being old for God's sake, he thought. She'll be an old woman herself one day, and I suppose she's got a mother, although she's never mentioned her. And Frank Mathews wasn't that old. Nor was it clear he was gay; just because he lived alone you shouldn't damn him out of hand like that.

He brooded, remembering her way of treating Ted,

tormenting him more like. And remembering too his own childhood when his mother was still alive. When she'd died his childhood had ended; young as he was, he'd known without her he couldn't keep his father at bay; he'd soon left home, taken to the streets, become a member of what they called a rat-pack, had scrambled his way to the top of that particular heap. Probably Meg the Gypsy had similar memories, who knew; although since as far as he could tell Meg certainly liked men, it couldn't have been her father who was so bad! But for Hal personally, all the happiness he'd known in his young life had lasted only as long as his mother was alive

He turned back to his original train of thought. Frank Mathews might be gay, he thought, probably was, but she wasn't telling all the truth. It wasn't that or his age that made them jump at him. It was, he tried to concentrate, as if she had picked Frank out specially, and then expected them to gang up on him.

That's it, he thought, suddenly enlightened. A special victim. And we were brought there deliberately, as witness to part of some strange ceremony that she's got locked inside her head and which I'll never get the key to either. But if it's something odd, some battle between men and women, he thought, again frightened as if he were breaking some taboo; if it's some freakish sexual reversal, like the sort I've heard of, I don't want any part of it. It's, it's – he searched for the word – contaminating.

For when they'd actually seen the house, hadn't they all been awed, even he himself who hadn't wanted it; so big, so much ground, just as she'd described, just what they themselves would have dreamed of, if they'd been capable of dreaming. And when the van'd been hidden a fair way off (that'd been his job, he was good at that, empty, no identification marks, but close enough so they could get to it in a hurry); when the gates had been bolted with the bolts she'd had them filch from St Breddaford market; by then they'd all been so daunted by her that they'd been willing enough to help seal the doors and windows with wood brought from the farm. And after their duties had been allotted (she'd used him for that, too, making out he was still in charge, instead of what he'd really become, a figurehead, spouting what she told him to), when everyone had got tired of running through the different rooms and playing with the water taps, 'Now this,' she'd said. And making them all pick up the helpless figure, she'd had them drag the master of the house down into the dark cellar, stripping off his clothes and tying him naked to a post.

But before that she'd already persuaded Hal to two more things, cajoled him into what the police would call aiding and abetting. Frank's voice's easy to imitate, she'd told him when the police had first rung, all you have to do is hold your nose and swallow. And all you have to do is speak in the same voice and say the same thing, she'd said, when later the police had actually showed up in person; hide behind the curtains, don't panic – almost as if she'd been enjoying it, almost as if she'd been expecting them, two detectives on foot, racing up the drive and banging on the door as if they meant to break it in.

He fingered the red mat of hair again. When they'd knocked she alone had kept calm. As if on clue she'd produced the wig and beard, pulled the wig on him anyhow and coolly dabbed the gum round his chin. Up the stairs you go, she'd said, into one of the front bedrooms, tell them to sod off, they'll never know the difference. But for God's sake, don't let them in. They can't do anything if you don't let them in.

The questions, stupid questions about rackets and stuff,

had surprised even her, but she'd been quick to improvise. 'Questions, that's all they are,' she'd prompted from her place beside the door. 'They don't suspect, there's nothing to suspect. Tell them the truth, or more or less the truth: that the rackets were left because they weren't needed any more, that'll satisfy them.'

Coolly she'd whispered what to say as if he were an actor on stage and she the stage manager. And it had been easy. 'Just following up inquiries,' they'd said politely.

'That's how they speak to "real gentlemen",' she'd jeered when they'd gone and he'd ripped the wig off as if it burned, tearing off the beard to get the taste out of his mouth. 'And aren't we the lord of the manor? And don't we look the part!'

She'd dropped him a mock curtsey, speaking before he could say anything, defusing his anger, making all the others laugh, making him seem the fool again.

'How do you know so much?' he'd said, staring at her when she led the way downstairs and the others, those who were left, had all crowded round to applaud. 'Where did you learn about such things?' He might have been asking, 'Where do you go when you go off on your own – except into someone else's arms? Where do you go in your dreams – except into your past where I shall never find you?'

Yes, the police had been easy, Hal could handle them. But not the other one, the first visitor, the secret one, the one who had come prowling up alone by stealth. The hammering at the door, the footsteps crunching round the back, the silence that followed, had caught them all off-guard. And just because she hadn't set a watch as he'd warned her to. He didn't even have time to rub it in, to say, 'I told you so,' before they'd had to huddle in a back corridor, scarcely daring to breathe.

It had seemed a long while before that first intruder left, before Hal himself had peered from the curtained windows and stared down at the empty terrace. Afterwards the others had merely been relieved, had joked about it for a while, then dismissed it from their thoughts. Not a moment's curiosity about who the stranger was, nor the possibility that his visit might have caused the second; not a moment's fear that he might have tipped off the police. And that was really stupid. Because whoever that second visitor was, Hal had been sure he meant to come back. And that would be bad luck for them; he'd felt it in his bones.

And so in the end had she. That's when she'd first produced the revolver, holding it cocked in front of her, her finger on the trigger. 'If anyone else comes,' she said, 'we'll meet them with this.'

She'd found it in one of the cabinets, rows of hunting rifles behind glass panels in what must have once been the game room and was now, like the rest of the house, slowly rotting into dust. She'd picked up a poker and broken the glass, then chosen the revolver carefully, handling it with ease and finding the bullets in the drawers underneath. He hadn't had a moment's hesitation about her intention to use it, he knew at once she'd used guns before. And so had the others. He'd seen how their enthusiasm had suddenly waned, how they'd drawn back each into a shell. Shooting wasn't part of their scene. And that was why, when she'd finally given way and left the house at his insistence, there'd just been the two of them. The others had run away because they were frightened. So why hadn't he run before she made him her accomplice one final time?

'What are we scared of?' Her singing had changed, the

words a mocking refrain, while she rocked the baby on her lap. 'Aren't we all part of it? One for all and all for one.'

There's a truth, he thought even more despondently, that's why she doesn't care if we go or stay. The others may have escaped, perhaps, but they aren't really free. There isn't anything any of us can do now to free ourselves, not even talk, without incriminating ourselves; me most of all.

For before they'd gone, hadn't she made him go back down the cellar stairs with the light, and pick up the rope and carry it.

He stared in front of him, his mind blank.

The morning light brought no respite to the Incident Room. They'd worked all night, sifting through the many clues that had now been revealed. Some officers had gone to comb through Widow Penlore's cottage, dragging out her gargoyles and statues, searching along the corridor and the various littered back rooms, finding nothing new except the pitiful debris of a lifetime's hoarding, like that of some giant magpie. Equally her garden, when examined after daybreak, revealed nothing new, just a host of rotting and forgotten rubbish she thought of as treasure, where birds had made their nests. Only the remains of her collection of bottles, her brews and tinctures and ointments, brought any flicker of excitement, were collected into boxes and brought back for examination, together with the others Reynolds had previously selected.

Meanwhile another team had gone to Sam Trewithin's house. It was a surprisingly modest dwelling, a small cottage, two rooms up and two down, with a modern bathroom tagged on under a lean-to roof, where Sam and his mother had lived together for years and where after her death he still continued, his umbilical cord, as it were, to his former life. It was remarkably neat, nothing out of place, strange in a bachelor establishment; only the cupboards filled to overflowing with stylish clothes, among which the torn and bloodstained trousers and a ripped shirt were conspicuous. As for his office, here too the searchers drew a blank; no diaries, no 'black books' with names and telephone numbers, no secret letters hidden under floorboards, only dry office records and bank accounts (for the most part overdrawn) whose contents were carefully noted in Sam's neat handwriting. If his scheme to persuade the council to pay him rent for his empty houses really existed, he'd kept no notes about it, and the only mention of Marilyn Burns was a formal one in his engagement book dated, as he'd said, some eighteen months previously. (As was, incidentally, the name of the couple who had so irritated him when, to keep them quiet, he'd first shown them Hanscastle Farm.)

Come daybreak, the search intensified. Officers swarmed over Hanscastle Fort looking for the cave. They searched in vain. It was not until Sam himself was taken there to show them that they were able to climb into it, hidden so well in a gorse thicket that, unless one knew the very bush to start with, it would be impossible to guess its whereabouts. An interesting point this, suggesting again that if Sam were right, Marilyn Burns must have learned about the cave from the same person who had showed it to Sam.

Reynolds and Derrymore, bleary-eyed after a night of virtually no sleep, were the first to go inside. They stood still for a moment to grow accustomed to the dark. When a lantern was lit, they saw the cave much as Sam had described it, the blanket still spread on the floor, the overturned tumbler, the stain that could have been whisky or

215

blood. Overhead the cave was rounded like a beehive, the stones that formed it fitted together like cells in a honeycomb. 'This is no miner's cave,' Reynolds said. He tugged at Derrymore's arm. 'My God, it's a barrow, a prehistoric burial place, older than the fort by centuries. When there's time, get an expert to look at it. It's a masterpiece.'

But whether as old as he thought, or whether a burial place for some ancient Celtic chieftain, it furnished no further clues as to what other death had been planned here and carried out more recently. No one unearthed what Reynolds had been fearing, the remains of a decapitated head. And Sam's story was neither proved nor disproved.

Frank Mathew's house, the unloved, unwanted house that inheritance had burdened on him, had been searched all night but, as at Widow Penlore's, Clemow's fine-toothed comb revealed little of new interest. Whoever had been there (and obviously someone had), there were no strange fingerprints, no extra litter, nothing to suggest the presence of the Travellers for whom filth was a trademark. But then, as someone pointed out, Frank himself lived in such squalor – the kitchen knee-deep in old rubbish anyhow, and an upstairs study used for a midden – that even if the Travellers had been there, who was to separate their filth from his?

Of the Travellers themselves, there was still no sign: they seemed to have vanished into air. Although again and again, Derrymore and, after him, Reynolds, had tried to get Icky Penlore to tell them when the baby had been collected – the baby must have been collected before the Travellers left, they wouldn't have abandoned it, when had they come for it? – she would not or could not give a time.

'After he went,' she said, meaning Reynolds. 'Before the others came,' meaning Clemow's men.

Again later, just before dawn when he returned home to snatch an hour's sleep, Reynolds bitterly regretted his own impetuous departure. If only he had taken the baby with him, he thought, it would be safe; not that he knew anything about babies, he quailed at the thought. Better still, he should have waited with it at Icky's house. If he'd waited he might have caught them redhanded, as it were. As it was, his going had done poor Mathews no good and had probably permitted the Travellers to escape.

That none of this could be undone now didn't help much. As soon as Mathews was dead they must have driven from Mathews' house straight to Icky's, somehow by-passing him on the road. They had killed Mathews, had fetched the child away and disappeared, with a good enough start to make a clean get-away if they wanted to. The only hope was that, although Derrymore had put out a search for them, and police blocks had been established on all the main roads out of the county, and at the bridges over the Tamar River, stretching north to south between Devon and Cornwall, no one resembling their description had yet been seen.

Of course, if they had left the van and walked, or even rowed across the river, they could have found a multitude of smaller roads to use and be gone so far by now that they would be lost among the hundreds, or thousands of people like them, no one the wiser. Only Reynolds was convinced they'd not gone that far. But that again was after another drink or two seemed to make his brain work faster, as when he was young, and the warming taste and smell seemed to melt the frozen cold that threatened to encase him like a shell. For anything was better than that coldness, even the breaking of his abstinence which he'd fought so hard to maintain.

Chapter 14

Meanwhile the new suspects had also been detained. First of these was Sam, whose story, although improbable, was beginning to make more sense as time went on. But Sam was guilty of withholding evidence, if nothing worse. This he strongly denied, denying also any likelihood that he'd fathered Meg's child. ('I'm careful,' he said, unconsciously parodying Icky's verdict on him.) He also seemed dubious that either of the young women could have found more interest in each other than in him, part of his macho new image. But perhaps he might be forgiven, Reynolds thought, as Sam listed the times and places when he and his 'poppet' had met – the girl had certainly led an active life; no wonder she'd left her infant so often under Icky's care.

The second suspect was Icky herself. Her fate was sealed by another phone call, from the laboratories this time, revealing the contents of her jars. Just as Reynolds had suspected, her potions weren't just the time-honoured remedies of a village 'witch'. Whether she used them herself too was at this stage immaterial. If other people did, 'Look out,' was the official verdict, 'this stuff's lethal.'

The making of dangerous drugs brought her activities out of the bracket of cottage industry and into the harsh reality of drug-dealing. Pretended senility and real old age couldn't talk her out of that. Icky, the clever, who made fools of authority, had never belittled her ability with herbs, or her knowledge of finding, picking and blending them; she'd boasted once too often of her skill. Did she also know the effect of hallucinatory herbs on abnormality? Could she estimate the extent to which schizophrenia is stimulated by certain infusions, or paranoia heightened by them? These technical terms meant nothing to her: she blinked.

'I rest my case,' was all she would say. There was a certain dignity to her as she spoke, a kind of regal finality. She even seemed resigned to Toby's fate (although in fact one of the inquiry team finally took him in: Sue Henderson, with her bright smile at Derrymore. 'I like dogs,' she said).

Reluctantly, Reynolds decided it was only Icky's hatred for Di Rowan that had allowed her to give away as much as she had, that had made her bring her rival down with her – the hate which was also as strong as love. As for Lady Rowan herself, the third suspect, she also was charged with 'withholding evidence', although other charges might be levelled as the case unfolded. She scarcely understood the term. 'All she cares for is herself.' Clemow, once duped, was unforgiving. Remembering the anguished cry, the hidden fear, Reynolds was less certain. 'It can be hushed up,' she'd said. It wasn't herself she wanted to shield.

But these old friends, old enemies, must wait. It was well after midday when all the other evidence was discussed and analysed, and (such as could be displayed) spread out on the long counters in the Incident Room. Clemow himself stood fingering various pieces, or rather fingering the plastic bags in which they had been placed. He didn't say much, but overnight most of his uncertainty had evaporated. He still could not admit Reynolds' theory was correct, but he had come round part-way to it, sufficiently to let his original suspect go and to issue a statement, the longed-for statement, that hinted at 'new findings, hopefully soon to resolve this case.'

Now he looked expectantly from Reynolds to Derrymore. 'Well?' he said. When there was no reply, 'Don't tell me there's nothing more,' he said. 'Don't tell me this wild-goose chase has come to an end.'

'On the contrary,' Reynolds said, 'it's just beginning.'

But when he told Clemow what conclusions he'd come to, and where he suspected Meg and the Travellers might be hidden, when he suggested how to find them, the Chief Inspector frothed with anxiety. 'Impossible,' he spluttered. 'Would cost a fortune and get us nowhere.'

'Will certainly cost a fortune,' Reynolds agreed, 'if you go it alone. But the whole village'll be behind you. Get Derrymore to ask and they'll help.'

His grey-blue eyes bored into Clemow. 'It's your last chance,' he said. 'If it doesn't work, nothing else will.'

Clemow dithered. As Reynolds had intended, the 'you' and 'your' threw the burden back on him. Too late it must have come to him that in reality Reynolds had nothing to do with the case; it had just been too easy, almost natural, to defer to him. And in doing so, now he would be thinking bitterly, he'd got caught up again in the old hassle of budgets and costs, of probability versus guesswork and improbability – all the familiar problems which working with Reynolds in the past had made so maddening. But if he dug his heels in now, if he disagreed, he'd probably lose the chance of a lifetime and the murders would never be solved . . .

Reynolds almost smiled. Sometimes Clemow was too

easy, reading his thoughts was an open book. He waited nonchalantly. No one could have guessed how relieved he was when, 'All right,' Clemow said doubtfully. 'But how many? And how much?'

So once more Reynolds had his way. Derrymore, given the go-ahead, passed the word. Within the hour the green was crowded with villagers anxious to take part in what promised to be a search of unprecedented proportions. If it hadn't been so serious, Reynolds could have laughed as old men turned up, gaitered and hatted as if on a shooting party, and red-faced farmers rode in on their hunters, while their wives presided over tea-urns. Viewing the chaos, Clemow was in despair. 'Wait,' said Reynolds, 'they'll steady.'

And steady they did, while Clemow's map was spread out, the red circle that surrounded Hanscastle Farm serving as a starting point. Old Ted and others like him, even Bestwick, who knew the moors, were brought in to plot the routes to various locations. The moors were divided into segments, each under the charge of a local citizen who knew that area best. With Clemow's policemen to oversee correct search procedures, every foot of ground would be covered. Teams were selected, parties began to move out, striding away confidently as if on a hiking expedition ... until Derrymore explained in detail what their quarry was: an old van used by the Travellers, and a child with its deranged mother, who couldn't be trusted not to do it harm.

Although only Reynolds could (or again would) describe the baby (and he made a poor showing at giving evidence, again his ignorance of babies hindering him), Old Ted and Sam Trewithin could give full descriptions of the woman. As her slight figure, her intent look, her determination and wiry strength came alive before them, along with the realization of what she had done and still might do, suddenly the carnival atmosphere changed. Children who had run and squealed were silenced; their mothers drew them close.

'Ironic, isn't it?' Clemow said, with his braying laugh. 'After all, Lady R's got what she wanted, a village united against the Travellers.' No one laughed with him.

Reynolds himself drove up to Hanscastle Farm, parked in the lane and walked past the old farmhouse, sitting broodily in the hot June afternoon, its granite façade impervious to all the activity about it. On the hill above him he saw a line of searchers disappearing over the crest, making for the path that Old Ted had taken, while others were spreading out towards the fir woods. He leaned on the wall of the empty pig-pen. What would the old farmer who had lived here think of it all, he wondered, the God-fearing, kindly Farmer Hansard who'd always had a place for tramps and time for everyone. He sighed.

Old Ted was waiting for him. Ted had been given the task of showing Reynolds all the places he'd used for camping, just in case, an outside chance, the Travellers had found them and were using them themselves. Reynolds realized they were the old man's prized possessions, for him as private as homes are for other people. Opening up this secret world, these hidden haunts, would come hard, forcing him to do what was contrary to his nature. To everyone's surprise Ted had agreed. 'It's for a baby,' he'd said.

Now Old Ted was in his element. Smelling of honeysuckle and manure he sat in the front seat of Reynolds' car, playing with the gadgets as, to save time, he was driven from spot to spot. He was especially taken with the stereo, whose buttons he pressed like a child with a new toy, and equally enjoyed chatting direct with the Incident Room over the police intercom, a piece of equipment that Reynolds had been lent. Hearing his own voice when he gave directions brought a pleased smile. 'Could do with one of these meself,' he said.

Actually he wasn't much good at road directions – 'Avoid roads usually,' he said – but when he came close to places he knew and they continued on foot, it was amazing how quickly he took charge, moving swiftly and confidently over the rough ground. And it was amazing too how many hidden places there still were; how just yards away from tarmac and buildings, a narrow overgrown lane still existed, leading to a copse of trees, a grassy mound, even a river bank.

Looking at the way the water curled sparkling past one such site, with its line of overhanging alders for shelter, and its neat little circle of stones for a fire, Reynolds was struck by the beauty of it all. Old Ted might be homeless, he thought, in the real sense of the word may be poor, to be pitied; but here on a summer day he lives in a tranquillity a king could envy. The Travellers had not been to any of these places. Remembering the description of the Travellers' camp, Reynolds thought Ted was right to keep them out. The day was drawing towards twilight when they came to the last place, the one Ted had kept to last because he himself had scarcely ever used it. 'Too hard for me,' he'd said. 'I likes grass.'

There are many deserted quarries in Cornwall but this was the closest to St Breddaford. Here, as in others, the rough-hewn granite stones (once used for creating great bridges and buildings all over England) were lying where they had fallen, in massive rectangles, like monuments to a dead civilization. Between the stones, deep pools of oily water had gathered, scummed with leaves and grass. The machinery that hauled the finished stones up the track had rusted away into a tangle of wheels and spars, and the track itself, leading from the quarry to the road and once bustling with workers, was now overgrown. Reynolds could scarcely see the sleepers on which the trains which carried the cut stone used to run. The whole place had a deserted, bare look about it, but it was certainly secret; they'd have to walk into its centre to be sure no one was there.

'I'll take a quick look round,' Reynolds told Ted. 'And, noticing the old man's reluctance, partially due to weariness, 'You stay here,' he said. And Ted seemed glad enough to sit in the driver's seat, eyes closed, enjoying the last of the evening sun and listening to soft music on the stereo, while Reynolds squelched ahead towards the quarry proper.

He could see tyre tracks, but it was impossible to judge when they'd been made: the grass and brambles had grown in such a way as to spring back quickly. As he drew further into this wilderness, he felt the futility of his search. No one's been here for years, he thought. But when he came to what could be called the central area, where the stone dressing had taken place, a new unease came upon him, especially when the large expanse of the quarry and the enclosing semi-circle of cliff from which the granite had been cut became apparent. Plenty of room for hiding here, he thought.

The height of the cliff was astonishing; it towered overhead like a vast wall. He felt pinned beneath it, hemmed in. He had the strangest feeling that he was being watched, that he had run into a trap, that someone was creeping up behind him.

He dropped on all fours. He'd known the feeling before, but not for a long time now, the sixth sense that hunters get when they are closing in on their prey. Or when they themselves are being hunted! Keeping his head down, he began to circle the clearing, taking advantage of every cover, thanking his stars that, by instinct over long years of practice, he'd made his approach quietly, again by instinct keeping out of sight.

The clearing itself was mainly open, consisting of stretches of granite chippings, interspersed with more bushes and boulders, these shaped and ready for hauling away. He could see the old chisel marks on some of them. Around the edges, wild rhododendron bushes were clumped in profusion, as thick as trees; he used these to conceal his progress towards the cliff face where creepers cascaded down from the top like a hanging garden. He could even see other trees sprouting at impossible angles from narrow ledges, proof of how long ago the quarry had been abandoned. He was about to turn away when something caught his attention, a green clump of bush among the many green clumps at the base of the cliff – except the leaves were just beginning to curl in the sun.

As an old soldier he knew enough about camouflage to recognize it. He felt his blood tingle. He was unarmed, of course, but he suddenly wished he had a gun; he actually bent and picked up a fallen stick. Even more warily he began to approach, moving stealthily until he was close enough to see the cleverly woven mat of branches. He was about to pull it back to reveal the van underneath when he heard the gun-shot. The sound reverberated off the rocks above him in a series of echoes.

He was sure it came from behind him, from the car where he'd left Ted. Dropping his stick, he began to run, openly now, across the chippings. But when he came to the spot where he'd left the car, it was gone, its intercom system with it, and Ted was lying on the ground.

He wasn't dead. She'd hit him in the arm.

'She could've killed me.' Old Ted, at first incoherent, became remarkably calm as Reynolds carried him out of the sun and tried to make him comfortable. 'Walked up to me, set the baby down and raised the gun. "So comfort's got the better of you, after all." She laughed. She was always laughing, Meg. "My, haven't we come back in style?" '

He lay silent for a moment, as if summoning up energy. 'I knew she meant to kill me,' he whispered, 'could see it in her eyes. I just stared back at her.' Suddenly proud, he added, 'Show a wild animal you're not afraid, you bend it to your will.'

Whether that was it, or whether there was some other reason, Meg had made Ted get out of the car – to spare the mess, she'd said – then, after deliberately pointing the gun at his head, at the last moment had shifted aim. After which, Ted said, she'd stepped over him and settled the baby in the back seat. It had begun to cry, frightened perhaps by the noise. She'd got in herself, started the engine, and driven off, as calm as anyone returning from an ordinary afternoon outing.

'She did it for fun,' the old man insisted, 'to make a mock of me. At that distance she could have hit me anywhere.'

If she'd had a modern high-powered rifle, for example, which thank God she didn't, Reynolds thought, she would have killed him, fun or not. And now she was armed with something more than a knife, she had to be taken even more seriously; a modern weapon somehow brought her back into the mainstream of modern crime. Suddenly he was overcome with the magnitude of what they were against: cold-blooded murder 'for fun' was even worse than he'd envisaged.

But after Reynolds had made sure that Ted could be left, after he'd run to the main road to flag down a passing motorist, after a call from the nearest phone box alerted an ambulance and Clemow's men, Reynolds had time to make a more thorough search. He found the van. And he found Hal.

Hal lay in the undergrowth not far from the van. He was curled up as if asleep, face down in the blood-soaked grass. Perhaps he had been asleep when she came up to him and so knew nothing; perhaps he had heard her coming and sat up and cried out before she raised the gun. Looking down at him, Reynolds remembered what Old Ted had said of him, that he wasn't all bad, and hoped he'd never known.

Once more the bustle of police disturbed the silence of the old quarry. While Ted was driven off, Reynolds, now joined by Clemow, went over the contents of the van, leaving others to see to the body. The van itself was remarkably tidy, its back seats stripped out to make room for two beds, incongruously if cheerfully covered by tattered Union Jacks. There had been little on the body, a few coins only, no identification papers, but under the dashboard they found a dog-eared notebook with a driver's licence in it, presumably showing Hal's real name.

The notebook, scrawled in the large sprawling script of a schoolboy, was where Hal kept his accounts; debits for petrol and bread, punctiliously detailed, as well as credits. Among these were several bland mentions of thievery: 'Took a tenner today by pickpockiting', and the records of Sam's 'gifts' of money, a considerable amount overall, in return for which the Travellers were supposed to have formed the nucleus of Sam's 'Homes for Homeless' scheme.

Had Hal ever believed in it? Had he just gone along with Sam to take Sam's money? They would never know, but at the back of the notebook there were actually long columns of names, presumably of other Travellers who might be contacted to become part of the plan, suggesting that Hal had taken his part of the bargain seriously.

Although these names reminded Reynolds of the Middle Ages – every other one was John of Northampton, or Richard of York, as if he had no other identity – they would help modern-day police draw up their own lists of suspects for questioning about the killings, though increasingly it looked as if Meg was ploughing a lone furrow. Remembering again what Ted had intimated about Hal's band, Hal would have been sorry, Reynolds thought, to see his carefully drawn record being used against his own followers.

The only other obvious finds of personal interest were a child's book on *Natural Life*, initialled J.B. and well thumbed: Hal had obviously been fond of country living (again, Reynolds thought of what Ted had said: that Hal had loved the countryside); and a pile of freshly laundered baby clothes, spread on one of the beds.

'Cost a bomb, those,' Clemow said, letting them ripple through his hand. And, remembering how married friends were always complaining of the cost of children's clothing, Reynolds at first wondered where the money had come from: perhaps her dead lover had given it to her. Then, remembering Lady Rowan's remarks about an inherited income, her husband's 'only mistake', he at once recognized what some of the inheritance had been spent on.

And hadn't Trewithin hinted that she might be rich? All these things would have to be looked into in time, but again he was saddened by the waste; to have so much and misuse it angered him.

There were no other weapons; the knife Sam had mentioned was gone, as was the revolver that had killed Hal and wounded Ted. (And by this time its probable source had been identified from the broken glass in the game room in Frank Mathews' house, where, with typical ignorance or effrontery, Frank Mathews had kept the arsenal he must have inherited without bothering about licences or permission.)

The two inspectors were about to leave when one of the officers gave a cough, the sort that inferiors in the Force use to draw their superiors' attention. Beside the bed, a loose piece of panelling had revealed one other find – a group of drawings, mostly black and white, labelled with a slanting, almost satirically large 'M'. Some were grotesque, on a level with the caricature Lady Rowan had received. Others, less of these, were delicate: a group of flowers, a flock of birds, an unfinished sketch of a baby's face. Reynolds recognized it.

'My God, here's a psychopath.' Clemow stirred them with a distasteful hand. 'Quite mad.'

An idea came to him and he guffawed. 'Save us all a lot of trouble, and the taxpayers a packet, if we get rid of her.' He cocked his finger. 'Bam, bam.'

Again when no one said anything, 'Just joking,' he said. But looking at the pages spread side by side on the gaudy counterpane, Reynolds saw the pity of it, the two sides of the same person nakedly revealed. A wave of compassion passed through him that what should have been lovely – what was Di Rowan's name for her? Belle, the beautiful –

had become so bestially deformed.

It was already evening when Reynolds left the hospital where Ted was recovering – although not 'comfortable' as the saying goes. ('A bed!' Ted's outrage at where he'd have to sleep was only surpassed by the indignity of having to take a bath.) The searchers, summoned back, were already making their way home, the horror of the third murder dulled by the fact that the victim was unknown to them. Dulled too by familiarity, Reynolds thought wearily, as he too was driven back in a police car. Familiarity breeds contempt. His original contention had not changed, however; had, if anything, become even more certain. 'She's still out there somewhere,' he told Clemow, 'she's still got the child. And she means to kill it at Midsummer.'

Once more he stared at Clemow. 'We don't know exactly when,' he said, 'although it'll be sometime tonight. And we do know where. She'll come to Hanscastle, she's bound to come to Hanscastle. We'll wait for her there.'

'But she's got herself a car,' Clemow said, ever practical. Reynolds saw the effort the Chief Inspector was making not to say, *Your car.*

'She could be anywhere,' Clemow went on. 'The road-blocks were looking for a van, so she may already have slipped through and be miles away. In any case she must have been able to listen to us on our own damn system; she'll know where we are.'

Again Reynolds saw his heroic struggle not to add, *Handed to her as a present, while you were creeping about in some bloody quarry like a bloody tenderfoot.*

Reynolds accepted the justness of the unspoken remark, and did not try to refute it. It was partly true. It was also partly true that he'd talked so often of a third murder; he'd been so sure what the third one was meant to be, that this one had been unexpected. It broke the mould.

Whether it would break the mould for her, would deter her, was another matter. He hoped so. But he couldn't be sure. It was not being sure that made him speak so definitely.

He said, 'We can't waste time looking for the car. She'll have abandoned it or, if she's still in it, will have hidden it somewhere safe. But we've a killer on our hands. She's dangerous. You must issue a warning. Now. Place a curfew on the villagers and on all the surrounding farms; keep people under cover. Use your men to enforce it. If you have to, call in the army, damnit, but make everyone stay indoors. Because my guess is she's not gone anywhere, she's waiting to come back tonight.'

He said even more urgently, 'Listen. I've shot a tiger when it came out of the dark, but it wasn't hunting me. It was hunting the man beside me, the man it'd missed the day before and had set its sights on.'

He went on, 'Have you seen a big cat before it attacks? Its eyes lengthen, its head juts out, its whole body focuses. Nothing changes that focus, nothing interferes, it's fixed. Like an obsession,' he said. 'And for whatever reason, this young woman is obsessed. Perhaps it's due to drugs, perhaps Icky Penlore's poisons alone are the cause, but I doubt it. We know drugs can increase aberration, sometimes even give supernatural strength, make people do crazy things. But if the craze is there already, if the focus is already fixed, she'll go ahead, with or without drugs.'

'But why?' Clemow's cry was almost despairing. He meant, 'What made her be like that to come bothering me?'

'We may never know,' Reynolds said soberly. 'Why is it

in an ordinary happy family one child goes astray? He's treated like the others, there's no difference in his life, and yet he can't adjust like his siblings, he drops out. This young woman's led a sheltered life, brought up with every luxury, surrounded by beauty and wealth. Something went wrong. Something spoiled. It may have been a specific incident, or a number of specifics. We know she was close to her father, his dying may have unhinged her. And her relationship with her mother was certainly strained. But it may be something quite different. In any case, she probably doesn't know either, and will never know unless some long-fangled therapy pulls it out of her. All that we can say is that what went wrong turned her away from the normal road and brought her to this obsession: that she has to kill to worship, that she has to hurt what she loves best, that hate's all that's left. And that in some twisted way all men are scum, dirt under women's feet.'

It was a longer speech than he usually made. He was almost embarrassed at its length. And he wasn't sure what made him say these things; they came welling out of his mind with some primeval force that was stronger than he was. For a moment it was almost as if he had got inside her head. He was silent.

In the Incident Room, the circle of men around him grew unusually silent too. They didn't look at each other, they didn't look at him. Outside, the long summer twilight was closing down, steadily engulfing them. They stood together under the harsh modern lights that finally Clemow had had installed, closing ranks, as it were, a circle of men, a brotherhood, united against an older force.

Then someone coughed. Someone else mouthed at him, 'Well done.' The tension was broken; there was a homely clatter of tea mugs. But his long speech had had its effect.

Slowly, as if against his will yet spellbound, Clemow nodded agreement.

'You'll take charge?' was all he asked, after a spurt of violent energy on everyone's part had made sure the message was broadcast and that police cars had circled all the isolated farms to warn the inhabitants. Other policemen had already been sent to Hanscastle, directly by the main road, under instructions to conceal themselves in the old farmhouse or along the track that led to the fir woods. If by some chance she came that way, they were to let her pass. They were not to interrupt or hinder her, but to follow carefully out of sight, letting her set the pace and route. They were only to take action if she stopped for some reason, or seemed about to hurt the child. Whatever happened, they must try to protect the child.

Clemow wasn't meaning charge of all these arrangements. He was speaking of the most important part, the hardest, perhaps most dangerous part, at Hanscastle Fort itself where, if Reynolds was right, the facing of the murderer and her disarming would take place before she completed her bloody intention.

It wasn't only Clemow's attempt to safeguard himself (so that if things went wrong; if, for example, Reynolds had cocked it all up or subsequent events proved his theories wrong, he, Clemow, wouldn't be held responsible, wouldn't be blamed), it was also common sense. Reynolds had the training, Clemow hadn't. And given that finding someone else with similar experience would be almost impossible at this late stage, it was better all round for Reynolds to carry on. After all, Clemow could think, in the safety of the Incident Room, it was Reynolds' theory, not mine.

Which is why Reynolds and Derrymore left the village

together in Derrymore's car, to put that theory to the test, and why, in the end, Reynolds would be left with the solving or not solving of the case.

There was no one to be seen in the village, except lonely blue-uniformed figures at every corner and crossroads, sentinels on watch, again as Lady Rowan had once envisaged. Few lights were visible; those houses which faced the green had drawn their curtains; some people were rumoured to have hunted in their attics for old World War Two blackouts which they draped across the windows in spite of the moth-holes. At the bridge, an officer saluted and waved them on. They turned up the lane leaving the village behind them, a village under siege.

They said little as they drove along, crossing the cattle-grid in silence and entering the open moors. The road wound ahead of them like a silver track. A line of poetry ran in Reynolds' mind, as if it had become stuck: 'The road was a ribbon of moonlight'. In that poem, he recalled, the hero was shot down on the highway in his own blood; not a good omen.

Actually, there wasn't much of a moon yet, but the sky was clear, and against the deepening blue the faint light from stars shimmered over the grass. Suddenly Reynolds understood why many people disliked the moors, dislike shut down round him, not exactly fear, but a shivering along the spine, as one had when one went out on some night patrol, knowing the enemy was waiting in an alien countryside.

Derrymore must have felt it too. 'Feels queer, doesn't it,' he said, 'to be out like this, unarmed? Sometimes I wish we all had guns.' He thought about that for a moment. 'Mind you, it probably doesn't help in the long run,' he said tactfully.

Privately Reynolds had considered arming himself, although uncertain what his position would be if, as an ex-policeman, he was found carrying a gun. In the end he'd decided against it. The thought of one woman armed, even a mad woman, was enough complication. It wasn't male superiority either, no relying on the 'little woman' giving way easily. He was sure this woman wouldn't give way, and knew how to shoot. But, as Old Ted had put it, 'There's the baby to think about.'

They drove quietly past the turn-off to Icky's cottage, passed the gates leading to Frank Mathews' house where lights were on, showing that officers were still at their work, turned right, past the cut-off that Trewithin used, and parked well back off the road. Slowly they circled round to what Trewithin had called the cul-de-sac, walking lightly over the grass. Both men wore dark clothing, Derrymore out of uniform; even their running shoes were black.

Derrymore dropped behind Reynolds now as they started to climb, naturally taking up the rear as Reynolds did the van. Neither was puffing or panting as they'd both done the first time they'd climbed the bank; they never disturbed a stone. With something like thankfulness, Reynolds knew he hadn't mistaken his man: sometime in his past, Derrymore had also been used to night patrols.

As they suspected, the climb was much easier on this side, and they had no difficulty getting up to the first ditch. There they waited for a moment or so, listening, before crossing towards the gorse bushes that hid the entrance to the cave. Going inside it, sliding noiselessly into the darkness, was about as frightening as anything either man had done. But the cave was empty. They explored its dim recesses; no one had been there since this morning, but probably traces of their searching would have frightened away anyone who knew it well.

They left it, climbed up further, and so came at last to the top of the fort with its flower-covered enclosure and its sacrificial stakes.

Chapter 15

The starlight was brighter here, the high open circle seemed bathed in it, and the shadows of the bushes were darker by contrast. There was no one there and nothing had been touched. The white wood gleamed dully; between the stakes the stone made a grey shape. As they moved towards it, their feet dug into the bluebells, releasing their special scent, both acrid and sweet, and somewhere ahead of them a bird whirred. They froze.

It whirred again, then settled back, probably a pheasant; they could hear it moving among the heather clumps. It wouldn't settle like that if there were anyone else here.

Reynolds looked at his watch. The luminous dial showed barely eleven. A long night ahead. He jerked with his head and together they slid back into the bushes that surrounded the bank.

Derrymore had thoughtfully brought a flask of tea; they had a quick drink while they made their plans and prepared for the long wait ahead. Now they were here they had to decide what they actually should do, a relatively simple choice. They'd lie under cover not to scare her off, watch until she came, then try to talk her round. But there were complications. For one thing, although it seemed most likely she'd take the easy route, they couldn't be sure, would have to separate, each watching a different entrance. Nor could they be certain when would be the best moment to reveal themselves, or what they would then say and do. They'd have to play that by ear when the moment came. Discussing these details they lingered, as if reluctant to take up their positions. It was as if, even now, they hoped there would be no reason to, that she wouldn't come and it would all turn out to be what Clemow had called a 'wild-goose chase'.

'What I still don't understand,' Reynolds said at last, as if that might explain it all, 'is how so little was known of her. You've lived here all your life. Hadn't you heard of her?'

The question came out more accusingly than he meant, but Derrymore answered it good-naturedly. 'There was talk,' he said, 'among the older folk; always was talk, then nothing. There was some hint, years ago it was, I don't remember what, that she'd gone away or died when her father did. They lived a pretty insulated life, of course – secretive, you could call it – until Lady R began to meddle in village affairs.'

He added in his mild way, 'People from the village aren't in the same league as a millionaire's daughter, you know. Probably none of us ever had contact with her at all. And she was quite a bit younger than I was, so I wasn't interested.'

He frowned, trying to work things out. 'And when she was small I doubt if she ever came into the village; there'd be no point. Lady R wasn't about to trot her round, not wanting to call attention to her own self – how did you put it? – wanting to conceal her own background. And then when school age came Lady R would shut her daughter up, in some posh school, I suppose, out of sight. I believe

Lady R said she didn't come back even for holidays. But for all that,' he added thoughtfully, 'at some point the girl must have criss-crossed the countryside pretty thoroughly; she's got the sort of knowledge that only comes from poking about on your own.'

'A lone explorer.' Reynolds nodded. 'That makes sense. An only child, petted and cloistered to suffocation, who escapes as soon as she's old enough into the forbidden territory she's been shut off from. Turns it into her own world.'

A world of books, he thought, a world of secrets and hiding places, a magic old world, as wild as any Ted dreamed about. Until it too went sour. Aloud he said, 'I like that version of her; pity that she didn't stay like that.'

He sighed, stretched. 'Well,' he said, 'too late for that. We've got to deal with what we've got. I'll take the right side, shall I, you the left?'

Gorse bushes make prickly cover, but eventually each found a good place at opposite sides of the enclosure, close to either entrance, near enough to get out when or if anyone came, far enough back not to be immediately spotted themselves. There was a slight rustling as they pushed their way in, a barely muffled curse as a thorn caught; they crouched down, silence again.

Reynolds could just make out the outline of the bushes where he knew Derrymore was ensconced, although he couldn't see Derrymore himself. He felt better knowing where he was. Now he could admit to himself what a tricky business the moment of apprehension was going to be; that's why he'd asked for Derrymore rather than someone more senior. Partly because Derrymore deserved it – he'd worked hard and should be present at the denouement – but mainly because Reynolds wanted someone stable whom he could trust, not some hysterical idiot who'd either make the wrong move too soon and frighten her off, or else rush in and force her hand.

And that's why he'd decided against the use of a gun. He knew in situations of this sort, all depended on diplomacy not force, on careful, cautious argument, on advance and retreat, like persuading a man dangling over a parapet not to jump. Matching force with force was bound to end in disaster, was fraught with possibility of error. He didn't want a blood-bath.

But as the night wore on, he began to regret his decision. As Derrymore had said, it would have been nice to have been armed. He began to worry. He and Derrymore should have prearranged some way of signalling to each other from time to time. He had to force down the awful presentiment that she had already come up to the fort, seen Derrymore and attacked him, silently, slit his throat perhaps, or stabbed him with the same knife she'd used against Trewithin; he wanted to jump up to make sure Derrymore was all right. He shook himself. This isn't real war, he told himself, and Derrymore's a big man. He can take care of himself. But so had Sam been big. So had Hal.

The minutes passed; he counted their passing. Thoughts slid like shadows through his mind: his book that he hadn't even looked at since the evening Derrymore had first come to his cottage, his subsequent meeting with Lady Rowan, his feelings about her now mercifully dimmed, his feelings about all women, his past life. He thought too of poor Marilyn Burns, and her last moments; of Mathews; of Hal, the modern-day tramp who, if Ted had had the training of, wouldn't have been 'all bad'. Most of all he thought of the woman, the girl, who had killed them. Life isn't only a battle between men and women, he thought, there's more to it than that. When a real shadow crept across the bank he had to stop himself from jumping up. But it wasn't a human shadow. The scratching of badger claws and then the snuffling and crunching of bluebell roots made him smile in relief. Somehow seeing a nocturnal creature, a rare creature, restored an innocence, brought this watching back to proper proportions. He wondered if Derrymore had seen it and what Derrymore was thinking. More and more he was coming to like the way Derrymore thought.

The night didn't last long; in fact there never was darkness in the strict sense of the word, merely an indeterminate grey. Towards four the wind grew chill and the bushes rustled. Dew fell like rain. Then almost perceptibly the grey began to fade. Shapes hardened, took on edges, when he lifted his hand he could see it. Close to his ear a bird chirruped and another answered. The dawn chorus. Cautiously he stretched his legs and flexed them.

Light crept in stealthily; without his noticing he could see beyond the enclosure. To the west, over the Atlantic, the clouds were massing, but in the east the sky still was clear. Red streaks grew. The horizon parted, heaving up a golden ball. Bars of gold touched the rocks on top of Bolventor, the dawn of Midsummer, the summer solstice, sacred to all the ancients, worshipped by them as the most splendid of natural occurrences. Of course, he thought, dawn: that's when she'll come.

He tensed, ready to spring. As yet, the enclosure where they crouched remained in gloom, still outlined in palest grey. Then, like a dagger stab, the burst of sun spread across the bank, lit up the spiderwebs with diamond drops, gilded the grass. The bluebells were stiffened, the stakes leapt out, between them the granite stone caught fire, its flat surface streaked with wet.

Half paralysed in wonderment and awe, Reynolds saw her coming up the path they'd used. She was carrying her child, bearing it on what looked like a white cushion, the christening robe draped over the side in a fall of silk and lace, a sacrilegious christening planned for it, a travesty. She moved quickly, gliding through the brambles with her mother's grace, barefoot, her long white dress trailing, her hair bound with white flowers.

She was small but fiery. Eager. Reynolds caught a glimpse of her head thrown back. When she appeared, framed in the entrance, silhouetted against the sun, radiance seemed to stream round her, the priestess, the goddess, returning to her high altar. She seemed to float off the bank into the enclosure like thistledown.

By then, as they had planned, he was standing up, as was Derrymore, trampling down the flowers in their eagerness to get out, the gorse bushes restraining them, holding them back with spiky arms. She must have heard or seen them; they might not have been obvious as she came up the pathway but were certainly in her line of vision when she stepped off the bank. Yet she seemed to look straight through them, like a sleepwalker, Reynolds thought.

Rooted to the ground again, once more he found his throat and mouth were dry, even his tongue felt numb. If she were a priestess, he had become a follower, part of her congregation. A thousand, two thousand years of worship: who was he to break its hold?

But Derrymore could. Derrymore took a step forward, ponderous, sensible, not given to fancy. 'Now then, Miss,' he said.

Somehow his flat way of speaking broke the spell. Reynolds too stepped towards her, keeping himself between her and the sun. He saw the glint of it upon the knife-blade. Of course she'd use a knife, a gun wasn't part of this world. He held out his hand. 'We'll have that,' he said.

She stopped, smothered down a little scream as if they'd startled her. Or as if she really were sleepwalking, and they'd broken through her sleep, had roughly torn the veil of unconsciousness away and brought her back to reality.

She dropped the cushion, clutched her baby closer to her, grasped it as a miser does his treasure that someone threatens to take away. That gave them their chance. She needed two hands for the baby, she couldn't use her weapon until she put the baby down. As if she recognized that, she twisted, her dark hair flaring, looking frantically for a way of escape, pivoting like a dancer on her bare feet. Meanwhile, the child, who until then had been quiet, began to fret, struggling in her grip. They heard its wailing like a sob for help.

'Now then, now then.' Derrymore was admirable, slowly but carefully closing the gap. He might have been speaking to a child, a wayward child playing with something danger-ous that an adult would have to take away. 'No need to be frightened. We're here to help.'

By then she had recovered enough to recognize them. Derrymore perhaps she didn't know, but his way of speak-ing told her at once what he was. Reynolds she had seen before. 'Still spying,' she told Reynolds. She sneered. 'Spies deserve what they get.'

A spate of obscenity broke from her, indecent: it was like hearing a child curse, or picking a flower and finding it rotten inside. 'Keep off,' she screamed, 'get back. Don't interfere. You're not welcome.'

She suddenly began to whine, 'No one invited you.'

Before they could stop her she had made a leap, her white dress caught and ripped. She brushed past Reynolds, he couldn't have said how, but afterwards he remembered the touch of her lithe body, the scent of the flowers in her hair. He remembered too how he had laughed at Sam Trewithin for not stopping her. 'A big man like you,' he'd scoffed.

That one fast leap had gained her the few yards she needed. It brought her to the stone; she slid the baby on it so roughly it began to scream. Reynolds saw its little feet thrash as she ripped the covers off, then the upward motion of her arm.

She was outlined in red and gold, fire itself. She was the goddess of fire and sun. The sun transfixed her, she offered herself, her arm came down to make the final stab. Scarcely knowing what he did, scarcely feeling the slice of the knife, Reynolds leapt after her, bearing her to the ground.

There was a confusion, the sun was in his eyes, he was aware of a locking of bodies, a sensation of warm flesh and cold, a mingling of red and white. Off somewhere out of sight a baby was crying and someone was screaming. 'Can't you stop the screaming?' he heard himself say thickly. His tongue had grown too big and he couldn't get words round it. Then later he said, 'Where's the child?'

By now the enclosure seemed full of people, all sorts of men smashing down the flowers; for one curious moment he thought it was the colour of the broken flowers that had dyed their uniforms blue. The air was rank with the odour of crushed leaves and the white cushion had been trampled on. He closed his eyes on what seemed sacrilege. Then he was sitting up and they'd put a bandage round him. It hurt like hell when he moved, but if he sat still he could cope. Clemow's men were still milling round the enclosure; they must have come up from the farm, he caught the familiar crackle of intercoms.

The sun was not so blinding now, already patches of cloud obscured it, later it might rain. The air had cleared, a breeze had got up and was blowing, cold and fresh. The girl was gone. But he still thought he could hear her screams. A long way off he heard a door slam and a car start up.

He turned his head painfully. Seated on the stone, Derrymore was holding a white bundle on his lap. He held it with awkward skill, grinning sheepishly. 'Just look at that,' he said.

The baby had grasped hold of his hand, had wrapped its fingers round his huge paw. When Derrymore tried to pull away it held on tightly. 'Tenacious little beast,' Derrymore said, making an effort to hide his emotion. He stared down at the baby, as if attempting to guess what was going through its mind; if it had any awareness of the peril it had faced, or the way it had been saved. He jogged the baby up and down, making it gurgle. His face showed the strain: dark streaks under the eyes, a shadow of beard along the jaw. Any moment now he might break down himself: the aftermath of shock takes people that way. But in his own fashion, Derrymore was resilient.

'Makes you feel good,' Derrymore was continuing, controlling himself. 'I mean, most times, say in Ireland, you came too late. The bomb or whatever it was had gone off, you were left with the clearing up. Nice for a change to think you've prevented disaster.'

Couldn't have put that better myself, Reynolds thought. At least as far as the baby is concerned. As for its mother, I'm not so sure. I hadn't meant it to end this way. Where did I fail? Where, come to that, did we all fail her somehow, that wild and wanton girl? He closed his eyes.

When he sat up again, Derrymore was still playing with the baby. He'd taken off his jacket and made it into a kind of nest, put the baby in it. He didn't look at Reynolds when he said, 'We didn't make the choice, it was forced on us. We did what we had to, the best way we could,' but he meant it for Reynolds. He smiled. 'So that's that,' he said. Tidied and finished with, his smile said, all neat and done with. Just as you said.

It still didn't feel tidy or neat to Reynolds, it felt blurred, disjointed, unfinished. But then, he thought, Derrymore's right, what other way could it have ended?

Derrymore was saying in an apparent non-sequitur, 'They're sending someone up to take you down. And to take care of the child. I hope it's Henderson.'

Reynolds made an effort, smiled himself in turn. 'Good work,' he said. 'And certainly all neat and finished with, except for one thing. You've forgotten one thing.'

At Derrymore's look, Reynolds' grin spread. 'Lady R's flower-pots,' he said, laughing, although his ribs felt as if they were being sawn apart. 'Her bloody flower-pots smashed after her bloody meeting.'

'My God,' Derrymore said, 'I'd forgotten about them.' He stopped playing with the baby's fingers, sat up stiffly, feet together. 'So who do you think it was, sir? Any clues?'

'Not a one,' said Reynolds, 'but I've got a hunch.'

Again he looked at Derrymore, sitting at attention. 'All I've got are ideas,' he said, 'theories, premonitions, guesses. For what they're worth, I put my money on Peter Burns. His last act of defiance, his little spurt of anger when he came home and found his wife gone and decided it was Lady R's fault. But I haven't any proof, of course. I never have.'

A selection of bestsellers from Headline

OXFORD EXIT	Veronica Stallwood	£4.99	☐
BOOTLEGGER'S DAUGHTER	Margaret Maron	£4.99	☐
DEATH AT THE TABLE	Janet Laurence	£4.99	☐
KINDRED GAMES	Janet Dawson	£4.99	☐
MURDER OF A DEAD MAN	Katherine John	£4.99	☐
A SUPERIOR DEATH	Nevada Barr	£4.99	☐
A TAPESTRY OF MURDERS	P C Doherty	£4.99	☐
BRAVO FOR THE BRIDE	Elizabeth Eyre	£4.99	☐
NO FIXED ABODE	Frances Ferguson	£4.99	☐
MURDER IN THE SMOKEHOUSE	Amy Myers	£4.99	☐
THE HOLY INNOCENTS	Kate Sedley	£4.99	☐
GOODBYE, NANNY GRAY	Staynes & Storey	£4.99	☐
SINS OF THE WOLF	Anne Perry	£5.99	☐
WRITTEN IN BLOOD	Caroline Graham	£5.99	☐

All Headline books are available at your local bookshop or newsagent, or can be ordered direct from the publisher. Just tick the titles you want and fill in the form below. Prices and availability subject to change without notice.

Headline Book Publishing, Cash Sales Department, Bookpoint, 39 Milton Park, Abingdon, OXON, OX14 4TD, UK. If you have a credit card you may order by telephone – 01235 400400.

Please enclose a cheque or postal order made payable to Bookpoint Ltd to the value of the cover price and allow the following for postage and packing:

UK & BFPO: £1.00 for the first book, 50p for the second book and 30p for each additional book ordered up to a maximum charge of £3.00.

OVERSEAS & EIRE: £2.00 for the first book, £1.00 for the second book and 50p for each additional book.

Name ....

Address ....

....

....

If you would prefer to pay by credit card, please complete:
Please debit my Visa/Access/Diner's Card/American Express (delete as applicable) card no:

Signature .... Expiry Date ....